The Chase
or
A Long Fatal Love Chase

Also by Louisa May Alcott

LITTLE WOMEN
GOOD WIVES
JO'S BOYS
LITTLE MEN

The Chase
or
A Long Fatal Love Chase

Louisa May Alcott

ARROW

Published by Arrow Books in 1996

1 3 5 7 9 10 8 6 4 2

First published in the United Kingdom in 1995 by Century

Arrow Books Limited
20 Vauxhall Bridge Road, London, SW1V 2SA

Random House Australia (Pty) Limited
16 Dalmore Drive, Scoresby
Victoria 3179, Australia

Random House New Zealand Limited
18 Poland Road, Glenfield
Auckland 10, New Zealand

Random House South Africa (Pty) Limited
Box 2263, Rosebank 2121, South Africa

Random House UK Limited Reg. No. 954009

ISBN 0 09 966411 9

Typeset by Keyboard Services, Luton
Printed and bound in the United Kingdom by
BPC Paperbacks Ltd
a member of The British Printing Company Ltd

Contents

CHAPTER I

Fair Rosamond

'I tell you I cannot bear it! I shall do something desperate if this life is not changed soon. It gets worse and worse, and I often feel as if I'd gladly sell my soul to Satan for a year of freedom.'

An impetuous young voice spoke, and the most intense desire gave force to her passionate words as the girl glanced despairingly about the dreary room like a caged creature on the point of breaking loose. Books lined the walls, loaded the tables and lay piled about the weird, withered old man who was her sole companion. He sat in a low, wheeled chair from which his paralyzed limbs would not allow him to stir without help. His face was worn by passion and wasted by disease but his eyes were all alive and possessed an uncanny brilliancy which contrasted strangely with the immobility of his other features. Fixing these cold, keen eyes on the agitated face of the girl, he answered with harsh brevity, 'Go when and where you like. I have no desire to keep you.'

'Ah, that is the bitterest thing of all!' cried the girl with a sudden tremor in her voice, a pathetic glance at that hard face. 'If you loved me, this dull house would be pleasant to me, this lonely life not only endurable but happy. The knowledge that you care nothing for me makes me wretched. I've tried, God knows I have, to do my duty for Papa's sake, but you are relentless and will neither forgive nor forget. You say "Go," but where *can* I

1

go, a girl, young, penniless and alone? You do not really mean it, Grandfather?'

'I never say what I do *not* mean. Do as you choose, go or stay, but let me have no more scenes, I'm tired of them,' and he took up his book as if the subject was ended.

'I'll go as soon as I can find a refuge, and never be a burden to you anymore. But when I am gone remember that I wanted to be a child to you and you shut your heart against me. Someday you'll feel the need of love and regret that you threw mine away; then send for me, Grandfather, and wherever I am I'll come back and prove that *I* can forgive.' A sob choked the indignant voice, but the girl shed no tears and turned to leave the room with a proud step.

The sight of a stranger pausing on the threshold arrested her, and she stood regarding him without a word. He looked at her an instant, for the effect of the graceful girlish figure with pale, passionate face and dark eyes full of sorrow, pride and resolution was wonderfully enhanced by the gloom of the great room, the presence of the sinister old man and glimpses of a gathering storm in the red autumn sky. During that brief pause the girl had time to see that the newcomer was a man past thirty, tall and powerful, with peculiar eyes and a scar across the forehead. More than this she did not discover, but a sudden change came over her excited spirit and she smiled involuntarily before she spoke.

'Here is a gentleman for you, Grandfather.'

The old man looked up sharply, threw down his book with an air of satisfaction, and stretched his hand to the stranger, saying bluntly, 'Speak of Satan and he appears. Welcome, Tempest.'

'Many thanks; few give the Evil One so frank and cordial a greeting,' returned the other, with a short laugh which showed a glitter of white teeth under a drooping black mustache. 'Who is the Tragic Muse?' he added under his breath as he shook the proffered hand.

'Good! She *is* exactly that. Rosamond, this is the most promising of all my pupils, Phillip Tempest. The "Tragic Muse" is Guy's daughter, as you might know, Phillip, by the state of rebellion in which you find her!'

The girl bowed rather haughtily, the man lifted his brows with an air of surprise as he returned the bow and sat down beside his host.

'Ring for lights and take yourself away,' commanded the old man, and Rosamond vanished from the room, leaving it the darker for her absence.

For half an hour she sat in the great hall window looking out at the waves which dashed against the rocky shore, thinking sad and bitter thoughts till twilight fell and the outer world grew as somber as the inner one of which she was so weary. With a sigh she was about to rise and seek her own room when a sudden consciousness of a human presence nearby made her turn to see the newcomer pausing just outside the old man's door to regard her with a curious smile. An involuntary start betrayed that she had entirely forgotten him, a slight which she tried to excuse by saying hastily, 'I was so absorbed in watching the sea I did not hear you come out. I love tempests and—'

He interrupted her with a short laugh and said in a deep voice which would have been melodious but for a satiric undertone which seldom left it, 'I am glad of that, for your grandfather invites me to pass the night, and I shall do so willingly since my young hostess has a taste for tempests, though I cannot promise to be as absorbing as the one outside.'

In the fitful light of the dusky hall the newcomer's face suddenly appeared fiery-eyed and menacing, and, glancing at a portrait of Mephistopheles, Rosamond exclaimed, 'Why, you are the very image of Meph—'

Tempest strolled to the picture which hung opposite the long mirror. Looking up at it, a change passed over his face, an expression of weariness and melancholy which touched her and made her repent of her frankness.

With an impulsive gesture she put out her hand, saying in a tone of sweet contrition, 'I beg your pardon; I've been very rude, but I live so entirely alone with Grandfather, who is peculiar, that I really don't know how to behave like a well-bred girl. I had no wish to be unkind, will you forgive me?'

'I think I will on condition that you play hostess for a little while, for your grandfather begs me to pass the night and gives me into your care. May I stay?'

He held her hand and spoke, looking down into the beautiful face which was so unconscious of its beauty. A hospitable smile broke over her wistful face and with a word of welcome she led him away to a little room which overhung the sea. Placing him in an easy chair, she stirred the embers till a cheery blaze sprung up, lighted a brilliant lamp, drew the curtains and then paused as if in doubt about the next step.

'I always have tea here alone and send Grandpapa's up. Will you take yours with him or with me?'

'With you if you are not afraid of my dangerous society,' he answered with a significant smile.

'I like danger,' she said with a blush, a petulant shake of the head and a daring glance at her guest.

Ringing the bell, she ordered tea and when it came busied herself about it with the pretty earnestness of a child playing housewife. Lounging in his easy chair, Tempest regarded her with an expression of indolent amusement, which slowly changed to one of surprise and interest as the girl talked with a spirit and freedom peculiarly charming to a man who had tried many pleasures and, wearying of them all, was glad to discover a new one even of this simple kind. Though her isolated life had deprived Rosamond of the polish of society, it had preserved the artless freshness of her youth and given her ardent nature an intensity which found vent in demonstrations infinitely more attractive than the artificial graces of other women. Her beauty satisfied Tempest's artistic eye, her peculiarities piqued his curiosity, her

4

vivacity lightened his ennui, and her character interested him by the unconscious hints it gave of power, pride and passion. So entirely natural and unconventional was she that he soon found himself on a familiar footing, asking all manner of unusual questions, and receiving rather piquant replies.

'So, like "Mariana in the moated grange," you are often "aweary, aweary," and wish that you were dead I fancy?' he said, after a series of skillful questions had elicited a history of the solitary life she had led. To his surprise she replied with a brave bright glance that betrayed no trace of sentimental weakness in her nature, but an indomitable will and a cheerful spirit.

'No, I never wish that. I don't intend to die till I've enjoyed my life. Everyone has a right to happiness and sooner or later I *will* have it. Youth, health and freedom were meant to be enjoyed and I want to try every pleasure before I am too old to enjoy them.'

'I've tried that plan and it was a failure.'

'Was it? Tell me about it, please.' Rosamond drew a low seat nearer with a face full of interest.

Tempest smiled involuntarily at the idea of recounting his experiences to such a listener, and said, in answer to an imperious little nod, as he paused, 'That history would not interest you; but of this I can assure you, one may begin with youth, health and liberty, may taste every pleasure, obey no law but one's own will, roam all over the world and yet at five and thirty be unutterably tired of everything under the sun.'

'Are you so old as that? I didn't think it,' was Rosamond's reply.

'Does five and thirty seem venerable to fifteen?' asked Tempest curious to learn her age.

'I am eighteen,' she answered with an air of dignity which was very becoming; then returning to what interested her, she said thoughtfully, 'I don't understand how one can ever tire of pleasure. I've had so little I know

I should enjoy it very much, and I can imagine nothing so delightful as to have entire liberty as you have.'

'There is very little real liberty in the world; even those who seem freest are often the most tightly bound. Law, custom, public opinion, fear or shame make slaves of us all, as you will find when you try your experiment,' said Tempest with a bitter smile.

'Law and custom I know nothing of, public opinion I despise, and shame and fear I defy, for everyone has a right to be happy in their own way.'

'Even at the cost of what is called honor and honesty? That is a comfortable philosophy, and having preached and practiced it all my days I've no right to condemn it. But the saints would call it sinful and dangerous and tell you that life should be one long penance full of sorrow, sacrifice and psalm-singing.'

'I'm so tired of hearing that! In the books I read the sinners are always more interesting than the saints, and in real life good people are dismally dull. I've no desire to be wicked, but I do want to be happy. A short life and a gay one for me and I'm willing to pay for my pleasure if it is necessary.'

'You may have to pay a high price for it, but sooner or later I am sure you will have it, for a strong will always wins its way.'

'Thank you for saying that. It's the first word of encouragement I've had for years. I comfort myself with hopes and dreams but cheery prophesies uttered by friendly lips are far better,' she said gratefully.

'Tell me your hopes and dreams.'

'You would laugh at some of them, but I'm not afraid to own that I hope to be free as air, to see the world, to know what ease and pleasure are, to have many friends and to be dearly loved.'

The last words fell slowly, softly from her lips and the brilliant eyes dimmed suddenly. As the ruddy blaze shone on the slender figure in the simple gown and the drooping face framed in clusters of dark hair, Tempest thought that

6

the little room held the sweetest piece of womanhood he had ever seen. Most men would have been touched by the innocent confessions of the girl, but this man's heart had grown hard with years of selfishness and he merely enjoyed her as he would have done a lovely flower, an exciting book, a passionate song. Rosamond sat listening to the wind that now raved without and the rain that beat upon the windowpane. Tempest listened also and smiled a curious smile; the girl saw it and asked with an answering smile, 'You like storms as well as I?'

'Yes, but I was thinking of something peculiar. Whenever I enter a house where some adventure or experience is to befall me, I invariably bring a tempest with me.'

'Of course you do, if you bring your name. But do you really mean it always storms when you pay visits?'

'The omen never fails, and I'm growing superstitious about it. For that reason I seldom make visits or come ashore,' he answered, as she looked up laughingly into his face.

'Why, where do you live then?'

'Cruising about in my yacht.'

'Then it was you I watched coming gallantly into port today and wished a bon voyage?'

'Thanks, I seldom have any other. For months I have led the life of a sea king, floating to and fro with no society but books and my Greek boy, Ippolito.'

'How charming! What a delicious life it must be! Tell me about it, please. I love the sea so dearly that everything concerning it delights me,' and Rosamond plied him with questions till he was irresistibly roused from his ennui and incited to recount the pleasures and perils of a summer voyage. The girl listened with an eager face, a breathless interest more flattering than words, and when he paused exclaimed with a sigh of satisfaction, 'You tell it so well it seems as if I saw all you describe. Where are you going when you sail away again?'

'I shall cruise about among the islands of the Mediterranean if no other whim seizes me. You know there is no winter in that lovely climate but one long summer all the year round; this suits me as a change after our fogs and winds, so when you sit here next January with sleet beating on the window and snowdrifts whitening the rocks below, you can imagine me lying among violets and primroses under the orange trees of Valrosa.'

'What is that?' asked the girl, drinking in every word.

'My little villa near Nice. I've not seen it for two or three years and have a fancy to revisit it. A pretty place in a nest of roses; just the spot to spend one's honeymoon in.'

'Did you spend yours there?'

'Do I look as if I ever had one?'

Undaunted by the sudden sharpness of the question, Rosamond bent forward and gravely scanned the face opposite. It was inscrutable, and all she discovered was that Tempest had magnificent eyes and a mouth which betrayed a ruthless nature.

'No, I think you never did,' she said decidedly. 'You haven't the look of a man who has a wife to love, or little children to take upon his knee. You don't care for such things, do you?'

'Not I; no bonds for me of any kind. You read faces well.' He indulged in a noiseless laugh that had more of mockery than merriment in it.

'Do I amuse you?' asked Rosamond, looking piqued.

'Delightfully. I've not laughed so much for an age. I wish I could persuade your grandfather to try a voyage with me and let me enjoy your gay society.'

'Ah, I wish he would! But it is impossible. He never stirs out and I am almost as much a fixture as he.'

'Do you never go away?'

'Never. Till you came I had not seen a strange face for weeks, and when you go the dreadful loneliness will return. *Must* you sail in the morning?'

'The word "must" is not in my vocabulary. I go and come as I like, and lead the life of the Wandering Jew;

8

with the comfortable difference of knowing I have the privilege of dying when I like.'

'You don't look as if you ever could die, you are so strong and—' she did not finish her sentence but looked at the vigorous figure before her with genuine womanly admiration for a manly man.

'I have been very near proving I *could* die more than once; but my hour has not come yet so I must bide my time.'

'Was that wound received on one of the occasions of which you speak?' inquired Rosamond, touching her own smooth forehead to indicate the scar on his.

A transient glitter shone in Tempest's eye, and his powerful hand closed like a vice, but his voice betrayed no emotion.

'Yes, I have to thank a friend for that and a year of suffering. The debt is paid however, and I'm none the worse for the wound. I'm told such scars are an improvement as they give an heroic air. Do you like it?'

'Not now. If you had received it in a real battle I might admire it, but duels are not heroic.'

Tempest smiled at her decided mode of speaking, yet passed his hand across his forehead as if *he* did not consider the scar an ornament, and asked with some curiosity, 'Where did you get that idea? Not from your grandfather, I'm confident; he has fought too many himself to condemn the practice.'

'I got it where I get most of my ideas, out of books. The house is full of them and I've nothing to do but read. Was Grandfather very wild and wicked when he was young? He never speaks of himself, and during the ten years I've been with him I've discovered nothing about his past life except that he never would forgive Papa for marrying as he did.'

'He is kind to you?'

'Yes, in his own way. He gives me a home but nothing more. I never understood why he did it, because he was angry with Mama and yet at her death he took me in.'

'I can tell you why he did it.'

'What do you know about it?' Rosamond's dreamy eyes flashed wide open as she turned to him.

'I never saw your lovely mother but once, yet I do not forget her. I was your grandfather's pupil even then, though only a lad, but he was a gay old man and we saw life together. Your mother would have inherited a fortune had she not displeased her father by marrying a poor man. Her sister has the fortune, but when she dies it will come to you. Therefore the old man keeps a hold upon you.'

'Is that it? I knew he did not love me, but I thought there might be a little pity in his cold heart. I hope that fortune will come quickly so that I may be free sooner than I planned.'

'You mean to go away then?'

'Yes, I can bear this life no longer, it is so purposeless and lonely. I care for nobody and nobody cares for me; the years drag on and nothing changes.'

'Except that the bud becomes a rose.'

'A very thorny one, for there is no kind gardener to tend and train it,' she said sadly.

'Wild roses are fairest, and nature a better gardener than art.'

She looked a rose indeed as she blushed brightly under the glance he gave her, and frankly showed that his admiration pleased even while it half abashed her.

'I never had a compliment before, but I think I like it, though I don't deserve it,' she said, so naïvely that his satirical mouth softened with a smile of genuine amusement.

'I seldom pay them, but tonight I feel as if I had got into a fairy tale, sitting here in an enchanted tower while the storm raves without and Fair Rosamond entertains me hospitably by her fire. You know the old ballad?'

'Oh yes, and like it very much. I often make romances when I'm tired of reading them. Shall I sing you a little song I made about my namesake?'

'If you will. It is just the time and place for such music.'

Turning to the old instrument that stood near, Rosamond poured into the simple lay all the passion and the pathos of her fresh young voice. Tempest listened with the indolent satisfaction of a man whose senses, those ministers of pleasure, had been cultivated to the utmost by years of indulgence. Yet when she ceased he did not thank her, but sat looking moodily into the fire as if the music had conjured up memories of other short-lived roses who had lent sweetness to his life.

Before either spoke there came a sharp peal of thunder and a vivid flash of lightning followed by a heavy crash. The man never stirred but the girl sprang to her feet, exclaiming, 'It was the cedar on the cliff! I thought it would be struck some day,' and she went to the window.

'Come away or you will share the fate of the tree,' said Tempest commandingly. But Rosamond remained in her dangerous position till a second flash showed that her surmise was correct; then she resumed her seat, saying sorrowfully, 'That was my favorite tree. Papa planted it when I was born and I always called it mine. It is a bad omen, for the superstitious say when the tree dies I shall follow soon. Do you believe in such things?'

'No,' was the brief reply, but Tempest muttered to himself, 'My coming was a worse omen than either storm or thunderbolt, if the child did but know it.'

At this moment a bell rang sharply and an instant after a servant appeared to summon the guest to his host's room. Tempest obeyed reluctantly, bade Rosamond good night, and with a backward glance at the bright little nook and its charming occupant he went away, leaving her to dream dreams of the new hero who had come to play a part in the romance of her life.

CHAPTER II

The *Circe*

All night the gale blew, the rain poured and the sea thundered on the coast. But at daybreak the wind lulled a little, the rain ceased and the sun shone fitfully. Tempest left his room early, paused an instant before the picture in the hall, eyeing it with a curious expression, and strolled about the great, silent house, wondering if his young hostess had yet left her room. A gust of air blowing downward from an open door led him to look up. A flight of winding steps led to the flat roof, and noiselessly climbing them he found Rosamond. A stone balustrade ran round the roof and in the angle which overhung the sea stood the girl, her dress fluttering in the wind, her hair blown back from cheeks rosy with its keen breath, her eyes intently fixed upon the horizon where the ocean seemed to meet the sky.

'Is Hero looking for her Leander?' asked Tempest's resonant voice.

'My Leander has not yet been found,' she answered, glancing over her shoulder with a sudden smile.

'What were you looking for so intently then?' he said, going to lean beside her.

'Your yacht. I dreamed I sailed away in it but before we reached a lovely land lying in the distance I woke. Can we see her from here?'

'No, the *Circe* lies in a little bay behind the cliffs, and there she must lie till the gale abates.'

'I'm glad of it!'

'Why?'

'Because I want you to stay. I'm so dull here I should welcome even—' she paused for a word and he supplied it – 'Mephistopheles.'

'Don't remind me of that rudeness or I shall think you have not forgiven it. I don't see the resemblance now.' Holding back her hair, she looked up at him with a frank, confiding glance which would have softened the most relentless heart.

'Who would not linger when welcomed by such a sweet Miranda?' he said, with a look which made her flush and change the subject suddenly, as if some womanly instinct warned her that his compliments were dangerous.

'Isn't it splendid up here? I always come when there is a storm, and long to be a seagull to float away on the wings of the wind as they do.' She spread her arms with such an impetuous motion that Tempest involuntarily put out his hand to arrest her for she looked as if she would in truth 'float away on the wings of the wind'. She laughed and drew back from the detaining hand.

'No fear of that; if I'd wanted to make a romantic end I should have done it long ago.'

'Then you don't approve of suicide?'

'Not I; it's a cowardly way of ending one's troubles. Better conquer or bear them bravely.'

'I like that.' Tempest gave an approving nod which pleased her more than the most graceful compliment, and made her talk on freely.

'I used to amuse myself by testing my own courage in many ways. Up here I began by walking round on the top of the balustrade, and when I could run along it without fear I tried the ledge outside.'

'Faith! That was a dangerous test,' and Tempest leaned forward to look at the narrow ledge which projected over the rocky shore, for the house was built on the very verge of the cliff.

'It was very foolish and I *was* terribly afraid at first,

13

but I never give up, so I kept on and now can go all round without touching the balustrade.'

'Can you?' He looked politely incredulous.

'Is that a wreck?' said Rosamond, suddenly pointing to a speck far out at sea. Tempest turned to look; an instant after a laugh recalled him and he saw the girl outside the low railing.

'Don't touch me or I'll let myself fall,' she said, and folding her arms, with a fearless smile and a steady step she went rapidly along the perilous path. The stones were wet, the wind blew strongly, the sun shone in her face, and Tempest, as he walked inside with his eye on her, his hand ready to clutch her if she slipped, felt his pulse quicken as she turned corner after corner till she reached her starting point; then he drew a long breath and exclaimed, 'Bravo! That was a feat to be proud of. Didn't it make your heart beat?'

'No, I think not. I'm never conscious that I have one.'

Tempest smiled at a simplicity which had no touch of coquetry in it, and said, with a tone of pity in his voice, 'You will find it soon enough, and perhaps regret the discovery. Now come out of danger, a gust may blow you away.'

'I like danger, there's excitement in it and that is what I want.'

'Very well, then you shall have it. Will you come back?'

'Yes, when I'm ready—' she began, with a defiant little gesture, for his air of command displeased her. But the words were hardly spoken when Tempest bent suddenly, took her by the waist and set her down inside the parapet.

'How dare you!' she demanded, scarlet with surprise and anger.

'I dare anything,' was the cool reply.

'Don't boast, you dare not do what I did,' said the girl petulantly, though rather afraid of him.

'I dare try it,' and he put his hand on the railing with

14

such an evident determination to make the attempt that Rosamond held him back, forgetting her resentment in alarm.

'No, no, you must not! I know you are brave, there is no need to prove it. Don't frighten me and endanger yourself for such a foolish thing.'

'Yet you did both and added disobedience to the folly. I will be more docile. Sit here and recover from your fright.'

He spoke in a masterful way which subdued the girl's willful spirit and she sat down on the stone seat to which he pointed, heartily ashamed of her freak and its consequences.

'It was my fault,' she said with an air of mingled dignity and humility. 'If I behave like a child I must expect to be treated like one. I'll try to be a woman and then perhaps I shall receive the respect which is due a woman, according to the books.'

Tempest made her a deferential bow and said penitently, though a mocking smile lurked in his eye, 'I beg pardon, I won't forget myself again. Now to assure me that my offense is forgiven will you come and see the *Circe* before she weighs anchor?'

Rosamond forgot her dignity and clapped her hands with delight as she answered, with no trace of anger in face or voice, 'With all my heart! I wanted to see it very much, but did not like to ask. When can we go?'

'There will be another shower before it clears, so we must wait till afternoon, which will give me time to put my floating home into holiday trim in honor of your visit.'

'How charming it will be! I was longing for something to happen and was quite desperate, but now you have come and everything is changed.' She stopped with a shy glance, and added abruptly, 'I am forgetting that you have had no breakfast; come and let me give you some.'

Tempest smiled his inscrutable smile and followed, idly asking himself if it was worth his while to linger and amuse himself for a time with the beautiful, impetuous creature who seemed to have reached a point when a word would make or mar her future.

He breakfasted and remained shut up with the old man for several hours, then departed, promising to return in the afternoon. Meantime Rosamond watched the sky, counted the hours, and when the sun broke out brilliantly she beguiled her impatience by making herself as pretty as her scanty wardrobe allowed. Youth and beauty supplied all deficiencies, for the lithe grace of her girlish figure set off the simple gown, and the little old hat with no ornament but a garland of red autumn leaves shaded such a blooming face that one forgot to look farther. When ready a sudden whim took her into the drawing room. It had long been disused and was half dismantled, but a great mirror still hung there, and standing before it in a streak of sunshine she examined herself with unusual interest. Something seemed amiss, for she shook her head and was turning away with a listless air when she caught sight of another face in the tall dark mirror. Not a whit abashed at being found there she nodded to it, saying with brightening eyes, 'Shall we go now, Mr Tempest?'

'If you please.' Then, as they walked away together, he asked in a tone that would have daunted many young girls, 'Were you admiring yourself or looking for your fate as in old times, Miss Rose?'

She did not answer but said softly, as if to herself, 'I like that name; no one ever calls me so now.'

'Rosamond means "Rose of the World", you know. The name suits you and I unconsciously gave it to you. But you do not tell me what you saw in the glass.'

'I saw myself – and you.'

'Well, were you satisfied with your fate?'

'I was not thinking of my fate but of my old straw hat.' Then, like an inquisitive child she asked, 'Did you ever see a magic mirror?'

'Yes.'

16

'And read your fate in it?'

'That remains to be proved?'

'I wish I knew what you saw.'

'A lovely dead woman, an old man mourning over her and myself standing near with an expression of remorse and despair such as I am quite incapable of feeling. Is that sufficiently mysterious and romantic for you?'

'But did nothing like that ever happen to you?' she asked, stopping to look up at him with her great eyes full of interest and wonder.

'Nothing resembling it in the slightest degree. The mirror lied and the dead lady has never appeared to me except as a part of that melodramatic farce.'

'Where was it?'

'In Venice.'

'How long ago?'

'Four or five years. A friend had a fancy to visit the magician who was amusing the idlers there so we went.'

'What did your friend see?'

'Her husband.'

'Oh, it was a woman, was it? That must have pleased her.'

'On the contrary, it alarmed her extremely as she particularly desired *not* to see him.'

'Didn't she love him?'

'Not a whit.'

'Then I hope her fate proved as false as yours.'

'It proved exactly true. She saw her husband three days afterward and went raving mad by way of a pleasant welcome.'

'How terrible! Was he angry or wicked, that she feared him so?'

'He was an amicable fool enough, and not at all angry when she saw him, but quite calm and comfortable with a bullet through his heart.' Tempest spoke carelessly but there was a sinister glitter in his black eyes, and an involuntary motion of the hand across the forehead betrayed that the scar and the story had some connection. Rosamond looked troubled, for even her innocent heart felt by instinct the darker tragedy that remained untold.

'Why do you tell me such things?' she said, watching him askance as he walked beside her with an indolent gait curiously out of keeping with his athletic figure and bronzed face.

'You said you pined for excitement so I'm trying to give you some. Don't you like it?'

'Yes, but I think that perhaps it's not good for me, at least this kind. One more question and then we'll talk of something else. Aren't you afraid that your vision may yet be fulfilled as your friend's was?'

Tempest shrugged his shoulders with his peculiar laugh, noiseless, brief and mirthless, a sound that made the listener sad because it seemed to mock not only at others but at the laugher himself.

'I have some curiosity on that point,' he said. 'So much has been written about remorse and despair that I sometimes think I should like I taste of them. I've tried almost all the other passions and sentiments and this would have the charm of novelty at least. There is the *Circe* curtsying to her master.'

Rosamond's face cleared as she eyed the little vessel in its holiday trim. Pennons streamed from the mast, a gay awning was spread on deck, and several foreign sailors in picturesque costume stood ready to receive her. Like a delighted child she looked about her, breaking into merry exclamations and enthusiastic praise of all she saw as Tempest did the honors of his floating home, which was as perfect as skill, taste and money could make it.

'I do not wonder you seldom go ashore. I'd never land if I were you, except to make this more charming by contrast. Ah, I wish I had such liberty as yours.' Rosamond was standing at the bow, looking across the boundless waste with an expression of intense longing which made her young face tragical.

'Shall I weigh anchor and sail away with you in the free fashion of the sea kings?' asked Tempest.

'I wish you would,' and her eyes shone with merriment at the playful proposition.

'Should you regret nothing that you would leave behind?' he asked, alert to catch the changes of her expressive face.

'Nothing,' she said, decidedly, then with a gesture as if she put aside some unwelcome subject she added, 'Let us forget all that; I want to enjoy my holiday undisturbed by a sad thought. Can I go below?'

He led the way to the luxurious little saloon and showed her all the appliances for ease and pleasure which it possessed, finding much amusement in her demonstrations of delight.

'Why didn't you have more of these charming nests so you could fill your yacht with friends sometimes?' asked Rosamond, putting her lovely head out of the daintiest of the two dainty state rooms which opened on the saloon.

'I never want but one at a time. I am as fickle as a woman and often change.'

'All women are not fickle. I never had but one friend, yet I loved him faithfully and have not filled his place though I lost him six years ago.'

'Ah, then you did find a Leander once? You are young to be such a constant lover.'

'It was not a person but a dog.' The tone of tender regret made the fact that her only friend had been a brute touching instead of ludicrous. Tempest turned abruptly to the door and called, 'Ippolito!'

A light step came bounding down the cabin stairs and a slender, handsome boy of twelve in Greek costume appeared on the threshold.

'Here is a friend for you, Miss Rose, a safe and faithful little friend. Will you have him?' said Tempest,

19

as the boy pulled off his embroidered fez and stood regarding her with a glance of admiration in his bold bright eyes. Before she could reply he smiled and nodded approvingly as he said to Tempest in prettily accented English, 'She is to stay then? Of that I am glad for she has more of beauty than Señora Zoe. Do you—'

'Do *you* remember what I told you, young marplot?' demanded Tempest laying a heavy hand on the boy's shoulder as a quick glance arrested further words on his lips. Ippolito held his peace, but he looked quite undismayed and leaned against his master with the air of a favorite who was more accustomed to caresses than reproofs.

'Yes, I'll have him and thank you heartily,' said Rosamond, charmed with the grace and beauty of the boy.

'Do you think your grandfather would allow me to leave him in your care for a time? I want a safe home and someone to be kind to the young rascal.' For the first time Tempest's face betrayed a trace of emotion as he stroked the short gold curls that shone above the boy's dark eyes and classically molded features. The girl saw the momentary softening of that hard face and was touched, but shook her head, saying regretfully, 'I am sure Grandfather will not let me keep him, he hates children. But why not let him stay with you if you are fond of him?'

'It is too wild a life for him, and I am too rough a master. Hey, Lito?'

The boy's only answer was an eloquent look and a closer grasp of the hand that still lay on his shoulder. Tempest smiled a genuine, warm, soft smile which changed and beautified him wonderfully as he said, 'He's a pretty plaything, isn't he? I found him in Greece and took a fancy into my idle head that I could make a fine man of him. Well, what is it, Mademoiselle?' he asked suddenly, for Rosamond was looking intently at the boy.

'I was trying to think who he resembles. I never remember seeing anyone like him, yet his face looks so familiar it quite puzzles me.'

'Sharper eyes than I gave her credit for,' muttered Tempest, adding aloud, as he put the boy away, 'Some picture probably; Lito has a classical head and is a direct descendent from some of the Greek gods I daresay. Now come and amuse yourself with these trifles while my Ganymede prepares supper.'

Opening the drawers of a cabinet, Tempest entertained his guest with rare and curious spoils gathered from many lands, keeping her intent on corals, cameos and antique coins till Ippolito thrust his blond head between them with the announcement, 'Master, it is ready.'

'It is I who feel as if I'd got into a fairy tale now,' said Rosamond, as she sat at a table covered with foreign dainties, drinking her host's health in choice wine from a slender-stemmed Venetian glass, while the pretty boy served her like a page, and everything about her heightened the romantic charm of time and place. As the words passed her lips she paused suddenly, conscious for the first time of the unusual motion of the yacht. 'How it rolls! The wind must be rising. Why does he laugh and why do you look so wicked? Have I said or done anything very absurd?' she asked, glancing from one to the other.

'Come on deck and you will see why we laugh at you.' Tempest rose, Rosamond followed, and one look explained everything. The yacht was flying down the harbor before the wind, and land was already far behind. She stood a moment half bewildered, while Lito danced with delight and Tempest watched her face.

'What are you doing? Where are we going?' she demanded.

'I am taking you at your word, and we are going out to sea,' Tempest replied so gravely that her smile faded and she looked a little startled.

21

'Not far I fancy. It's a pleasant joke, but you would tire of it first.'

'We shall see,' and turning he gave some order to his men.

'Do you mean what you say? Are you in earnest, Mr Tempest?'

'Quite in earnest. Do you like this sort of excitement better than housetops and magic mirrors?'

Rosamond eyed him keenly, but his face betrayed no sign of relenting and she grew pale with anger, not fear. 'You said you dared do anything and I can believe it, but I wish I could be sure whether you really mean what you say now.'

'Why not? I am simply gratifying your wish; you want to be free, I want a companion, Lito a playmate. I'm fond of wild exploits and have a fancy to try this.' He certainly did have the air of a man who was capable of any freak regardless of consequences.

'Will he take me back, Ippolito?' she asked anxiously.

'If he wants you he will keep you as he did—' A hand on his mouth silenced the boy and Tempest swung him over the boat side, holding him there with one strong arm while he emphasized his words with the other. 'You imp! Will nothing silence your unruly tongue? Shall I drop you and try that cure again?'

'Yes, if the Master wishes another grand fright,' answered the boy, laughing in the ireful face bent over him.

The child's apparent peril made the girl forget her own. She clung to Tempest's arm, imploring him to take the culprit out of danger, till, with a relenting smile, he complied, saying, as he swung Lito back to the deck and fixed his eyes upon her, 'You see of what I am capable; are you resigned to your fate, Miranda?'

The act, the look, the name reassured Rosamond; her face brightened and she gave him a confiding glance which would have conquered Tempest had his threat been made in earnest.

22

'Yes, I do not fear you now, for I remember that brave men are not cruel. I trust you because I know you are too honest to steal a poor little girl, and I am sure that your love for Lito will make you kind to me.'

'Well for you that you submit; if you had opposed me I think I should have kept you, for I never yield to another. You took it so seriously I wanted to try your mettle. What would you have done had I persisted in stealing the "poor little girl"?'

'Gone overboard; I never yield to injustice if I can help it,' and Rosamond's resolute mouth and flashing eyes proved the truth of her words. Tempest's face betrayed redoubled admiration as he said with his emphatic nod, 'I think you would. Now we will enjoy ourselves and go back by moonlight. No one will be anxious about you at home and you have no neighbors to gossip over our improprieties.'

For an hour Rosamond paced up and down the deck reveling in the breezy motion of the boat, the delicious sense of freedom which possessed her, the atmosphere of romance which surrounded her. Tempest lounged beside her, watching her beautiful face, listening to her happy voice, and enjoying her innocent companionship with the relish of a man eager for novelty and skillful in the art of playing on that delicate instrument, a woman's heart. When she wearied of walking, he placed her in a nest of cushions under the awning, wrapped her in a soft silken cloak (at the appearance of which she wondered much but said nothing) and sitting by her beguiled the twilight by telling the tales girls love, while Lito up aloft sang song after song in his clear, boyish voice. Slowly the moon rose, bathing sea and sky in her magical splendor, and slowly the *Circe* floated homeward along that shining path. The air was balmy, the heavens clear, the ocean beautiful after its wild unrest, and Rosamond felt like one in an enchanted dream as she lay there conscious of an intense desire never to awake but to go floating on forever. All too soon the moonlight voyage ended and the girl reluctantly rose to go back to the dreary life which now seemed doubly dreary.

'Good-bye, Lito; I wish you could stay and be my little friend, for I need one very much,' she said as the boy followed her with wistful eyes.

'Good night, not good-bye, we shall see you soon again I well know,' he answered, kissing her hand in his pretty foreign fashion with a last 'Addio, bella Rosa.'

As her foot touched the shore, Rosamond sighed and cast a lingering look behind.

'Are you tired?' asked Tempest very gently.

'Not tired but sad because I've been so happy and now it is all over.'

He made no reply and they walked a moment in silence, then Rosamond broke out with sudden energy, 'Mr Tempest, you know a good deal of the world and you take a little interest in me perhaps for Grandfather's sake, so I will venture to ask you what I can do to earn my bread in peace and freedom when I can bear this dreadful life no longer?'

'Turn governess and drudge your youth away as most indigent gentlewomen do,' was the brief reply.

'I don't know enough and am too young, I think.'

'Be an actress, that's a free life enough.'

'I've no talent and no money to start with if I had.'

'You can stitch your health and spirits into "bands and gussets and seams" as a needlewoman. How does that suit?'

'Not at all, I hate sewing and know very little about it.'

'Then marry some rich old man who will let you have your own way in everything and die by the time you are tired of it.'

'A rich man wouldn't care for a poor girl like me and I should not like money without love.'

'Bewitch a young man and let him make an idol of you – for a time,' he added under his breath.

'I don't know any,' she said in a tone of artless regret that made the listener smile.

'You might be a companion; I think you'd make a charming one for some people.'

'I like that, and will gladly try it if I can find anyone who wants me. Don't you know of anybody who would have me?'

'I know a dozen people who would take you in a moment, but you wouldn't like them.'

'Why not?'

'Too gay and too free even for you,' and Tempest laughed.

'Don't do that, but tell me what you mean,' said the girl, peering up at his face as she spoke, half impatiently, half pleadingly. 'You look as if you had some plan in your head yet would not tell it. You need not be afraid if it is humble work, I'll do anything to get out of my prison.'

'Anything?' He looked at her keenly.

'Yes, I mean what I say. Now will you tell me your plan?'

'Not yet; I have one, but must prove its practicability before I propose it. Wait a little longer, you impatient bird, and do not try to fly too soon.'

Something in his tone made the girl draw nearer and say confidingly, 'I knew you'd help me, you are so kind and know so much. When I saw you standing in the doorway last night I was glad and welcomed you as the captive ladies used to welcome the brave knights who came to free them. You will try to free me, won't you?'

'I'll think of it. Good night, little Rose.'

They stood in the old porch now; he took her hand as he spoke and bent on her a look that made her heart beat, for the powerful hand pressed hers, the fine eyes were full of pity for her loneliness and the deep voice made her name doubly sweet. The moon shone full upon him, but his hat brim hid the sinister scar and as she glanced shyly at him Rosamond thought this bronzed face the comeliest and kindliest she had ever seen. In her impetuous way she said, warmly, gratefully, 'Thank you very much for this day's pleasure and your promise to help me. I wish I could do something to show how grateful I am, but there will be no time.'

'Why not?' he asked suddenly.

'Because you go so soon; at least you said you must.'

He watched the innocent face an instant, then said almost sternly as if to himself, 'Yes I *must*. *Addio, bella* Rosa,' and bending his head he imitated the boy's act as well as his words.

'Good night, good night!' cried the girl, and lingered till he disappeared, leaving her with a kiss on her hand, a soft name in her ear, a happy memory at her heart and on her lips the eager, longing question, 'Will he go or will he stay?'

CHAPTER III

A Companion

He stayed; not for a day but for a month; and for Rosamond that month was a long holiday. Autumn seemed changed to summer, her dreary life grew full of interest and delight and her future shone before her, for the hero of her girlish fancy had become a living man and she had found her heart at last. As Tempest had said, there were no neighbors to gossip, for there was no other house upon the Island, and no friend ever came to watch over or warn the girl of what she was too ignorant and innocent to know herself.

Many another voyage did the *Circe* take her, and each time she returned with increased reluctance, for soon the yacht seemed more like home than the prison on the cliff. Often the three roamed away into the wood, or spent hours among the caves along the shore. When storms forbade these pleasant wanderings, they sat in the little room beguiling the time with music, books and conversation. Or they strolled about the great, solitary house, filling it with laughter and gay voices, for Lito followed Tempest like a shadow and soon loved Rosamond with boyish devotion. All day they were happy, but when evening came the old man claimed his guest and Tempest seldom denied him, though the girl's eyes silently besought him to remain and Lito openly lamented, for neither of the young ones were admitted and they found the hours very long without 'the Master'.

'What is it that they do? They do not talk I know, for

27

one evening as I passed I could not resist stopping an instant because the room was so still, though they were there. I waited several minutes, but heard not a sound except Mr Tempest's laugh once and an odd chink as of silver or glasses. I *must* find out.' Rosamond said this one evening as she and Lito were waiting for Tempest, who had gone to the mainland for a day as he often did. They were in the drawing room, which the girl had tried to make habitable with a cheery fire in the great chimney place, the few pictures she owned, and some ancient furniture covered with faded damask. The two were walking up and down in the twilight talking confidentially, for the boy had much endeared himself to the girl by his affection and the happiness he found in her society.

'You never will unless you peep and that you are too honorable to do,' said Lito, feeling proud to have her on his arm.

'I shall ask Mr Tempest.'

'He will not answer and he will be angry.'

'I'll make him answer and I should like to see him angry.'

'Ah, you'd not say that if you had ever seen one of his rages. He is terrible then.'

'How does he look?'

'Like that.' The boy pointed to the face of Mephistopheles, which looked singularly menacing as the fitful firelight played over it.

'Yes, I can fancy that, but it won't frighten me and I shall ask him.'

Before the boy could answer the clang of the great door startled them.

'Hark, he is come! I hear his step in the hall. Quick, let us be dancing or he will know that we have been talking of him.'

Catching her round the waist he whirled her away in the waltz he had taught, for he made an excellent little cavalier, being nearly as tall as she and an adept in the graceful pastime. As they circled round the room they saw Tempest enter noiselessly and seat himself on the couch by the fire where he leaned watching them till they paused. Lito, being rather conscience-stricken, affected to be absorbed in settling the loose velvet jacket which was the most picturesque part of his costume, but Rosamond, who knew no fear, went straight to Tempest with her question ready on her tongue.

'You told me to ask for anything I wished, may I now?'

'Well, what is it, little Eve?' He motioned her to take her usual place beside him. She did so looking very gay and lovely with the glow of exercise in her cheeks and a gleam of mischief in her eyes as she said persuasively, 'Lito says you will be angry if I ask, I should rather like that so I'm going to venture. What do you and Grandpapa do every evening when you shut yourselves up and leave us dismally alone?'

Still hovering in the background, Lito watched anxiously to see how this was received, and was much amazed when 'the Master' merely laughed, and answered blandly, 'We have discovered the philosophers' stone and we make gold.'

'I'm not satisfied with that; tell me the truth, Mr Tempest,' she said imperiously, for now she sometimes ruled.

'It is so, I assure you.'

'Then let me come and see you do it.'

'The old gentleman will object to it.'

'Not if you present our petition.'

'Do you think I have such power over him?'

'I know it. Please grant my wish and I'll grant anything you ask of me, if I can.'

'Will you?'

'Yes, try me.'

'Not now, wait till tomorrow.'

'There is the bell, can we go up with you?'

'You can, persistent angel.' He offered her his arm.

'Not without Lito, he wants to see also,' she said.
'Do you, boy?'

'If the Master permits that I go, I am glad to see.'

'Come then, I am in a good humor tonight and disposed to be gracious. I shall not forget your promise, Rose, but hold you to it. Will you gratify your curiosity on these terms?' he asked, pausing.

'Yes. Won't it be pleasant, Lito, to go in and stay with them all the evening instead of moping here alone?'

The boy did not answer, but followed with a troubled, curious face as Tempest led her away to the old man's room.

He was waiting in his easy chair; a shaded lamp burned on a small green-covered table on which lay cards and some pieces of gold. He looked up impatiently, but his face darkened as he saw that Tempest was not alone.

'Why do you bring those children here?' he demanded angrily.

'Because they wanted to come and I had a fancy to gratify them,' was the cool reply.

'I shall not play if they remain.'

'And I shall not play if they go.'

For an instant the two men looked at each other and the children drew back alarmed at the fierce glance of the old man, the scornful sneer of the young one.

'Your play will be the worse for it, but I yield,' said the old man, with a visible effort at meekness.

'You are wise to do so, for it's your last chance to make any play, good or bad. Sit here, Rose, and enjoy yourself if you can.' Tempest drew a chair beside his own and sat down with a defiant air which made his host clench his thin hand and vent on the boy the wrath he dared not vent upon the master. 'Don't skulk behind my chair that you may telegraph the contents of my hand to my opponent, you young villain. Go opposite and play pranks if you dare. Rosamond, come here, I'll have no flirting in my presence. Now, Phillip.'

Rosamond obeyed and the game began. What it was she did not know and dared not ask, but soon was absorbed in it as her quick eye followed the cards and gave her some clue to its mysteries. She felt that the players were both excited, though neither spoke often or betrayed any emotion beyond an impatient gesture now and then. But their eyes were terrible, for there the passion showed itself. In the old man's a rapacious expression glittered when he glanced at the gold which lay between them. In the young man's was a cool, relentless purpose which nothing could thaw out or soften, and in both that concentrated look which only gamblers wear.

Game after game was played and Tempest always won, yet the old man always said sternly, 'Go on, I'll try again, fortune may favor me at last.' They did go on till late into the night and the young pair still sat there fascinated by the baleful spell which held the players, till Tempest threw down his cards with a triumphant smile and the one, emphatic word, 'Mine!'

The old man sat silent with his eyes on the girl who was watching Tempest with evident satisfaction in his success. With an air of relief he said slowly, 'Be it so. I've done my best, but the pupil outwits his master by the very tricks he taught him.'

'You will keep your word?' asked Tempest suddenly.

'Ay, we shall neither of us profit by the bargain and the devil will get his own in time. I have done my part. I leave the rest to you, see that you keep your word regarding the one condition and trouble me no more about it. Take these children away. I'm tired.'

'Very good, here is the paper; I shall settle the rest tomorrow. Come infants, the revel is over.' Tempest went to the door, followed by Rosamond and the boy. But as the handle turned in his grasp the old man's voice arrested them. 'Child, come here.' Rosamond turned to see her grandfather stretching his hand toward her with an expression which amazed her as much as his altered

31

voice. She went to him, he looked up into the blooming face with a troubled glance, drew it down to his and kissed it, saying in a broken tone which changed suddenly to its usual sharpness, 'Good-bye, God bless you, my girl. Go, go!'

Dumb with astonishment she followed Tempest, who broke into a peal of laughter which completed her bewilderment.

'What does it mean? He never did so before. It quite frightens me. Don't laugh but speak,' she said as they reached the drawing room and Tempest's eyes still danced with that uncanny merriment.

'He has lost heavily and that has affected his mind perhaps. Or he is touched with late remorse at his neglect now that he is about to lose you.'

'Lose me! Am I going to die?' cried the girl.

'No, I hope not, but you are going away. I forgot to tell you I'd found a place for you as companion.'

'Have you? Many thanks, but—' there Rosamond's voice failed her for the granted wish was no blessing now, since it took her from him.

'It's a middle-aged person who wants you to sing, read, talk and make yourself agreeable. Salary and the rest of it can be arranged when you meet tomorrow, for I want it to be settled before I go.'

'Are you going!' All the light and color faded out of the girl's face and she clasped her hands together with a gesture of despair.

Still looking indolently at the fire as if quite unconscious of her emotion Tempest went on, 'Yes, we are off at noon. I've stayed too long, but now that you are happily provided for I must get the *Circe* into her winter berth as soon as possible. Shall you miss me, Rose?'

'Yes!' Only a word but there was a heartbreak in it.

'I think you will a little. You'll come down for a last look at the yacht in the morning, won't you?'

'I'll come.'

He rose and strolled away to the picture which hung

32

opposite the long mirror. Looking up at it, a dark smile passed over his face and he said low to himself, with a glance over his shoulder at the girl's drooping figure and pallid face, 'Poor little Margaret, no hope for you when Faust and Mephistopheles are one.' He came back, touched her bent head with a caress, and said kindly, 'I'm going now, you are tired and so is the boy. Come down early and we will talk over everything before I go.'

He pressed her passive hand. Lito, half dead with sleep, whispered a kind 'Good night,' and she was left alone to lie on the desolate little couch all night long, weeping the bitter tears that aged her more than years.

She did go early, looking so wan and weary that her little friend cried out when she appeared, and Tempest needed no confessions to assure him of her love. The anchor was up and only a hawser held the *Circe*, which seemed eager to be gone. All was ready, and as the girl looked her last, traitorous tears dimmed her eyes; Tempest saw them and looked well pleased but offered no consolation.

'Come into the saloon and let me tell you about the place. Time is going and that must be settled.'

Listlessly she followed, too wretched to be curious, and sitting where he placed her listened to his words with eyes that saw nothing but the tall figure pacing to and fro before her, ears that heard only those sad words, 'I am going,' and a heart that ached as only young hearts can.

'This person is going abroad and you are to accompany the party. You will like that,' he said as he walked.

'I'll try to.' She stifled a sob before she could speak.

'Your duties will be very light and you can demand any salary you choose. Odd, isn't it?'

'Rather.' She had hardly heard the question.

'The person is hard to please, but you will suit exactly and I think you will be happy.'

'I hope I may,' and she pressed her hands together in mute despair.

'When can you go?'

'Any moment, after you are gone.' The meek voice broke there and hiding her face in her hands, Rosamond tried in vain to control the passion of grief which overwhelmed her.

'Nay, don't be tragical, my child. You asked me to find a home for you and now you look at me as reproachfully as if I had proposed some hateful scheme.'

'No, no, forgive me, I'll be good and grateful, indeed I will!' And, choking back her sobs, the poor girl tried to smile upon him as he stood beside her with a curiously excited look on his usually impassive face.

'You do not ask where your new home is to be; have you no wish to know?' he asked abruptly, being satisfied.

'Yes, tell me,' but there was no curiosity in her tone.

'It is here.'

All the coldness was gone from his voice, the calmness from his manner as with a sudden gesture he gathered her into his arms and held her fast, saying so tenderly she could not doubt an instant, 'My little Rose, did you think I would leave you? I only waited to be sure you loved me and to win the old man's consent. I know this tender heart is mine and I have bought this little hand by its weight in gold. Look up, my darling, and begin your pleasant work at once, for you are *my* companion now. Will you have Phillip Tempest for your master, sweetheart?'

'I will! I will! Oh what have I ever done to be so happy, so beloved?' and Rosamond forgot her tears, her heartache, her despair and clung there radiant with the bliss which comes but once in a lifetime.

Seating himself, Tempest drew her down beside him and when her first glad excitement was a little calmed, amused himself by answering the questions she poured out, often pausing to caress the lovely head that leaned upon his breast with the confiding abandon of a child.

'What did you mean by saying you had bought my

hand?' She looked at it with a charming air of bewilderment.

He took it in his own, and drawing from his pocket a circlet of diamonds smilingly fettered one slender finger as if to claim the hand, perhaps also to soften the hard truth, for he said slowly as she watched the glittering ring with girlish pleasure, 'Your grandfather, little Rose, was once a skillful gambler, for having spent two fortunes he made another by dice and cards. Riotous living brought ruin and sickness and now in his old age he is helpless and poor. You may never inherit the fortune of your Aunt, a young and healthful woman, and he is tired of waiting. He told me he was just beginning to think of disposing of his one valuable possession, yourself, when I came. I loved you, I wanted you and this saved him time, expense and trouble, for I am rich and thought no price too high for such a companion.'

'Did you play for me?' suddenly asked the girl, with a frown of shame and pain.

'Yes, he would have it so. It began in jest, you see, but the old appetite awoke in him and while I wooed you I amused him with his favorite pastime. I excel him now and he lost heavily; this angered him and when he said he could never pay me for he had staked and lost all he possessed, I answered half in jest, 'Stake Rose and if I win I'll forgive the debt.' He took me in earnest, yet as the game went on he seemed to dread losing you and a strange touch of remorse or cupidity came over him. I played with all my heart and won, forgave the debt and added a gift which will keep him above want if he plays no more. That is the truth, forget it and be happy, dear.'

'Then you bought me?' A shadow fell on the girl's happy face.

'I ransomed you as knights did captive damsels in the romances you love, and now shall you leave the lonely island, the stern wizard and the sad life behind you forever.' So stated the ungracious fact grew bearable, for

35

the master was a lover and the slave an inexperienced, tenderhearted girl.

Rosamond sat silently recalling many things, among them the words she had heard spoken between the two men the night before, and when she spoke it was to ask curiously, 'What was the condition which Grandfather bade you remember?'

'You recollect that, do you? Wait a little, I've some questions to ask you first. The night I came you said to me as we sat talking by the fire, "Everyone has a right to happiness and sooner or later I *will* have it." Are you happy now?'

'Supremely happy.' Her face shone with the intense joy which filled her innocent heart.

'Good; do you remember saying also, that you were willing to pay a high price for it?'

'Yes, and I *am* willing!'

'One more question and then I'll answer you. Another thing you said was this, "Law and custom I know little of, public opinion I despise, shame and fear I defy." Now prove it.'

'I will, what must I do?'

'You will soon see. The condition upon which I was to have you was that I should marry you.'

'Is that so terrible?' Rosamond turned her blushing face to him with eyes full of soft surprise.

'Yes, to me; I hate bonds of any kind; I want you to go with me as my little friend whom I love and who loves me. Pay this price for your happiness and defy public opinion as I do. Will you not, my darling?'

Voice and eyes and tender lips pleaded for him and he thought that she would yield. But the instinct of a maidenly heart rose up to oppose him in spite of love and sorrow. Innocent and ignorant as she was, the books she had read gave her some hints of the existence of sin and her woman's nature warned her when no other voice was near to save. Amazement, terror, shame and grief swept over her face and left it pale but steady as she shrunk away and stood up before him, saying brokenly, 'No, I will not! Let me go home, you do not love me, and I must not stay.'

'You promised to grant me anything—' he began, but she would not listen and, as if fearing her own resolution, she retreated to the door.

'Go then,' he cried, 'go and forget me if you can.'

'I will go, but I never can forget you,' and with one loving, despairing look she fled up the cabin stairs.

'Too late, too late!' called a mocking voice after her, and in a moment she saw that it spoke truly, for with all sail set the *Circe* was flying out to sea, and this time there was no return for Rosamond.

CHAPTER IV

Rose in Bloom

'More than a year since you stole me like a pirate, Phillip. How short the time seems, and how happy!'

'The shortest and the happiest year I've spent since I was a boy. You are a wonderfully accomplished companion, Rose, to keep me contented so long.'

'And you a kind master not to tire of me sooner. You are not tired of me yet are you, Phillip?'

'No, nor ever shall be I think. What the charm is I cannot tell, unless it be that for the first time in my life I really love.'

Few persons looking at his beautiful companion would have failed to see where the charm lay, or have wondered that after many counterfeits real love had come at last. They were together on the terrace of Valrosa. Tempest, cigar in hand, lounged on the wide steps which swept down to the garden, looking up at Rosamond, who leaned on the carved balustrade gazing with delight upon a scene of beauty in which she was unconsciously the fairest and most striking object. A mile away the blue Mediterranean rolled up to meet the curving shore, along which lay the white-walled city with its gilded domes, its feathery palms and lovely villas. Valrosa was the loveliest of all; in truth 'a nest of roses', blooming as luxuriantly through January in that climate of perpetual summer. Roses overhung the archway and thrust their sweet faces through the bars of the great gates, luring all passers-by to stop and long to enter there. Roses fringed the avenue that wound up through orange and lemon groves to the broad terrace that ran round the villa. Roses covered its walls with bloom, draped every cornice, climbed every pillar and ran riot over the balustrade. Every green nook where seats invited one to sit and dream was a mass of flowers; every cool grotto had its white nymph smiling out from a veil of blossoms; every fountain was fringed about with beauty, and nowhere could the eye fall without resting on some fair and fragrant sisterhood.

A fit queen for that nest of roses was the human flower that adorned it, for a year of love and luxury had ripened her youthful beauty into perfect bloom. Graceful by nature, art had little to do for her, and, with a woman's aptitude, she had acquired the polish which society alone can give. Frank and artless as ever, yet less free in speech, less demonstrative in act; full of power and passion, yet still half unconscious of her gifts; beautiful with the beauty that wins the heart as well as satisfies the eye, yet unmarred by vanity or affectation. She now showed fair promise of becoming all that a deep and tender heart, an ardent soul and a gracious nature could make her, once life had tamed and taught her more.

In the stately figure standing on the terrace one would have scarcely recognized the little girl who first met Tempest's eyes. The simple frock was replaced by costly silks that swept rustling about her, the loose curls were gathered up with a golden comb, the slender brown hands were snow white now and shone with rarer jewels than the diamond ring; the scarf that trailed behind her was of the richest cashmere, and the lace which ornamented her whole dress was worth a small fortune in itself. An exquisite taste was shown in her costume, and the careless grace with which she wore it proved how slight a hold the feminine passion for finery had taken upon her. As she leaned there with one hand lying on a cushion of thornless verdure, the other idly gathering cluster after cluster of tiny cream-colored roses, her eyes wandered with unwearied delight over the green wilderness below, and when she spoke a smile of genuine happiness touched her lips.

As he answered her, Tempest had looked up with a glance that took in every charm of expression, tint and outline, and in his face was a warmer, tenderer admiration than any woman had ever seen there before.

'I am so proud to have you say that; to think that I had power to make you risk your liberty, and after a year of wedded life to hear you own that you are happy.'

She stooped and laid a caressing hand on the dark head below her, but Tempest turned away and with a half-laugh replied in the tone of one not quite at ease, 'I risked my liberty because you left me no other choice. You remember I did my best to keep it and win love also, but that failed as I feared it would, and you had your way. I never shall forget how superbly defiant and determined you looked as you stood ready to dash into the sea when you found I had sailed away with you that second time. I know you would have done it had I not promised to atone by a speedy marriage and produced the Reverend at once, marrying you in less than an hour.'

'I should, Phillip, and I think I never could forgive you that insult if you had not proved your better knowledge of me by calling up the minister whom you had prepared in case I was rebellious. Let us forget it; I am your wife now and I want to respect as well as love my husband.'

With a sudden impulse Tempest kissed the soft hand that touched his lips when he would have spoken, and thought bitterly within himself, 'I wish to heaven I had found this girl ten years ago and saved myself from treachery for which I never can atone.'

'Why do you sigh, Phillip? What are you thinking of?' asked Rosamond as he sat with his head on his hand looking down at the golden-green lizards playing on the warm stones below.

'I was thinking what a curious thing love is; only a sentiment, and yet it has power to make fools of men and slaves of women.'

'It never will have power to make a slave of me.' Rosamond lifted her handsome head with the defiant air of some wild, free thing, indignant at the thought of bonds.

'I think it would, Rose. If you love me as you say you do, would you not prove it by doing anything for me, making any sacrifice at my bidding, and defending me against the world if there was need of it?'

'I would do anything that was right, make any sacrifice except of principle, and defend you against anyone who wrongfully accused you.'

'Where did you get your ideas of right and principle and all the rest of it? I never taught you that, nor did the old man. Perhaps it's instinct; women are often kept safe and made wise by that "wonderful thing", as Shakespeare calls it. Suppose I had committed some terrible crime? Would you stand by me? I merely ask to see how far your principle will carry you.'

'Yes, if you repented of it I'd cling to you and bear the disgrace for your sake.'

'Suppose it was a crime of a peculiarly black and damnable nature, the consequences of which would fall upon you, making it wrong for you to cling to me. Would you hate and desert me?'

'No, I would love you and leave you.'

'I doubt it. Take another case. Suppose you discovered that I did not love *you* and wished to be free. How then?'

'I'd try to win your heart back and be faithful to the end, as I promised when I married you.'

'Suppose I broke away and left you, or made it impossible for you to stay. That I was base and false; in every way unworthy of your love, and it was clearly right for you to go, what would you do then?'

'Go away and—'

He interrupted with a triumphant laugh, 'Die as heroines always do, tender slaves as they are.'

'No, live and forget you,' was the unexpected reply.

'Do you think that possible if you still loved me?'

'Everything is possible to a strong will. If it was right to cease loving you, I'd do it if I spent my whole life in the task.' She clenched her hand with a resolute gesture.

'By my soul I think you would! That is why I don't tire of you, Rose, you are submissive to a certain point but beyond that firm as rock. Could I break your will if I tried? I've broken many.' He got up and stood beside her, looking as if he longed to make the attempt. She eyed him intently, but smiled as she shook her head with an air of conscious power.

'You might kill me but not bend me if I had once decided to oppose you. Don't try any more tests, Phillip, for you would fail in spite of past success. They are dangerous for both of us.'

'I'll wait a little and keep that amusement for the time when others lose their charm.'

'You are in a singular mood today. What is amiss?' she asked, leaning on his arm.

'Nothing. I'm only prying into your heart as you pry into the heart of that poor rose. I'm curious but I don't tire of my investigations as soon as you,' and he pointed to the flower, whose petals whitened the stones at her feet. She looked at it a moment, then fixed her eyes on him with a strange expression as a foreboding chill passed over her.

'Promise me one thing, Phillip.' She laid a hand on either shoulder as if to enforce her words.

'Anything, sweetheart, promises are easily made,' he answered, smiling into the lovely, serious face before him, adding within himself – 'and broken.'

'You married me upon an impulse, suddenly and without much thought; perhaps I should say from pity if I did not have daily proofs that you love me. I am young and ignorant; you might easily weary of me and regret your hasty act. But do not deceive me; when you are tired of me tell me frankly and let me go away till you want me again. I never wish to be a burden, never will claim anything, or reproach you for what was a kind though perhaps an unwise act. Promise me this and I shall be happy.'

'I promise.'

'Thanks; now come for a drive, the sea breeze is rising and sunset along the shore is my favorite hour.'

'Mine also, not because of breeze or sunset, but because the Promenade is crowded then and I am proud to show my handsome wife. You know you are acknowledged to be the most beautiful woman at Nice this year?'

'I know one foolish man thinks so. There's a carriage coming up the avenue, we must wait a little. It is Grammont, I think.'

Rosamond paused with one hand over her eyes and looked across the orange orchard toward the lodge gates, which had just admitted a carriage containing two gentlemen. Tempest looked also and after a careless glance strolled down the steps to meet his guests, saying morosely as he went, 'Who the deuce has Grammont got with him? An Englishman, I know by the veil on his hat and the white coat. I told him not to bring any of the stupid, conceited, gossiping fellows here, I hate the whole tribe.'

'Behold me, my Phillipe! I come with news of Ristori,* and I present a friend who yearns to offer his homage to Madame,' cried the young Frenchman, skipping from the carriage the instant it stopped.

The other gentleman leisurely followed, throwing back the gauze veil which the dazzling sun and dust make a necessary part of everyone's walking costume at Nice. Before Grammont could introduce him, Tempest

---

* Adelaide Ristori (1822–1906) was a leading tragedienne of the European stage. One of her greatest roles was Medea, which Louisa May Alcott saw her perform in Nice in April 1866. – Ed.

fell back a step with a startled face and the inhospit-
able greeting, 'Willoughby! What the devil brings you
here?'

'Upon my word, that's a cordial welcome. Why man,
I came to see you for old acquaintance sake and to get a
peep at your charming wife, as Grammont says,' returned
the other good-naturedly.

'I beg pardon, you took me by surprise. Glad to see
you,' and with a face which belied his words Tempest
offered his hand, glancing up as he did so in hopes that
Rosamond had gone in. She had not, but was leaning
over the flowery parapet with the evening glow upon
her beautiful, expectant face. Tempest set his teeth and
the instant Willoughby released his hand after a true
English grasp and shake, he said quickly, 'Step on,
Grammont, and give Madame your news, we'll follow.'

Up pranced the agile Frenchman, hat in hand, and for
ten minutes poured forth news, gossip, compliments and
questions with the charming ease and spirit of his
gallant nation. People always loitered up the wide steps
that led from the drive to the terrace, for the enchanting
spot drew praises from the least enthusiastic and rap-
tures from the appreciative, therefore the delay of the
gentlemen caused no surprise to those who waited for
them. The change in Tempest's face caught Rosamond's
eye the instant he appeared, but there was no time for
questions as he spoke at once.

'Rosamond, this is an old friend from England;
Willoughby, my wife.'

The stranger bowed with a curiously confused air, but
Englishmen are proverbially bashful and awkward among
ladies, so Rosamond thought nothing of it, and
recovering himself in a moment he plunged into a lively
conversation, glancing often at his hostess with admiration and curiosity very visibly expressed in his face.
Grammont dragged Tempest away much against his will
to look at the horses and Willoughby profited by their
absence.

'I had not heard of Tempest for an age till, by the merest chance, I learned that he was here, and came up at once to see him, though I had no idea he was so charmingly situated.' The stout Englishman tried to execute a complimentary French bow with indifferent success.

'You are very kind. Our marriage was so sudden and we sailed so soon that no one knew of it, I believe. Since then we have been moving about the Continent till we came here in the autumn.'

'You will not be able to tear yourself from this little Paradise for a long while, I fancy, if the climate permits you to remain,' said Willoughby after a long pause and an odd look.

'It will not, the heat is intolerable by June. We shall take to the *Circe* in May and sail away again to some new Paradise. Phillip seems to have a gift for finding them.'

'And angels to inhabit them,' added Willoughby with a glance that annoyed Rosamond though she was accustomed to compliments even more direct than this. She did not like the man and chid herself for the causeless dislike, trying to be gracious, yet ill at ease.

'You are from the north of England, I think Tempest mentioned?'

'No, from the east; Hythe was my home.'

'Ah, now I understand; I've heard of the beautiful Miss St John of Hythe but never dreamed that Tempest had won her. He was always a fortunate fellow.'

'Not in this case, for he did not win the beautiful Miss St John; he contented himself with poor Rosamond Vivian. Do you see my pretty little page?' Anxious to turn the conversation, she pointed to Lito, who was watering a tame antelope at the fountain below.

'By Jove! He's the very image of – I beg pardon, yes, a pretty boy indeed. Some protégé of Tempest's, I take it?'

Again Willoughby looked confused and half bewildered, yet quite unable to restrain his curiosity, for after a moment's pause he added, 'How old is the lad, Mrs Tempest?'

'Nearly fourteen, I think.'

'Ah, yes, exactly,' and having indulged in a long meditative stare at the boy he asked another question again with the odd smile.

'Where did Tempest find him, if I may ask?'

'In Greece, when he was there some years ago. He is a faithful little friend of mine and I am very fond of him. You began to say he resembled someone, may I ask whom? I've often tried to think but cannot, and fancy it must be some picture I've seen.'

As she put her question, Willoughby looked up quickly, colored to the roots of his blond hair and seemed much disturbed; but as she spoke of the picture an expression of relief came into his face, and he replied eagerly, 'You are right, it is the *Piping Fawn* you have in your mind. The boy is very like it.'

'But I never saw it,' said Rosamond, with her eyes still on Lito.

'Then it's Ganymede or one of the antique statues. I had a dozen floating in my fancy when I spoke of the likeness.'

'Yes, I daresay it is. I shall find out some day.'

A look of pain and pity made Willoughby's pale eyes almost tender for a moment as he looked at the sweet, placid face beside him. His blunt manner softened, his tone grew respectful, and no more compliments left his lips. Something in the quiet assiduity with which he gathered up her parasol and scarf, took the little basket of embroidery which stood near, and offered her his arm to lead her in when Tempest beckoned, pleased Rosamond, and she began to think the odd Englishman more endurable.

'I am on my way to England. Can I serve you as bearer of dispatches to anyone at home, Mrs Tempest?' said Willoughby, as they sat in the breezy salon while Lito served them with fruit and wine.

'Thanks. Do you ever go to Hythe?' she asked wistfully.

'Often' – which was a friendly falsehood, by the way.

'Perhaps then you would kindly take a letter to my grandfather and post it safely in London. I have written several times but receive no reply and fear he has never got my letters, foreign mails are so irregular.'

'I will do so with pleasure and as soon as possible. It is singular that *all* the letters should be lost.' As he spoke, Willoughby glanced at Tempest, who stood apart apparently intent on something Grammont was saying.

'The cholera still continues in Paris in spite of the season; many deaths a day Dr Montenari tells me, though it is kept as quiet as possible lest the panic spread. I tell Willoughby not to stop there on his way home, he is just the subject for it. I have an ardent friendship for him, but I confide to you that he is a gourmand as well as an invalid and the cholera loves such victims.'

'He does not look ill, what is his malady?' asked Tempest, in the same low tone which the Frenchman used.

'Disease of the heart; it is hereditary he tells me. He is much better for his tour, but sooner or later he must drop away as his father and brothers have done. A sudden shock, a violent illness, or any intense excitement would kill him he tells me, so he resigns himself to indolence, grows stout, and supports his affliction with heroism.'

'Sensible fellow. How long does he stay, Grammont?'

'Only a day or two, which gives me no time to do the honors, for my wife is as yet too feeble to permit long absences on my part. Can you give him a day? He is anxious to see the lions but, pardon that I say it, like most Englishmen very slow to make friends when among strangers and so finds it dull.'

'I'll give him a day tomorrow; where is he staying?' said Tempest, with unexpected cordiality.

47

'At the Hotel des Anglais. Too noisy and fashionable for him, he says. He may decide to remain long, can you recommend a good, quiet hotel? You are an *habitué* and should know the best?'

'The Hotel de Ponchette is a plain, comfortable house and near the old town, which to me is far more interesting than the new.'

'Ah, but not so airy and healthful. The drains are abominable, and in the autumn, when cholera was here, seven persons died in that hotel, they say.'

'All gossip, my dear Grammont, and if it was not I could match your story with one of the Hotel de Lanure where you are; a dozen died there and the house was shut up for a time. These things are kept quiet because it is for the interest of the people to draw crowds here during the winter, which is their harvest time. Dr Montenari could tell you of cases now, almost daily down in the city and the hospital. Say nothing about it, but take care of yourself and keep out of the sun, it is unusually hot this year. Heat, ice, fruit and fatigue I warn you against.'

'I will remember; my poor Adèle would fly at once if she knew it, and the air is doing wonders for her so I shall be on my guard. Come, Willoughby, we must tear ourselves away if we would get back in time for dinner. I have good news for you: this amiable Tempest desires to devote a day to you and will show you in that time more than I could in a week, for he knows every nook and charming sight like a professional guide.'

The Englishman looked surprised but grateful, and with thanks and compliments the guests departed. Their host accompanied them to the carriage and as they drove away Willoughby said maliciously, with a glance at Lito, 'He is very like Ganymede, as I told your wife when she asked me who he reminded her of. By the way, who was the father of Ganymede, Tempest? My mythology is defective.'

48

'I'll look up the story and tell you tomorrow,' answered Tempest, with a look which caused Grammont to hasten their departure by a touch of the whip.

'I like that Englishman after all, he is so friendly,' said Rosamond as Tempest joined her.

'Very friendly,' he answered, adding under his breath an emphatic, 'Damn him!'

CHAPTER V

Cholera

The next morning when Rosamond was in the garden with her pets, Tempest went up to his dressing room and, closing the door with unusual care, opened a large, silver-mounted box which always stood in his room on shore, his stateroom when at sea. It was a medicine chest, and, selecting one of the little bottles, he poured a few drops of its contents into a glass of water and mixed it carefully, saying, as he swallowed the draught, 'Here's to your health, Willoughby.'

Pulling out a drawer in the box, he examined several small packets, reading the labels and directions on each with care. One he opened, and taking a pinch or two of the fine, aromatic powder which it contained he sprinkled it in his hair and among his clothes, smiling a wicked smile as he did so. Replacing bottle and packet he relocked the box, prepared himself for the day's expedition and went to bid Rosamond good-bye.

'I may not be back till late, do not wait up for me, Rose. You look forlorn; silly child, don't you know that it is well to part occasionally that we may have the pleasure of meeting and so not weary of one another? No, Lito, you are not to go with me today, I want Baptiste. Madame will need you when she drives; adieu.'

Baptiste was Tempest's own man; he passed for a Frenchman but was an Algerian by birth, a slender, swarthy, fiery-eyed young man who looked as much out of place in the sober livery of a servant as an Arab of the desert would have done. For some reason he served his master with the blind fidelity and unquestioning obedience of a dog, though cold, reticent and haughty to everyone else. None of the servants liked him, Rosamond had an unconquerable prejudice against him and Lito hated him intensely. With this man sitting in the little seat behind him motionless as a statue, Tempest drove away to give Willoughby his day of pleasure.

'You are late, I was ready at the appointed time and have been waiting half an hour,' was the punctual Englishman's first remark as Tempest drew up at the door of the Hotel des Anglais, which was all alive with the swarm of titled English who always haunt its splendid rooms.

'A thousand pardons. I stopped to book myself up a little so that we might economize time. We will take Villa Franca first, before it gets hot, because the glare from the sea, the sand and the rocks is blinding by noon. One of our vessels is wintering there and Captain Upshur, whom I met just now, begs we will go aboard and lunch; which is not an invitation to be refused if you care for capital wine and good company,' said Tempest.

Much mollified by the prospect Willoughby settled his overcoat, linen sun umbrella, blue veil and green glasses to his satisfaction and away they went. Tempest was in charming spirits, the day fine, the carriage luxuriously easy and the drive indescribably beautiful, so that by the time they reached the picturesque little town on the hillside with its dusky olive orchards, its red-trousered troops about the fortress, and the ships riding at anchor in the bay, Willoughby was in an enthusiastic state of delight and ready for anything.

The company was good, the wine excellent, the lunch all that an epicure could desire, and the young officers were never tired of pressing upon Willoughby the iced claret and orange salad of which he partook so copiously that there was a general shout of merriment when he at last refused more on the plea that he was an invalid. It was well past noon when they got ashore, and the sun blazed down on sandy road, glittering sea and granite boulders with dazzling brilliancy.

'Let us go home and rest till it is cooler,' panted Willoughby behind his veil and goggles.

'Not yet, I'll take you to a charmingly cool place where you can rest and amuse yourself the while with some really wonderful Roman relics. It is close by and in a moment we shall turn into a shady road away from all this glare,' said Tempest, unconscious of heat or fatigue.

'Where are they?' asked Willoughby, interested at once, for relics were his delight.

'At Cimiez; there's a fine old Franciscan monastery there with some good pictures in the chapel, antique curiosities in the crypts and the ruins of a Roman amphitheater nearby. It's the pet lion of Nice and you will enjoy it. I've been so often the monks know and welcome me, for a franc or two wins their hearts. Isn't this delicious?' and Tempest took off his hat as they whirled round a corner into a shadowy green road overhung by ilex and olive trees.

'It's a very imprudent thing to do, but I must follow your tempting example,' and off came the other hat as Willoughby resigned himself to the grateful coolness of the spot.

Driving slowly, they began to wind up a steep path between flax fields and orange orchards, with villas on either side and glimpses of the gray monastery far above. A sudden exclamation from Baptiste interrupted an interesting conversation and caused his master to pull up. The man sprung down, examined a wheel and with much gesticulation explained that an overturn would inevitably follow unless the damage was repaired, which might easily be done by applying to the smith nearby among the beeches yonder.

'Confound the wheel! Come, Willoughby, let us stroll leisurely on while it is set to rights instead of stopping here to be stared at,' said Tempest impatiently, as a flock of black-eyed peasants began to collect with flowers and fruit to sell and petitions for money and offers of assistance. Willoughby assented and walked on, glad to escape the staring and the beggars. Tempest joined him after giving Baptiste directions to follow, adding in English which none of the bystanders understood, for Willoughby was out of hearing, 'Leave the coat and don't hurry.'

Resuming the conversation, Tempest made it so absorbing that his friend forgot warmth and weariness and walked on faster and farther than he had dared to do for a long while. Failing breath and a warning pain in his side recalled the fact, and he insisted upon stopping for the carriage. It came before he had time to rest or cool and in a few moments they reached the monastery.

'Do the vaults first before other visitors arrive to interfere,' advised Tempest, and wiping the drops from his forehead, Willoughby descended into the deathly damp and chilly crypts where no sun had shone for centuries. Unconscious of his danger and absorbed in the rare and curious relics, he pored over them for an hour to the great wonderment of the monk, his guide. Tempest soon tired of them and went up to get the chapel and cemetery opened ready for his guest. Blue and shivering, Willoughby appeared at length and with a hasty examination of the pictures went out to bask in the sunshine, which shone warm and bright over the cemetery.

'Will Monsieur permit that I advise him to put on his overcoat if he has one here, and not sit still in the sun, it is dangerous after a chill,' said the meek monk, observing that Monsieur still shivered and looked pale.

With thanks for the warning Willoughby sent for his coat, rejoicing that he had brought it. But Baptiste returned with a despairing countenance to report that it had been left at the smithy, and calling himself a beast and a villain offered to fly and bring it to Monsieur.

'The mischief is done, I think, so we'll waste no time in complaining or "flying" anywhere. We will go, Tempest, and find the coat on the way. We'll leave the amphitheater for another day,' said Willoughby good-naturedly, and with a generous fee to the monk they rolled rapidly down the winding road up which the cool sea breeze was blowing as the tide came in. The coat was found and put on and as warmth returned hunger began to hint that it was dinner time.

'I'm going to take you to an excellent hotel and give you a dinner in honor of the day. Grammont says you may decide to stay and don't like Hotel des Anglais, so this will serve as a trial of Hotel de Ponchette,' said Tempest, and after driving through the dirtiest, narrowest and most squalid part of the city he came out upon a gay little square where stood the hotel, overlooking the sea.

'Wait an instant and I will see if we can dine here in private.' Tempest went in, procured a room, inspected it, dropped the curtains over the back windows (that opened on a courtyard where kitchens, stables, fish houses and all manner of accumulated filth produced an atmosphere such as can only be found in an Italian* city), set several pastilles alight to banish the noisome odors that haunted it and ordered a charming dinner to be served near the front windows, before which a glorious prospect of sea and sky was spread. Then Willoughby was invited up to make a hearty meal on every delicacy which could be procured, no matter how unfit for an invalid. When he hesitated, Tempest ridiculed his prudence unmercifully and by raillery or example overcame his self-restraint. Wine flowed freely and when they rose from table the chill was replaced by fever and the poor gentleman was fitter for his bed than for the moonlight excursion Tempest proposed.

* Although we tend to think of Nice (Nizza in Italian) as a French city, it was at this time owned by Sardinia, which claimed it after the fall of Napoleon in 1814. It was not restored to France until after 1860. – Ed.

'Now a quiet drive to Castle Hill for the view and to cool our heads, and then we will go home to supper.'

'I am desperately tired, Tempest; your energetic style of sightseeing is rather too much for me. However, as my time is short I'll make the most of it and leave as little as possible to less agreeable guides,' and, quite unconscious that the evening air was particularly dangerous to invalids, Willoughby allowed Tempest to drive him away along the shore.

The view was glorious and they lingered long, but even when they descended they did not reach home without one more adventure which completed poor Willoughby's destruction. Coming to the Cathedral, they found it all alight and astir as if some festival was afoot.

'What is it, Magnico?' asked Tempest of a peasant whom he recognized in the crowd as they paused to let a train of nuns pass in.

'A funeral, Monsieur. Prince Passati died suddenly on his way from Rome and desired to be buried in Nizza, his native city. It is superb; Monsieur should enter.'

Tempest turned to ask Willoughby if he cared for it and saw before he spoke that the news had shocked him.

'I knew the Prince in Rome, he was my best friend. I will go in, not for the spectacle but as a mark of respect to his memory,' he said briefly, with such honest grief in his face that Magnico pulled off his hat and Baptiste helped him out with unusual respect.

The church was packed and with the greatest difficulty they forced and bribed their way to a spot whence they could see the high altar and the glittering group before it. The dead man lay on a bier of flowers, his weeping family knelt around him, nuns and monks with lighted candles formed a barrier between them and the throng; priests went to and fro with holy water, fragrant censers and pious prayers; the great organ pealed solemnly and behind the golden screen a choir of voices chanted the Miserere for the dead. The heat was suffocating, the pressure of the crowd oppressive, the lamentations heartbreaking and the atmosphere indescribably horrible. Women fainted as they knelt and were passed out over the heads of the throng, men grew pale, and the most inquisitive stranger was soon satisfied. Even Tempest, hardy as he was, felt his temples begin to throb and his breath come heavily after half an hour of it. Willoughby forgot discomfort in grief for a time, but sudden dizziness roused him to the fact that he was half suffocated.

'Tempest, I must get out of this as quick as possible. I ought not to have come. For heaven's sake get me out!' he whispered anxiously as a fresh arrival of peasants caused a general movement toward the altar.

'I'm afraid it is impossible. Here's a poor girl quite gone and she'd be crushed underfoot but for my arm. Hold fast to me, I'll do my best,' answered Tempest. He did do his best, for leaving the girl to her fate he struggled toward the door, drawing his companion after him. But before he reached it, with a stifled cry of pain and a feeble clutch at his shoulder Willoughby fell against him quite unconscious. A look of grim satisfaction passed over Tempest's face as he caught him with one arm and fought his way out with the other. Fresh air and water from the fountain dashing in the Square soon restored Willoughby enough to whisper faintly, 'Take me home,' and home they took him with all speed.

'My dear fellow, I never shall forgive myself for letting you get into that pestilential place. How are you now? Can I do anything for you?' and Tempest bent over the exhausted man as he lay on his bed with an expression of solicitude that touched the other. Offering him his clammy hand, Willoughby said gratefully, 'Nothing, thank you, I shall send my man for a doctor if I'm not better after an hour of quiet. You must be very tired, go and rest. You've done enough for me today.'

'Don't say that, I'll gladly stay if I can be of use,' said Tempest quickly as he laid the pale hand down.

'I need nothing but quiet. Go to your Rose, and Phillip, be kind to her; she is so young, so trusting; for your mother's sake be gentle with the poor girl.'

The momentary softness vanished from Tempest's face and the sinister expression returned. Taking up his hat, he said in a friendly tone but with averted eyes, 'No fear of that. I love her as I never loved a woman before. Now good night, Robert, sleep well and let me find you quite yourself in the morning. Don't call in any of the Italian doctors if you can get on without; they all bleed their patients half to death and you can't bear that, so I warn you.'

'Many thanks, good night. Tell Madame I'll not forget her message when I go to Hythe.'

'No, I think you will not,' muttered Tempest as he left the room.

Having driven home, he bathed, changed every article of dress and went down to find Rosamond waiting for him in spite of his advice to the contrary.

'What now, my little bookworm?' he asked, as he threw himself down on the couch near the table where she sat reading and lit the cigar always laid ready for him.

She looked up with an excited, troubled face and pushing the book away said, with a sigh of relief as if the magic of some evil spell was broken by his presence, *The Wandering Jew*. It's a horrible book. Why do you have it in the house, Phillip?'

'It is a favorite of mine. I like horrible books if they have power. I thought you'd get hold of that and I left it about as a test of your taste.'

'It fascinates me but I don't like it. Do you think there ever was or could be so thoroughly wicked a man as

57

Rodin?' asked the girl, so interested in the book that she forgot to inquire about the day's adventures.

'Yes, I've no doubt of it. He was simply a man without a conscience. Do you know, Rose, I sometimes think I have none.'

'What a dreadful thing to say. What do you mean?'

'I mean that it is more natural for me to be wicked than virtuous; when I do a bad act, and I've done many, I never feel either shame, remorse or fear. I sometimes wish it was not necessary as I don't like the trouble, but as for any moral sense of principle, I haven't a particle. Many people are like me as their actions prove, but they are not so frank in owning it and insist on keeping up the humbug of virtue. You'll find that is true, Rose, when you know the world better.'

'I hope not; but why do you say such things, Phillip? You know I don't believe nor understand them.'

'Bless your innocent heart. I never thought you did. Now and then I like to say boldly what others dare hardly think. You do know that I'm not a saint, don't you?'

'Yes, I cannot help that, for you are constantly telling me you are not,' and Rosamond sighed as if some burden of regret oppressed her.

'Yet you love the sinner and—'

'But not the sin,' she added quickly.

'Of course not, that will follow in time. I'm a bad fellow, my dear, and I give up the hope of ever being any better. Since I have had the nearest approach to an angel that humanity can produce for a companion I have cherished a foolish fancy that I might develop a conscience as well as a heart; but today I discover that I am worse than ever, and the crowning sin is that I'm not sorry for it.'

'What have you done?' asked Rosamond, with the serious yet puzzled expression she always wore when he was in this mood.

'Nothing but devote myself to my friend, yet all the

way home I've been telling myself that I'm a villain and it makes no impression upon me as you see.' It certainly did not seem to, for he lay there smiling tranquilly as he watched the fragrant smoke curl upward, apparently with no regret of any kind to mar his luxurious repose.

'Perhaps remorse will come all at once when least expected, for atonement surely must be made here or hereafter,' said Rosamond with softly warning voice.

'I doubt that. When children inherit the sins of their fathers it is not just that they should make the atonement. My father was a wild, wicked, handsome man, Dare-Devil Tempest they called him. Fortunate, happy and lawless all his life. A lovely woman adored him till he broke her heart and when her pride could bear no more she killed herself. I remember her and I hated my father most heartily. He disowned me and I roamed about the world a homeless lad till your grandfather met and took a fancy to me. My mother's fortune was mine so I never lacked the power to purchase pleasure and I got on capitally. My father died peacefully yet unrepentantly in his bed, cordially detested by everyone who knew him, and left me nothing but his evil nature. I simply live out my real self and I don't think I shall be called upon to atone for my sins, as they are his. I never told you that story before; now you will understand your husband better, Mrs Tempest, and see how hopeless his redemption is.'

'No, everything is possible with God. I do not give you up. I pity you, and love can work miracles, so I shall still hope and work.' Her face was like the face of an angel as she laid a soft hand on that scarred forehead, as if in spite of everything she claimed him for her own in the firm faith that love would save him.

'If it is a human possibility you will do it, my Rose. But you do not know what I am, and there may come a time when you will cease to hope,' he answered, looking at her with strange wistfulness, for no man is utterly without a desire for virtue.

At noon next day Tempest went to inquire for Willoughby, and met Dr Montenari standing at the door of the chamber with an anxious face and a vinaigrette at his nostrils.

'How is he?' asked Tempest abruptly.

'Gone, sir, gone. Don't go in, it's cholera!' returned the doctor in a shrill whisper, drawing the newcomer away and sniffing nervously at his salts as he spoke.

'When? How? Did he leave no message? Good God, how sudden!' and drawing the doctor into an empty anteroom, Tempest dropped into a seat like one overcome with the shock.

'Calm yourself, my dear sir. I did my best for him, but I was not called till midnight and then it was too late. I don't say I could have saved him; the state of his heart complicated the case, but I *might* have kept him. He spoke of you, and of your wife and some commission which he had failed to execute. He briefly directed his man regarding his affairs, and after hours of mortal suffering became mercifully unconscious and so died an hour ago. This sad occurrence is to be kept as quiet as possible out of regard for the fears of the many invalids now in the house. Heart disease may truly be said to have caused his death, for he spoke of the shock he received at hearing of the Prince's demise. He will be removed at once and his man leaves for home tomorrow. I may depend on your silence, Mr Tempest?'

'You may, Doctor; I shall never speak of it.' Nor did he.

CHAPTER VI

A Hidden Grave

At five o'clock in the afternoon all the fashionable world at Nice may be seen on the Promenade des Anglais, so called because laid out and kept in repair by contributions from the English. It is a wide walk bordered by palms, roses, and tropical shrubs, with seats all along, bathing pavilions on the beach which it overlooks and a fine drive between the walk and the hotels and villas standing on the outer curve of the bay along whose edge the Promenade extends.

Every nation is represented, every language spoken, every costume worn, and of a sunny day the spectacle is as brilliant as any Carnival. Haughty English, gay French people, plain phlegmatic Germans, handsome Spaniards, uncouth Russians, meek Jews, free-and-easy Americans, all drive, sit or saunter chatting over the news and criticizing the latest celebrity, be it the wicked old king of Bavaria, the dusky queen of the Sandwich Islands or Princess Dagmar mourning for her lost Czarovitch. The equipages are as varied as the company, and attract as much attention, especially the low basket barouches in which ladies drive themselves, with a groom or page in the little seat behind, a pair of dashing ponies, a parasol, whip and a net to keep their voluminous flounces from overflowing the diminutive vehicles.

Many of these carriages were rolling to and fro one afternoon, some two or three weeks after poor

Willoughby's death, and one among them seemed to attract much attention. Lined with blue silk as daintily as a lady's workbasket, with a pretty lad in Greek costume on the perch behind, drawn by snow-white ponies in silver-plated harness with blue favors on their spirited little heads, and driven by a beautiful woman whose dress of blue velvet and ermine completed the charming effect, it was no wonder that many eyes followed it and more than one party of gentlemen paused to examine and admire.

Among the crowd was a small, dark, sharp-eyed man who watched the pretty turnout with unwearied attention. Twice it went up and down the mile-long drive and his eye never left it. At the third turn it drew up before one of the villas and handing the reins to the boy, the lady entered the house as if to pay a call. Instantly the stranger's lounging gait changed to a quick pace, his listless manner became alert, and crossing the drive he approached the carriage. With a quick glance about him he stooped as if to replace the white net which trailed in the dust and at the same moment thrust a letter into the boy's hand, saying authoritatively, 'Hide it, read it in private and tomorrow give your answer to Camille, the flower girl of the Jardin Publique.'

'But, Monsieur—' began the boy in amazement.

'Hush, I know you, Ippolito; do as I say and you will thank me. Hide it, and bring an answer tomorrow,' said the stranger and was gone.

Lito glanced at the letter, saw London on the postmark and was so intensely curious to learn who his unknown correspondent was that he would have read it on the spot if Rosamond had not appeared. Slipping it into the pocket of his vest, he leaped down to help her in and all the way home sat behind her in a fever of impatience. The instant they reached Valrosa he vanished and was seen no more that night.

Whatever the contents of his letter were they seemed to affect him strongly, for next morning he appeared with heavy eyes, pale cheeks and an absorbed air which caused the French maids to accuse him of being in love. He scarcely seemed to hear their badinage, though usually quick to resent such accusations. The few light duties given him were either forgotten or half done, and he showed no interest in anything till the hour for his mistress's daily drive approached. Then he seemed to wake up and become all devotion. The carriage was brought round fifteen minutes too soon and having hurried Rosamond into it by suggesting that they would be too late to hear the new band in the Garden, he begged to drive and did so at a dashing pace till they came to the Jardin Publique, where the band filled the air with fine music while the brilliant crowd sat about under the trees, or lounged in the carriages drawn up along the sidewalk.

'Madame will not descend?'

'No, Lito. I will wait here for the Master, he agreed to meet me at the gates.'

'Will Madame permit that I go a little nearer to see the famous band of the Crimea? I am gone but a moment.'

'Go, child, and stay as long as you will. We are too early for Phillip.'

Away sprung Lito and vanished in the crowd. Leaning back in her basket Rosamond's eye idly followed the little scarlet fez as she listened and saw it pause an instant outside the great circle which surrounded the band, then disappear in an acacia grove near the fountain, which was deserted now. Wondering why he went to that solitary spot she watched for his return, musing meantime on the curious mood in which he had been all day.

A fresh breeze was blowing up from the sea, rustling the palms and tossing the drooping acacia boughs. As Rosamond mused, her eyes still fixed on the entrance of the green nook, the trees were suddenly blown apart and standing in the shadow were Lito and Camille, the pretty flower girl. An involuntary smile came to Rosamond's lips and she looked away at once, unwilling to play the spy on the unconscious little lovers, if such they were. The boughs fell again and Lito appeared just as Tempest joined his wife. With a shy, self-conscious look the boy resumed his place and said not a word during the drive, though usually he chatted with the freedom of a favorite. Master and mistress chanced to be absorbed in their own conversation and neither observed his taciturnity. But after dinner, as they sat together on the terrace, Tempest observed that something was amiss, for when Lito brought the amber-mouthed Turkish pipe his eye did not meet his master's and he seemed in haste to be gone again, most unusual demonstrations from the petted lad.

'Why, Lito, what is amiss? Come and tell your master,' said Tempest detaining him with a hand on his shoulder.

'Nothing, nothing,' the boy answered hastily as he shrunk a little and still kept his eyes averted.

'Was Camille unkind?' asked Rosamond, smiling.

Lito looked up quickly, turned scarlet and demanded, 'Did you see her? How? When?'

'The wind betrayed you when you held her hand in the acacia grove. Never look so frightened, child, no one will reprimand you for doing what every one is doing all about you,' she said kindly as he looked dismayed.

'Flirting, Lito? Upon my life you begin early. So she frowns upon you does she; and you are driven to despair, which accounts for the melancholy to which Baptiste tells me you are a prey.' Tempest laughed aloud at the boy's confusion.

'Baptiste is a spy and a liar!' he burst out hotly.

'Tut, my little gallant, curb your tongue or we shall fancy that you are jealous of Baptiste. Is that the thorn that lacerates you, hey?' and still laughing, Tempest gave the boy a playful shake.

As if angered past endurance by the rough caress, Lito jerked himself away and as he did so from the pocket of his jacket fell a paper. He made a snatch at it but Tempest's quick eye had caught something that roused his suspicion, and as the paper fell near him he put his foot on it. Flinging himself upon his knees, Lito desperately struggled to recover his lost treasure; but the foot was firm as rock and his attempts were vain.

'Let me have it! It is mine, you have no right to keep it. I will have it! Make him give it up, Madame, oh help me! Help me!' he cried despairingly as he clung about Tempest's knees, breathless and imploring.

'Dear, do not vex the poor child. It is only some silly note from Camille. Let me give it back, Phillip.'

'Camille does not use foreign postmarks for a love letter which she delivers herself. Leave me to manage the little rascal; there is mischief afoot and I must sift it to the bottom. Get up, boy, and stop whining.' So stern and ireful was Tempest's manner that Rosamond dared say no more, but Lito still clung and fought and prayed to regain the paper. Lifting and holding him off with one hand Tempest secured the letter and coolly read it over the boy's head.

Rosamond had once wished to see him in a passion, her desire was granted now, for as he read Tempest's dark face grew absolutely livid with that terrible pale wrath so much more appalling than the sudden flash which comes and goes. His black eyes grew fiery, the scar became purple with the hot blood that rose to his forehead and faded, leaving his face very white except that dark line above the fierce eyes. A ruthless smile came to his lips and his hand gripped the boy as if he would crush him. When he spoke his voice was cold and calm, but there was an undertone of suppressed passion which made the hearers tremble.

'So! This is your new amusement is it? Well for me that I discovered it in time to put an end to such dangerous play. How dare you receive and answer letters without my knowledge, you young traitor?'

Pale and trembling but undaunted in spirit, Lito

looked straight at him and answered steadily, 'I had a right to know what that letter tells me. I'm glad I do, and though you kill me for it I'll not say I'm sorry.'

'I could find it in my heart to kill you, you audacious imp,' muttered Tempest between his teeth.

'But you dare not because I am—'

'Stop!' cried Tempest in a tone that rung through the garden startling the timid antelope and causing the tame doves to circle wildly round their heads.

'Rose, go in, I must deal with the boy alone. No, I'll have no intercession, no delay. Go at once and ask no questions, I'm not in a mood to be trifled with.'

In truth he was not, and Rosamond hurried in to hide herself lest she should see or hear the poor lad's punishment. Not a sound reached her, and when at length she ventured to lift her head from the cushions of the couch and steal a look at the terrace it was empty. For two long hours she sat alone and no one approached her but Baptiste, who came to get ink and paper. From his impenetrable face she could learn nothing, and when she ventured to ask where Tempest was the brief but respectful answer was far from satisfactory.

'In his room, Madame.'

'And Lito, where is he?' she asked anxiously.

'Madame must pardon me that I do not answer, for I obey the orders of Monsieur,' and with a regretful air he departed, leaving her to watch and wait.

Tempest came at last, looking pale and grim; the storm was over but its effects remained. Rosamond was standing at the window looking out onto the moonlight scene; as he entered she turned, longing to speak yet fearing to rouse his wrath again. He paused an instant, regarding her with a strange expression in which love, regret and resolve mingled, then came and drew her to him with an impulsive tenderness that touched and surprised her very much, for something in the look and act seemed to suggest that he had feared to lose her and yet defied fate to separate them.

'Have you discovered the mystery and forgiven the poor boy?' she asked, thinking the moment an auspicious one. Instantly his black brows lowered and he answered with an ominous smile.

'I never shall forgive him. Leave him to his fate, Rose, and thank heaven that the mystery was discovered in time. Now talk no more of it or him, both are forbidden subjects henceforth between us.'

'But, Phillip, why?'

'Because I choose it.'

'I must know one thing, where is Lito?'

'Safely out of the way.'

'Gone!'

'Exactly.'

'But he will come home again in time?'

'No.'

'Shall I never see him any more?' cried Rosamond, aghast at this sudden separation.

'Never.'

'Oh, Phillip, this is cruel, this is too hard! He is so young, so loving, so accustomed to indulgence and freedom. If you have shut him up in any gloomy place or given him into the keeping of any stern master it will break his heart and ruin him for life. Forgive him for my sake and let him come home.'

'I never pardon treachery. It is impossible for him to return. Plead no more, Rose.'

'Will he be happy? Has he any clothes or money with him? You should have let me say good-bye,' and tears flowed for poor lost Lito as she spoke.

'He has gone where he needs nothing. He sent you his farewell and this.' Tempest offered her a short gold curl as he spoke, but something in his sinister tone made her shudder as she took it and glided from his arms with a sad sinking of the heart at the thought of never seeing her little page again. Her tears, her silence, annoyed Tempest, and in a tone he had never used to her before he said emphatically, 'Rose, remember one thing. I am master here, my will is law, and disobedience I punish without mercy. I tell you the boy is safe and happy, more than that you cannot know. I forbid questions to myself or anyone else, so dismiss the matter from your mind and forget that such a creature as Lito ever existed.'

'I shall remember,' was Rosamond's quiet reply, but her eyes flashed and her heart rebelled against the tyrannical decree. She would ask no questions but she would watch, listen and if possible discover where the boy had gone, for it was not in her nature to submit tamely to any injustice toward herself or others. Baptiste was absent all the following day, and the next time she saw him she fancied she detected a gleam of satisfaction in his stealthy eyes, for Lito was no favorite of his because he was jealous of anyone whom Tempest admitted to his confidence or for whom he showed any affection. Baptiste evidently expected to be questioned and relished the prospect of baffling curiosity by mysterious replies. But Rosamond uttered not a word and the man seemed amazed and annoyed.

Taking advantage of an hour when Baptiste was away and Tempest engaged with a friend, Rosamond stole to the boy's room, hoping to discover something there. It remained exactly as he left it. His colorful garments hung in the wardrobe, his little purse lay untouched in his drawer, nothing was gone but a rude miniature of herself which he had painted, and his ivory crucifix. As she looked a cold thrill passed over her and Tempest's words returned with a new significance – 'He has gone where he will need nothing.' Could he be dead? Had his master killed him in a fit of passion and sent Baptiste away to hide the poor little body? No, that was too horrible, and she drove the thought away from her again and again but it would return with painful pertinacity.

Two days after the boy's disappearance her dark fear was augmented by a few words which she overheard.

68

Baptiste brought a letter to his master as he sat alone in the salon and as Rosamond was about to enter noiselessly she heard the man say, with a shrug and a glance toward a wooded dell a mile or more away, 'Rest tranquil, Master, no one will think of his being buried there.'

Unseen the girl stepped back, hurried to the garden and tried to quiet herself before it was necessary to face her husband, whose quick eye instantly detected any change in those about him. Who could Baptiste mean but Lito? Was he buried in the olive grove? And were all the assurances of his being well and happy only falsehoods? At first she trembled and grew pale, then her eyes kindled, her color rose indignantly and she clenched her white hand with a gesture of determination as she said within herself, 'I'll satisfy myself of this, and if it be so, much as I love Phillip he shall atone for it, to me at least.'

With one like Rosamond, to resolve was to do, but time and stratagem were necessary, for Baptiste seemed suddenly to turn sentinel. Another boy came to fill Lito's place, but his mistress, though kind, never took any interest in the sleek brown Italian lad. Another groom rode after Tempest, and Baptiste always remained at home when his master was absent. Hour after hour he sat on a sunny bench in a retired corner of the terrace which overlooked the drive, and no carriage entered the gates that he did not scrutinize its occupants and in the most natural, unobtrusive manner discover their names and business before they reached Madame. At night Rosamond saw him still there, and however early she went down in the morning he was already at his post. At first she did not mind this, but the instant she desired to escape unobserved she became conscious that she was watched. Not only did Baptiste hover about her, but Tempest grew more devoted than ever, for of late a little coldness had existed between them. He drove, walked, sat, sang and read to her as in the days of their honeymoon, and but for the black thought hidden in her heart she would have been very happy.

She never had been blind to the fact that Tempest was no saint, but like many another woman she hoped to save him through her love, and as time showed her more and more clearly the nature of the man, she tried to forget his sins to others and remember only his generosity, his tenderness to her. Lately he had been less kind, less just and generous, and it became impossible to forget. Many things had troubled and perplexed her since she married him, but the loss of the boy alarmed and roused her, and once in the field Rosamond was not a woman to be deceived or defeated by any adversary. One or two trials proved to her that she was no longer free to go and come as she liked, and her quick wit soon suggested a means of escape. All day she was watched. Night therefore was her only time, and though she shrunk a little at the thought of stealing away through dusky groves and lonely paths on such an errand, the intense longing to set her fear at rest drove her on.

'Are you ill or worried about anything, Phillip?' she asked anxiously one morning as they sat together.

'No, love, why do you ask?' and in spite of the tender words the tone was sharp.

'Because you are so restless at night and moan and mutter in your sleep. Forgive me, I forgot that I was not to ask questions.' She meekly went on with her breakfast.

'Do I? that's odd. What do I say, Rose? A sleeper's nonsense is sometimes amusing,' said Tempest, veiling keen anxiety under a careless air.

'You will be annoyed if I tell you, for it is a forbidden subject.'

'You mean the boy? Did I speak of him? You may tell me.' He fixed his piercing eye upon her.

'It was not much, only you sighed and seemed unable to sleep without dreaming of him. Once you called him and that waked me; then you said sternly, as if going through the sad scene of his last day, "Get up, boy, and stop whining," and after a time you groaned and cried out, "Bring him back, Baptiste, bring him back!" and added in a dreadful tone, "Is it too late?"'

'What melodramatic rubbish! Poor Rose, did I frighten you? I was tired and various things vexed me yesterday. If I disturb you, I can sleep in the red room on the ground floor. I've often thought it would be well to slip in there when I come home late. Let it be made ready today, for I've got more exasperating business to attend to and you shall have a quiet night, poor child.'

Very frank and easy was his manner and he laughed over the 'melodramatic rubbish', but Rosamond saw anxiety under the smile and the proposed change proved that he had something to conceal. It was what she had planned and desired however, so she yielded and the red room was prepared. That night she dared not go, for Baptiste was at home; on the following his master sent him to the city with letters for the midnight mail and bade him stay till morning.

'Now is my time,' thought Rosamond, and having exerted herself to be particularly charming all evening, she finished by singing Tempest into a drowsy state and sent him away to bed declaring that he should dream of nothing but angels chanting Scotch melodies. Till midnight she remained quiet, then, anxious to profit by the moon, she nerved herself to the task and like a shadow crept through the silent house, glided along the dusky paths and struck away toward the distant olive grove. The peace, the dewy softness, and the mellow moonlight made the night too beautiful for fear, and on any other errand Rosamond would have enjoyed the midnight walk, which reminded her of former pranks in the old house on the cliff. Nothing was stirring but the bats, no sound broke the hush but a late nightingale mourning musically from the rosy coverts of Valrosa, and the girl safely reached the grove through which a long disused and half-effaced path wound its way to the hills beyond.

71

Shadowy and still was the place as with a beating heart she passed through it, looking keenly about her. A sudden sound of footsteps made her start and spring away into the thick undergrowth, there to crouch like a hunted deer. As the steps passed she peeped out to see only a stray lamb trotting homeward. With a sigh of relief she rose to her knees and was about to seat herself for an instant on a low mound behind her when, as the moon shone full through the swaying branches, she saw with a cry of terror that the mound was like a new-made grave!

CHAPTER VII

A Woman's Shadow

For a moment horror held Rosamond motionless, then with the cool, desperate calmness of a strong purpose she recovered herself and drawing back a step examined the spot. Her eye measured the length of the mound, scanned the roughly cut sods that covered it, the broken branches heaped over it but disarranged by her hasty feet, and everything assured her that it *was* a grave. But whose? That she could not tell, for no woman, unless goaded to despair by some strong passion, could find nerve enough to disturb the earth that hid the dead from her sight.

Ghostly pale and cold as ice, she left the spot intent on reaching home unseen, but as she stepped again into the path a few paces before her the moonlight shone on some bright object in the trampled grass. Scarcely conscious of the act, she stooped and took it up, gave one look and fled out of the grove as if some phantom had confronted her. It was only a little ornament of gold filigree, but it proved her fear to be an awful truth, for this ornament her own hands had fastened on Lito's fez and it was too peculiar to be any other than that very one; of this she would have been sure without the shred of red velvet to which her stitches still held it fast.

How she reached home and spent that night she never knew; her maid found her in a high fever when she went to her after waiting vainly for a summons next morning. 'It is only a cold; I sat on the terrace too late. Rest and quiet will restore me. Tell Mr Tempest to excuse me from breakfast and let me sleep if I can.'

Justine went away and soon after Tempest stole in, full of anxiety. But Rosamond seemed asleep, for when he softly called her she did not answer and lay motionless with her face averted and half hidden in the mass of brown curls which had broken from the little cap and fell over white arm and flushed cheek. Leaving a note and nosegay of her favorite roses on her pillow, he drove away and became so absorbed in 'the exasperating business' (which, by the by, was billiards) that he did not return till sunset.

'Are you better, sweetheart?' he asked tenderly as he hurried to meet Rosamond, who, with a lace shawl wrapped about her head and shoulders, lay languidly reading in a hammock slung under the ilex trees.

'Thank you, yes,' was the quiet answer as she received his kiss without returning it.

'That is well, for I have a treat in store for you. Ristori is here, I have secured a box and if you are able we will go this evening.'

'To the theater!' exclaimed Rosamond, to whom the idea of pleasure seemed impossible. A second thought made her add, with a sense of relief at the prospect of escaping an evening alone with her husband, 'You are very kind to remember my wish. I am able and glad to go. Let us dine at once, so take me out, Phillip.'

Well pleased at the eagerness of which he little knew the cause, Tempest was unusually devoted and gay as if anxious to efface from her mind all disagreeable recollections. When they reached the theater Rosamond was annoyed to find their box the most conspicuous in the house, for she felt in no mood to be stared at, and having but little vanity she had long ago wearied of public admiration. She shrank behind the curtains, feeling as if the many glasses leveled at her must inevitably discover the secret fear that weighed upon her like a sense of guilt.

The pertinacious gaze of one gentleman particularly annoyed her, for his lorgnette remained up long after the play began. He was a small, dark, keen-eyed man who, in spite of his ease, looked as if he was rather out of his element. Now and then he leaned back and appeared to speak to someone concealed behind the red curtains of the box. Glimpses of a white arm and shoulder betrayed that his companion was a lady, and several times the glitter of a glass was seen at the inner corner of the curtain, as if another pair of eyes watched as well as his own. Being nervous and excited, Rosamond felt troubled by this strange scrutiny and found it difficult to forget it in her delight and admiration at Ristori's splendid rendering of *Medea*.

Tempest was leaning forward, apparently intent on the stage, when Rosamond, who was covertly studying his face, saw it suddenly turn deathly pale as he started violently and let his double-barreled glass fall with a crash. Her eyes followed his and saw the outline of a woman's figure just vanishing behind the curtain of the opposite box, where sat the imperturbable little man who now appeared absorbed in the play.

'Deuce take the glass! It's quite spoilt. Lend me yours, Rose,' and taking it hastily Tempest looked long at their inquisitive neighbors.

'Do you know that man, Phillip? He seems to take a great interest in us, for he has been staring ever since we came.'

'Never saw him before in my life. There's a lady with him, have you seen her?'

'Only her arm and a very handsome one it is. She keeps herself hidden from *me*. You saw her, I think?'

'A mere glimpse; she's not pretty, that accounts for her concealing her plain face and showing her fine arms. I daresay he is some bear of a Russian prince, they are all perfect savages as far as good breeding is concerned.'

'He looks like a Frenchman, small, subtle and sharp.

The Russians are all big, stupid and boorish like that immense Baron Lakvrefzki nodding yonder.'

'Perhaps he is, but no Frenchman would stare in that rude way unless he had some strong reason for forgetting his manners. Thank you, we mustn't talk, this is the finest scene and our whispering annoys others.'

Tempest gave back the glass and drawing his chair a little behind Rosamond's seemed to forget the man and see only *Medea*. The door of the box stood open for coolness, a brilliant jet of gas burned in the lobby nearby, and happening to turn her head to ask Tempest the meaning of an Italian phrase which puzzled her, Rosamond saw, clearly defined against the open door, the shadow of a woman. It was leaning forward as if the person tried to peep unseen, for the instant Rosamond spoke it vanished.

'Someone was watching us, I saw the shadow,' she said quickly in English. Before the words were fully uttered Tempest sprang up and was gone, closing and locking the door behind him. Obeying a sudden impulse, she looked over at the opposite box, it was empty and a curious feeling of disquiet took possession of her. Tempest's long absence did not lessen this, for the tragedy ended and the house was nearly cleared before he returned, looking like a man who had passed through an exciting scene since he left her. His face was flushed, his eyes shone irefully, his breath was quickened and his laugh forced as he said, while hurrying Rosamond's burnous about her, 'It was that absurd young Thoma. The boy is in love with you and thinks you an iceberg like most English women because you don't see the necessity of having a lover as well as a husband.'

'Did he come in masquerade costume? The shadow wore an opera cloak and had long curls,' said Rosamond with a very incredulous expression.

'He wore his own cloak and has curls, you know. A shadow would distort and magnify any object and you might be easily deceived. I told him there must be no

76

more of this nonsense and sent him home,' answered Tempest, looking her full in the face with his frankest air.

'Did it take you all this while to do that?'

'No, I went to find the carriage, for that Nicolo is a born blockhead and it is never ready. There is terrible confusion about carriages here and I had a long search before I found mine. Here it is. Home, Nicolo.'

Nothing more was said, Rosamond asked no questions but had her own suspicions. Tempest jested about young Thoma but looked horribly anxious next day, and Baptiste was on guard with redoubled vigilance. After dinner Tempest looked up suddenly from some newly arrived letters with the abrupt question, 'Rose, I am tired of Nice, are you ready for another cruise?'

'Yes.'

'Good! We will be off the day after tomorrow. Tell no one but Justine; let her get your personal effects ready, Baptiste will attend to everything else.'

'Yes.'

'We will go to Sicily for a month or two, would you like that?'

'Yes.'

The lack of interest, the spiritless docility of the three meek affirmatives struck Tempest and caused him to say with an anxious glance at her pale face, 'You need change, my darling; we have been too gay this winter and it is quite time that we went away to some quieter spot where we can forget the frivolities of this giddy place.'

'I never can forget Valrosa.' Tears filled Rosamond's eyes as she recalled the happy days spent here before her trouble began.

'You foolish child, we shall come again next winter and find everything unchanged. Where are you going, Rose?' he asked, as she went toward the long window opening on the terrace, where the glow of sunset still faintly lingered.

'To wander about the garden, Phillip. If I am to leave so soon I must enjoy my flowers while I can.'

'Shall I go with you?'

'No, thank you, I shall only roam about a little and you are busy. I'll not go out of sight of Baptiste if you fear I shall get lost.'

'Go where you like and come back my cheerful, happy-tempered girl if you can. You are not like yourself lately; but I'm used to feminine caprices and never break my heart about them.'

With that he returned to his writing and Rosamond went down into the garden wondering what he meant by calling out to Baptiste as she left the room.

'Is Nicolo at the gate?'

'Yes, Master.'

'And Giuseppe in the garden?'

'No, Master.'

'Tell him to go then.'

'I will, Master.'

'Once at sea and there will be an end of this surveillance, for there he can watch me himself, and there will be no dark secret for me to discover,' thought Rosamond, and wandering from one green nook to another she came at last to the grotto – a rocky little cavern where a spring gushed up crystal clear and icy cold from the mossy basin scooped for it. The roof was green with climbing vines and the walls covered with feathery lady-ferns. Having gathered a handful, she stooped to drink at the fairy pool, but as she raised her head again the rosy shell which served for a cup fell from her hand, for tall and dark along the sandy floor lay the shadow of a woman. One instant she stood motionless, the next she sprang out into the path and looked about her. Nothing was visible, and as she glanced behind her no shadow but her own fell on the grotto floor.

A second and a keener inspection showed her an object which proved that some foot beside hers had lately passed that way. When she came she had seen one of the gay scarlet anemones which spring up everywhere nodding in the middle of the path and had turned aside to spare it; now it lay bent and bruised by a hasty step, for as she looked it slowly lifted itself as if but newly pressed.

'Julie! Lucille!' called Rosamond, thinking it might have been one of the maids who had made a trysting place of the grotto and whom her presence had frightened away. No answer came, but the rustle of leaves at some distance caught her ear. With a rapid step she followed, peering into the fragrant gloom of the orange grove on either side; yet all in vain, for nothing human rewarded her search except the boy Giuseppe, whom she found lounging on the grass at the entrance to the only path that led to the grotto.

'Did you see Justine in the garden?' asked Rosamond, feeling sure the lad must have met the intruder whoever she was if she entered that way.

'No, Madame, I have seen no one but Mademoiselle Bahette, who comes to play with me,' and he showed his white teeth as he smilingly caressed the little antelope who nibbled the grass beside him.

'You are sure no one has passed, Giuseppe?'

'No one, Madame may believe me. There is no way but this to the spring and the maids never go at night; they fear it, a ghost walks there they say. Perhaps Madame saw the ghost?' The boy's black eyes dilated with such genuine curiosity and alarm that Rosamond could not doubt him.

'What is the ghost like?' she asked.

'A tall pale lady, all in black with a veil about her head, and she walks here weeping by the spring where she was found dead many years ago. They say her tears keep the basin full and fresh and that whoever drinks of the water will soon have cause to weep.'

'God forbid!' ejaculated Rosamond, remembering her own cool draught. 'I think I saw the ghost, but it is a happy one – I saw it last night also at the theater. Say nothing, Giuseppe, or they will laugh at us. I shall go in now; put Bahette to bed and go soon yourself.'

'What is the story of the ghost of the grotto, Phillip?' she asked as she entered the salon and began arranging her ferns and flowers in a marble urn upon the writing table at which he still sat.

He looked up and laughed. 'I send you away to recover your spirits and you come back with a dismal face demanding a ghost story. How did you know there was one?'

'Giuseppe told me. Please relate it.'

'He firmly believes in it. I don't, nevertheless here is the legend. Once upon a time a young Italian built this house for his lady-love, and here she reigned a queen till one day she unfortunately discovered that he was false to her. So, in the summary style of those days, she stabbed him in the dark, and cursed Valrosa with a dreadful curse, prophesying that henceforth no woman should make it her home without finding before she left it that the bright waters were bitter, the roses full of thorns and love all a tragical delusion. Then she very sensibly broke her heart, and very foolishly continues to go weeping and wailing about the place for her false lover.'

'I hope she will find him,' was Rosamond's sole reply.

The next day was a busy one, but by night all was ready for their departure next morning, and weary with her preparations Rosamond went early to her bed, leaving Tempest to give the last orders to such of the servants as remained. How long she slept she did not know, but woke suddenly with a vague consciousness that some noise in the red room below had startled her. Listening she heard no sound, and was about to drop asleep again when a chilly gust from the open window blew over her and she rose to shut it. A strong light from the lower room streamed out across the flowery lawn and a murmur of voices caught her ear.

'What can Phillip be doing so late?' she thought, and

stepped out upon the little balcony before her window, meaning to speak. Her hearing was remarkably acute and as she bent over the low railing with his name upon her lips she became conscious that one of the voices was a woman's. With strange vividness the legend flashed into her memory, the mysterious shadow that haunted them, and the new anxiety which had beset her husband of late. Never pausing to think of danger, she knelt down, thrust her head and shoulders through the widely parted bars of the balustrade and steadying herself with both hands leaned far over, intent upon seeing or hearing something of this nocturnal visitor. Well for her that her hold was a firm one, else she would have fallen with the start she gave when her eye fell on the window, for there, distinctly outlined on the white inner blind, was a woman's shadow.

CHAPTER VIII

Into the Night

A moment she leaned so, all eye and ear, then with an almost fierce expression she sprung back into her room, hurried on her clothes, noiselessly opened her door and crept to the stairhead. There she paused with an inward exclamation of despair, for Baptiste sat tranquilly reading in the hall below. Gliding to her chamber, she stood racking her brain to discover some private means of descent. That was the only staircase she could reach, for the servant's wing was shut off from the main house, which was long and low with many rooms on the ground floor. Once more she went to the balcony and looked down. It was not high, and could she have taken the leap without noise she would have dared it; that was impossible and she groped about the room for something by which she could lower herself.

In her search her foot struck against a long, strong, leather strap brought in to fasten about one of the trunks which stood ready for the journey. Snatching it up she carefully buckled one end about the railing of the balcony, muttering sternly to herself as she did so, 'My wild feats as a girl stand me in good stead now.' When the strap was firm, she swung herself down with the agile skill she had acquired long ago, and pausing till a gust blew up the valley she took advantage of the general rustling of foliage to creep under the rose trees that grew thick and tall close about the house. Crouching there she listened with every sense alert; but though the window was ajar and the conversation in English, which none of the servants but Baptiste understood, so low and rapid were the voices that she often lost a sentence and could have cried out in her desperate suspense but for the fear of losing everything.

'Since you have been mad enough to come here in spite of all my warnings and promises, you must answer my questions before I answer yours. How did you know I had come back,' said Tempest's voice savagely.

'Willoughby told me,' replied the woman in a clear firm tone.

'Willoughby! The man is dead.'

'I know it, but the very evening he first saw you he wrote to me telling me where and with whom you were.'

'Curse his precipitation! Had I known that I might have spared myself and him. When I heard he was dead I said, "Fortune favors me as usual," and never dreamed the mischief was already done. Well, he'll meddle no more, that is a consolation. So you came on at once?'

'Yes, Dovenant promised to inform and secure the boy unsuspected, but I so longed to see my Lito I came also and remained concealed while Dovenant worked. He did give Lito my letter and I got his answer, then you discovered the plot and spirited away the boy. Phillip, I *must* have him. It is my right and I claim it.'

'No court of law will grant it to you, nor will I. Might makes right with me and you shall never have him, never! I swear it and I'll keep the oath.'

'Oh, be merciful! Think what I have suffered, how patiently I have waited, how long I have clung to the hope that in time I might have the child for a little while. Even when I wrote I did not blame or betray you, though you say he knew you were his father. He felt or guessed it, I never told him.'

'You told him enough to separate you forever. He is as much lost to you as if he were in his grave.'

A sudden cry broke from the woman as if in his face as well as in his somber voice she saw some ominous hint of loss or danger. 'Is he dead, that you look and speak in that horrible way? Have you killed the boy in one of your savage moods? If so I'll have justice, though I hunt you through the world.'

'He is not dead, better for him if he were, I speak the solemn truth, Marion, you may believe me.'

'I will believe nothing, there is no truth in you. Where is the boy? Tell me that and prove it or I will rouse the city till he is found.'

Here a sudden gust drowned both voices and when it passed the answer had been given. Whatever it was the mother seemed appeased by it, for the time at least.

'I know the place, dark and dreary but better for him to be there than here with you.'

'Let that pass, I'm tired of the everlasting rehearsal of my sins, I know them well enough and need no catalogue. What will you have next?'

'I might say my own rights and justice for myself, but I gave up all hope of that long ago; I do claim it for this poor girl. From the lips of strangers I learn that she passes for your wife; is that true?'

'Yes, why not?'

'And she consents to the lie?'

'She thinks it a truth. There was no other way; the old man knew nothing of you and made me promise to marry Rose. I knew it was impossible and tried to win her without, but she was firm and to satisfy her I prepared a convenient friend to play the parson on board the yacht. She knew nothing of such matters, trusted me blindly, and has been as happy as an angel till you came to mar our Paradise.'

'Poor child, poor lost unhappy girl! Man may forgive you for this, Phillip. God never will, and the punishment will come dark and dire when least you look for it. Has she no suspicion of the truth? Does she still believe and trust?'

'She begins to frown a little at times, but that only makes her lovelier, and she still trusts me or she would not be glad and ready to fly away again tomorrow. We need not go now as you leave, for the danger of your meeting her was what I have been guarding against. Why did you show yourself at the theater where there might have been English people who know us both?'

'I wished to see you and this girl. I found her so young, so lovely, and in her face such innocence that I could not resist the longing to say one word of warning in her ear. You thwarted me, but I'll say it yet; she shall be saved if I work a miracle to do it.'

'The same defiant spirit, the same indomitable will and bitter tongue. Time does not soften your hatred, Marion; nor lessen my aversion to the chain you make me wear. Is there no desire on your part to break it and let me do poor Rose the only justice in my power?'

'Would you marry her if I freed you?'

'I think I would.'

'Then you must truly love her, or is it but a ruse?'

'I do love her as I never thought to love any mortal creature, believe it or not as you please.'

'Will you give up the boy forever if I consent to the divorce?'

'No.'

'Then I will not give up the only hold I have upon him. The law gives me the power to keep *you*, I will until you yield the child to my sole care. The poor girl may be saved for a better fate than that of your wife.'

'As you please, so long as I love her and she is happy I care nothing for law or gospel, and defy your power to win for you the one thing you want of me. It is late, Dovenant will be tired of waiting and as your errand is accomplished will you allow me to see you to your carriage, Mrs Tempest?'

'Give me something of the boy's before I go; any trifle that my darling used. Is there no picture of him as he looks now? I've only the baby face. Oh, Phillip, do you remember how many bitter years have passed since I saw my son?'

85

'Yes, yes; don't cry and make a scene for God's sake. Here take this, I always wear it but it's sentimental folly and I'm willing to be rid of it. Now come, I've told you where I've sent him, be satisfied and give me another long holiday if you wish for any peace yourself.'

Here the voices ceased and soft steps passed through the guarded hall, down the stone steps and away into the garden, but Rosamond did not hear them. White and cold and still she lay among the broken roses, the saddest wreck of all. No one saw her in the moonless night, no one dreamed of the presence of the very person against whom all precautions had been taken, and fortunately for her Baptiste was too weary with many nights of watching to go his rounds again, so nothing was discovered.

When the chilly wind and falling dew at length aroused her, the first thought that came into her bewildered mind was escape. Not another day or hour would she remain, no help was possible, no atonement could retrieve the past, no love or pity, pardon or excuse should soften the sharp pang of reparation for the guilty man. To go instantly and forever was her only thought, and this gave her strength to rise and look about her. It seemed an age since the last words fell upon her ear, yet it could not have been many minutes, for the door still stood open, the lights still burned, and from the garden came the sound of steps and voices. Baptiste had gone to meet his master and they were returning together. The hall was empty and like a shadow she darted through it, up the stairs safely to her room before they reached the terrace.

Locking the door, she dropped into a seat and clasping her hands over her throbbing temples she compelled herself to think. Not of the terrible affliction which had befallen her, the blight upon her life, or the death of confidence and love; these sharp griefs would come later and years would not end their pain; now she must think how to act, and her strong will ruled the weak body, the

86

broken heart royally. Soon her plan was made; a glance at her watch by the faint gleam of a match showed her the hour; half-past twelve; at one the mail train to Paris passed through Nice that must take her away if she could reach it in time.

The house was dark and still now, all abed and asleep, and her brief preparations were so noiselessly made that they would not have disturbed a wakeful ear. Choosing the plain black silk in which she meant to travel on the morrow, she added a dark cloak, pulled the delicate flowers from a black lace bonnet and put on a thick veil. One change of linen and a few relics of the happy past she put in her small traveling bag; the purse in her pocket was always well supplied and the rings on her fingers would keep her long from want. When all was ready she had but fifteen minutes, and wasting no time in lamentation or farewells she dropped again from the balcony and hurried away to the station by a little path which led through the vineyard and lessened the distance materially.

She reached the station in time, bought her ticket and was about to step out of the bright *salle d'attente* lest someone should recognize her, when young Thoma came rushing in with a lady all in black and closely veiled. He did not see Rosamond and she glided out, hoping to secure a carriage to herself. Two trains came thundering in, one for Genoa, one for Paris. She had forgotten the southern train and had there been time would have changed her plan, thinking Rome or Naples a safer refuge than Paris. It was too late now and stepping into an empty carriage she hid herself in the darkest corner, alone with her misery.

Could she have known that Mrs Tempest and her friend occupied the coupé next her it would have added another sting to her suffering. She was mercifully spared that knowledge and so, almost side by side, these two heavy-hearted women were borne away into the night.

CHAPTER IX

The Chase Begins

High up in the sixth story of one of the tall old houses in the Rue Napoléon at her attic window sat a woman sewing. Not a *grisette*, for the bare, neat room showed none of the ruling tastes of that industrious but coquettish sisterhood. No birdcage, no pot of flowers at the window, no bit of cheap muslin festooned with pink cambric rosettes over the tiny mirror, no gay picture of some favorite actor or lover opposite the crucifix at the bed's head, or any glimpse of Sunday finery on chair or table. A glance at the woman would have settled that point at once, for, though beautiful, the face was pale and worn, the mouth almost stern in its lines, the eyes absent and mournful, the whole figure suggestive of one burdened with a heavy sorrow against which she struggled bravely.

It was a dull November day, 'the month of suicides' as they call it in Paris, and if ever sad, solitary women, worn out with ill-paid labor or driven to desperation by want or sin or wrong were to choose a day for ending hopeless lives that would have been a fitting one. Bleak, cold and foggy, there were frequent showers that made the street a sea of mud and those who walked there forlorn objects. Nothing was visible from that high window but a leaden sky and a row of squalid houses opposite, but as her eye turned from her work Rosamond saw only the sunny gardens of Valrosa or the blue waves of the sea beating round her tower on the cliff.

Nearly nine months had passed since she fled away and faced the world alone. On that dreadful night as she went on and on to meet her fate she had done her best to be prepared for it as far as possible. In Paris was a kind old woman who had taken her fancy on a former visit and whom she had served by procuring her work, thereby earning her gratitude. Mother Pujal, as her neighbors called her was a lace-mender; a cheery, busy, honest, little woman and to her Rosamond resolved to go, for to none of the delightful friends of an hour would she confide her downfall.

The old woman had welcomed her, given her a refuge, and as time went on without any alarm, she ventured out. Being unwilling to spend her little all in idleness, Rose took up her needle, thinking sadly of the time when she had rejected 'bands and gussets and seams' as unbearable. Now she earned her bread by them, and when the first shock of her double loss had been lessened by absence, time and labor, she fell into a dull, cold mood, and like a beautiful machine sat at her work day after day with no hope, no fear, no care for anything.

Yes, one wish she did cherish, to know where Tempest was. Why he had not followed and found her was a mystery, for he was not a man to submit tamely to any loss, however well deserved, without a struggle first. Was he dead, did he still search vainly, or had he forgotten her? These questions she brooded over daily and lay awake long, tearful nights endeavoring to answer, for in her heart yet lingered love for the hero of her early dreams, not for the man who had deceived and wronged her. Back to him she would never go, but in her lonely life still lived the sweet memory of that happy time when she believed in him and he was all in all to her.

As the last stitch was finished she folded her work, put on a gray cloak and bonnet with the thick veil without which she never stirred abroad, and with a little basket on her arm went out into the dreary street. It was dark when she returned, and wearily groping her way up the long unlighted stairs she unlocked her door, entered and groped for a match. Turning with a candle dimly burning in her hand she uttered a loud cry and rushed to the door, for there seated in her one chair was Phillip Tempest.

'At last, at last, my little truant, I have found you!' he said, rising with a laugh of triumph and a welcoming gesture as he advanced to meet her.

'It is fast, Baptiste is without, so be quiet for escape is impossible, and if you raise the house I'll swear you are mad and carry you away by force. Be wise, my little Rose, and tell me why you so cruelly deserted me. Come, I will listen patiently, and we may find some foolish trifle is to blame for this wearisome separation.'

He was right, the door would not yield to her desperate hands and finding flight vain she composed her startled nerves by remembering that he had no power over her now. This thought steadied her and gave her courage to confront him with indignant eyes but unfaltering voice.

'The "trifle" which separates us forever is your wife.'

Contempt embittered the brief answer and a defiant look warned him back. He paused with a black frown, though still his eye rested exultingly upon her and he wore the air of a master who has recovered a runaway slave.

'Ah, my suspicion was correct then, you heard us when that cursed woman came to Valrosa that last night?'

'Yes, thank God, I did!'

'And you believed her?'

'Every word.'

'But if I tell you it was false, and prove it?'

'I should echo her speech, "I'll believe nothing, for truth is not in you." Your own lips convicted you, my own senses are to be trusted, and that night's work cannot be undone.'

'It shall be! I'll not have worked so long in vain. Rose, sooner or later you must come back to me.'

'Never alive.'

'Bah! Let us avoid heroics and talk rationally. Sit here, sweetheart, and give me a kinder welcome than this.' He spoke in a softened tone and gently taking the candle from her he placed it on the table, drew up the chair and motioned her to come and take it with unfeigned tenderness in voice and eyes. But she never stirred; with one hand on the door, the other half hidden under her cloak as if some weapon were concealed there, she stood erect, and fixing her steady eyes full upon him she said in a tone of calm determination, 'Do not touch me or I will end this interview sooner than you wish.'

'Fire or stab as soon as you choose. I'm bullet- and dagger-proof or I should have been dead long ago,' he answered with a scornful smile.

'*You* are safe, I had no thought of killing *you*,' she began with a smile as scornful as his own.

'Yourself? Did you not once affirm that suicide was cowardly?' he asked, with secret anxiety at her threat.

'I did, but there are times when it is braver and better to die than to live. This is one of them.'

'Upon my soul, you are complimentary! Why, most unreasonable and hardhearted of charming women, I have gone far and wide for many months searching for you and when at last I find the desire of my eyes you turn upon me like a tiger. It is very becoming but meekness is better. Don't be thorny, little Rose, it will avail nothing, for love must conquer in the end.'

'Leave sentiment; I'm sick of it as I know its worth. How did you find me?' The contempt of her glance, the stern command of her voice stung his pride and for a moment subdued him, for he had never seen her thus and the new charm arrested him.

'I'll tell you. Pardon me if I sit while you stand but I

91

have been ill and your five flights of stairs rather exhausted me.' That hint of illness touched her as he knew it would; her eye scanned his thin face anxiously and grew pitiful, for marks of wasting disease were there. Seeing that this stroke succeeded where violence failed, Tempest assumed a quiet, serious air and simply told his story.

'When I found you gone, Rose, I was in despair. The balcony explained the manner of your flight and I at once bethought me of the night trains. Which way you had gone was the mystery. Two clues were found and unfortunately I took the wrong one. I learned that my wife, as I must call that woman, and her fellow conspirator had gone toward Paris together; also that young Thoma had joined a tall, veiled lady at the station and gone toward Rome, I could not think you would join Marion; woman's pride would forbid that. I did think you might have gone with that infatuated boy. But in order to explain this you must have made some plot beforehand, as there was no time to find him after you left Valrosa. How was it?'

'You thought I was false as well as yourself? A natural conclusion for a man like Phillip Tempest.'

'Say what you will, Rose, I'll hear it, for the joy of seeing you again outweighs the pain of your hard words and cruel accusations.'

'Finish, if you please,' was her only reply to the plaintive speech and the reproachful look which accompanied it. He bit his lip and went on with an inward resolve that she should expiate her present defiance by redoubled devotion hereafter.

'I knew that all women were fickle, false and easily won by youth, money and sweet promises. You had been cold and shy of late; unlike yourself, too obedient and meek to be quite natural, and when I spoke of Thoma you always turned the conversation. These things I recalled after you were gone and fancied that you had heard nothing but had hurried your flight because of my proposed departure. I followed, growing surer as I went on that it was you, for everyone confirmed the story of the enamoured youth, the lovely woman, and the evident fear both evinced of being overtaken. Some rumor of pursuit had reached them and they fled before me till I had I chased them all over the Continent. Ah, that pleases you, revengeful girl! You enjoy the thought of my fruitless fatigue, my bitter disappointment.'

'I do; it was a just punishment, though too light for your offense.'

'Thank you, amiable love. Do you know, I think I like this new tone of yours; it's stimulating, and as a change really charming now I am accustomed to it. Thoma it seems had run away with a pretty English girl by way of consoling himself for your coldness. He thought I was her father pursuing them until we met, when I gave him my blessing and advised them to go to Egypt. I had sent Baptiste to Paris when I went toward Rome and he soon reported that Marion (I won't use the offensive word, we both hate it) had returned to England. It seemed as if fate was against me, for all trace of you was lost, precious time wasted, and to complete my despair I fell ill with a fever which would have finished me but for my faithful Baptiste. Don't you love him for that?' he asked with a sneer.

'I love truth and fidelity in anyone. How did you find me at last?'

'By the merest accident. When I was able to travel I went to Hythe, thinking you were there. But the old man knew nothing of you and after a stormy tête-à-tête I returned to Paris feeling sure you must be here. Most men would have employed a detective, but I dislike them for they make inconvenient mistakes sometimes and bring to light things that are better forgotten. Baptiste was my spy and would have ferreted you out as surely as a hound had he not seen you in the street and recognized you in spite of the veil. Tonight when you went out we came in, and now nothing remains but for you to forget and forgive and come away with me to enjoy the gay, free life you love.'

'Dare you ask me? Yes, you dare anything! My only answer is, if my grave stood open on one side and you upon the other I'd go into my grave before I would take one step to meet you. Now leave me; you have no right to stay, no power to force me away, and alive I will not go.'

She expected a burst of wrath or some violent demonstration, but Tempest was too wise for that; he knew her too well, and looking at her with the one genuine passion of his life eloquently expressed in his fine eyes, he said in the tender tone few could resist, 'Do you no longer love me?'

She would have given worlds to have been able to answer 'No,' but she could not; he saw her hesitation and knew that her heart was traitor to her will. Feeling sure that she would yield if he did not press her too strongly, he concealed the satisfaction this betrayal gave him and without waiting for her reply said gently, 'You do, and in that fact is my hope. I have no right I know, for I have deceived you; I will atone by lifelong devotion but I cannot give you up. It is too late to undo the past, it is wiser to forget it and be happy. The fault was not yours, so why should you destroy your peace and mine by trying to atone for it in this stern way?'

'The sin is yours, but the shame and sorrow are mine; the past I cannot retrieve, the future is still unspoiled and I will not embitter it by any willful sin. Before I was innocently guilty, now I should be doubly guilty if I went back to the "gay free life I love". Atone for the wrong you have done me by ceasing to tempt and trouble me. I will not yield, though you hunt me to death.'

'Nor will I, Rose. If I were free, would you be my wife?' he spoke with sudden purpose and watched the effect of his words with covert anxiety. An instant and indignant refusal rose to Rosamond's lips, but a second thought checked it and made her say coldly, 'You cannot do it unless you give up the boy.'

'I *have* given him up.' An angry flash of sharp pain passed over Tempest's face.

'When and how?'

'I'll tell you nothing but that the boy is dead.'

She asked for no proof of this assertion but dropped her traitorous eyes and concealed the detestation that filled her heart, for necessity taught her dissimulation.

'Then you deceived your wife when you refused to exchange your son for your liberty?'

He shrunk and put up his hand. 'Yes, yes; let it go, it worries me! It was no fault of mine, they exceeded my orders; it cannot be helped now. Marion will free me willingly, since the boy is gone, and then I will marry you, Rose, I swear it.'

'Give me till morning to think of this; it is too sudden. I must have time. Go, Phillip, I'll answer you tomorrow.'

'You promise me, and you'll not do anything tragical meanwhile? Escape will be impossible, for I shall engage the room below lest you try your old plan, and Baptiste will guard the door. We have a plausible tale for the curious, and you will be wise to think quietly and give me a kind answer tomorrow.'

'I'll not kill myself, I promise that, for now I wish to live.' He did not see her face, her voice was low, her whole air changed and he believed she would yield if he was patient. Going to the window, he looked out; nothing but a narrow slope of tiled roof lay between it and a fall into the street far below.

'That is safe if she's not a bird,' he said with a smile, and opening the door he departed, saying hopefully, 'I shall come early for your answer, let it be a happy one, my little Rose.'

He did come early, but the answer was an empty room.

95

CHAPTER X

Mademoiselle Honorine

In the gray dawn Pauline Laurent was startled from the hour's sleep which she allowed herself after a long night's work, by a hand upon her shoulder and a breathless voice whispering in her ear, 'Wake and help me, I'm in danger!'

Up she sprung with her quick wits all about her in an instant. Her window stood wide open and by her bed knelt a girl with bloody hands and a white, resolute face that would have daunted any woman.

'Great heavens what is this? Mam'selle Ruth, how came you here, my door is locked?' she exclaimed.

'I came by the window. Shut it softly and let me tell you the sad strait I am in,' whispered the other as she glanced apprehensively about her as if fearing that the walls had ears. Pauline closed the window, made 'Ruth' sit upon the bed and, while she listened, bound up the torn hands.

'Forgive me that I came to disturb and ask favors of you, but you are my only hope, for Mother Pujal is too far away,' began Rosamond, who had assumed a false name in coming to these lodgings, where no one knew her story, though Pauline had gathered hints of it.

'My poor child, confide in me, I am at your service soul and body. I too have had dangers and been helped in my need. Speak freely, I listen.'

'Many, many thanks! I told you in one of our little

tête-à-têtes from our windows that I had left my husband and hid myself from him; Pauline, he has found me and now waits at my door to take me back. I will not go, for I detest him and he has wronged me. I begged the night to think of his proposal; he put a guard at my door and slept below himself, but I escaped as I had resolved to do when I asked for delay.'

'But, dear Mam'selle, it is incredible that you came along the roof! It was a frightful danger; I always tremble when my cat walks there. How could you do it?' cried Pauline, amazed and half incredulous.

'I scarcely know. It *was* frightful, but I had rather be dashed to pieces on the stones below than go back to that man; better destroy the body than the soul.' There was a dread of something worse than death in the girl's wild, woeful eyes.

'Long ago, when a daring, restless child, I learned to walk steadily along a more perilous place than this; but I find I have lost my steady nerves, firm foot and brave heart. The way was very short between our windows but I was forced to crawl and cling and drag myself along the dizzy edge where once I should have walked without a fear. Now I must get away immediately, but where can I go?'

'Not to Pujal, she is known to be your friend. Wait a little, I have ideas, I shall devise something. Lie down and rest; I'll think while I pack my work.'

Worn out with a sleepless night and reassured by the friendly sympathy of the kind soul, Rosamond lay down, not to rest but to think also as she watched Pauline fold several heavy velvet mantles and trains lined with mock ermine and evidently intended for some actress. As Pauline worked she knit her brows, muttered, shrugged and nodded in a way that would have been ludicrous had it not been so heartily earnest. Suddenly she flung the drapery down, ran across the room and lifting the lid of an immense wicker basket pointed to it with a theatrical gesture, crying joyfully,

'Behold the means of escape! I have a superb idea, an inspiration! See now, I go today early with my costumes to Mademoiselle Honorine; she is an angel, adores romance, is true as steel and a friend to the unhappy. You would vanish and leave no trace behind; the window was a grand stroke, mine shall equal it. I will leave the trains and take you in my *corbeille*, which Pierre comes for with his covered cart. I go with you, we give Mademoiselle a charming surprise, interest her in you, she is your friend at once, and Monsieur, *vôtre mari*, is outwitted. Say is it not superb?'

'But it is impossible; I am too large, too heavy; the basket is not strong enough, they will suspect, and this Honorine may be offended at my boldness.'

'Bah! I do not listen to your fears. See here,' and in skipped the lively Frenchwoman, dropping the lid and calling out from within, 'It is luxurious, airy and charming; the bottom is of wood, strong as iron, and the basket firm enough to hold another of your English Falstaffs as in that so droll play.' Here she skipped out again, still talking and gesticulating in a most inspiring manner. 'No one will suspect me; I go every week; sometimes my load is heavy, sometimes light; Pierre is a *stupide* and I can manage him with ease. Mademoiselle Honorine will be delighted, not annoyed; I know her well, I assure you of this and I implore you to let me have my way.'

It was impossible to refuse, for her goodwill and confidence were irresistible. Rosamond yielded and when all was ready she stepped into the great basket, caring little whither she went if she only escaped the keen eyes of Baptiste and his master. Pauline laid a tulle dress over her as a screen if by any mischance the lid was lifted, and calling up Pierre and the concierge she bade them be very careful, for the *corbeille* contained Mademoiselle's most costly velvets. So full of jests and compliments and odd merriment was she that the men went laughing down the long stairs scarcely conscious of the unusual weight of their burden. Once in the covered cart, with Pierre whistling on the seat outside and Pauline sitting near her with the lid half open to give her air, Rosamond's spirits rose and the two women talked in whispers as they rolled briskly away toward Versailles, between which place and Paris stood Mademoiselle's little villa.

Honorine was at breakfast in a charming room surrounded by every luxury a Frenchwoman could desire. She was thirty but looked barely twenty, so carefully had she preserved the beauty which had made her fortune. Rosy, petite and plump, she was altogether charming in her white cashmere dressing gown with its trimming of swansdown and rose-colored ribbons as she sat sipping her chocolate and studying a new role.

'Always punctual, my good Pauline,' she said gaily as the basket was set down and the two were left alone.

'Ah, Mademoiselle, I have a thousand pardons to beg that I disappoint you for a day. The costumes are ready but I do not bring them, because I know your infinite goodness and I assure myself that a kind deed will give you more happiness than the most ravishing toilette in Paris. Behold, I bring you one who needs the help you so delight to give,' and flinging back the lid, Pauline lifted the dress and discovered Rosamond.

As the girl rose to her feet with a gesture of mute appeal, Honorine uttered a little cry of surprise, followed by a glance of recognition, and hastened forward with extended hands, saying in a tone of mingled astonishment and welcome, 'Madame Tempest! In truth I am charmed that you visit me even in this so un-expected and romantic way.'

'Hush, I am not Madame Tempest – it is at an end and I am alone – oh, Mademoiselle, for the love of charity, befriend me.'

Overcome by conflicting emotions of gratitude and grief, surprise and shame, Rosamond covered her face and threw herself at the feet of the actress, whom she now remembered to have seen at Nice though the name had entirely escaped her memory.

Divining the sad truth with the quickness of a woman, Honorine proved that she deserved the praises of Pauline by the tender sympathy, the delicate respect, the cordial welcome she gave the innocent outcast. Lifting her, she laid the beautiful tearful face on her kind bosom, and said with softened voice and the pressure of a friendly hand, 'My friend then, if I may call you so. Believe me you are doubly welcome if I can serve or comfort you. Tell me all that afflicts you and let me help you as I have been helped in times past.'

Here Pauline broke in, for seeing that her work was done she was anxious to be gone and serve elsewhere, 'Dear Mademoiselle, I go to watch and report tomorrow when I bring the costumes. You are safe, my poor child, for this angel will guard you. Confide in her and the good God bless you both.'

Waiting for no reply, she seized her big basket and vanished, dragging it behind her sobbing and laughing as she went. Then Rosamond opened her whole heart to Honorine, feeling the indescribable consolation of sympathy after months of loneliness.

When all was told the actress said, after a thoughtful pause, 'You love this man, he offers to marry you; it is but justice, why not consent and be happy?'

'Because I can never forget nor forgive, and happiness is impossible with such a memory as this to poison all my life. I will not love him, I will learn to hate him, I will make the future one long penance for the past.'

'You will return to your grandfather perhaps?'

'No, I could not bear that house now. He does not love me; I never was a pride or joy to him. I cannot return now to be a disgrace.'

'What then will you do, my friend? Tell me your wish and it shall be done.'

'I only want a safe and quiet place to hide in, where I may work and wait till God sees fit to end the life that is

100

now a burden to me. I foresee but little peace while Phillip follows me, and follow he will until he tires of the chase. Neither of us will yield and he will hunt me down wherever I may hide.'

'No, that would be too cruel! Surely he has some pity; or if not, continued defiance will weary him at last if he is like most men.'

'You do not know him. He has no pity, and my defiance will but increase the excitement of the pursuit. I am solitary, poor and a woman; he powerful, rich and a man whom all fear. The world which rejects me though I am innocent will welcome him, the guilty, and uphold him. I am helpless and must go my way as best I can, praying that it be a short one.'

'Nay, that is too melancholy a future for a lovely young creature like you. See, I have a charming plan, or if that does not please you there is still another refuge to which you can fly. I am to play this winter in Berlin; for this I am preparing and in a week I go. Come with me as my friend, and if, when you have seen the gay yet innocent life I lead, you will share it, I will help you, and with beauty such as yours the future may yet be a brilliant and a happy one.'

'You are too kind, too generous! I will go, but tell me of the other plan before I decide on this.'

'Ah, that is only the last resort for those whom the world wearies or ill treats. I have an Aunt in the convent of St Annunciata near Amiens. She often implores me to come and share her tranquil life, but I refuse and she laments over me. If you choose this she will welcome you and fit you for Heaven. It is a safe and quiet place, and one might be happy there if one liked shadow better than sunshine. Think of both, I give you a week to decide; meantime we will enjoy each other and defy Monsieur.'

To this Rosamond agreed, and so cheering was the society of the lively and friendly Honorine that each day grew brighter as hope and courage returned and the possibility of happiness and peace began to comfort her, for at twenty the heart is wonderfully gifted with the power of outliving trials which later would break it at once or burden it for life.

Pauline reported that a grand explosion had taken place when Tempest discovered that Rosamond had gone. Both houses were searched, Pauline cross-examined and evidently strongly suspected of having some knowledge of the missing girl. Nothing could be proved, no one had been seen to enter or leave her room, and the merry soul convulsed her listeners with laughter as she recounted the scenes which had taken place between herself, Baptiste and Tempest.

'They are gone now,' she said on her second visit, 'but they leave spies behind I fancy, and it is well that you start so soon else that fox would surely discover your retreat before long. I shall come no more; it is not wise, but I will see you the day you leave and report the last news.'

Sunday came and on Tuesday they were to start. More than once Rosamond had nearly chosen the convent rather than the stage, for a sense of safety came over her as she thought of that sacred seclusion and shrunk from the gaiety and glare of a theatrical life. But Honorine could not part with her and used every inducement to fix her choice as she would have it.

They had been talking of the two plans as they sat together that sunny afternoon when the sound of music in the courtyard made Honorine look out. Two young lads with harp and pipe were singing at the gate, looking wistfully in the while with tired, hungry faces.

'Poor children! They must not go from my door unfed,' cried Honorine, whose kind heart overflowed with pity for every unfortunate she saw. Opening the window, she smiled and beckoned as she said hospitably, 'Come in, come in; I like your music well. But first go down and eat and rest, then return and play to me. Adolph, see that the little ones are cared for below.'

Pulling off their caps, the boys murmured grateful thanks as they smiled back at the sweet face above and followed the man away.

'Kind soul! What pleasure you take in helping others. It is this which keeps you young and good and gay. Dear Honorine, I used to pity you at Nice, thinking myself your superior, now I respect and love you more than any woman I have ever known,' said Rosamond, as the actress turned from the window well content.

'Yes, you have my secret for keeping young and happy. I envy no one, I am free as air, I earn my bread honestly and make success sweet by sharing it with the poor. Ah, it is so beautiful to give,' she answered, with an indescribably expressive gesture of her pretty hands.

Soon after, the boys came up to return thanks. One was a Savoyard and looked ill and very tired; the other an Italian and his beauty struck Honorine at once.

'See, Rose, the charming lad with his brilliant black eyes, his thick mass of dark curls, his pretty mouth and the grace of his carriage. Yes, he is a perfect picture—'

Rosamond looked up, started, sprung forward and caught him close, crying joyfully, 'Lito! Lito! Can it be you?'

CHAPTER XI

One More Unfortunate

'*Bella* Rosa! *Bella* Rosa!' was all the boy could answer as he clung to her sobbing with joy in spite of all his efforts to control any unmanly emotion.

'But Lito, how came you here? Where have you been? I mourned you as one dead. Dear child, sit here and tell me all,' cried Rosamond, forgetful of everything but the delight of finding the boy, the relief of knowing that the sin of his death did not burden Tempest's soul.

Bidding the Savoyard wait below, Honorine would have followed had they not kept her to share their happiness.

'Yes, I shall tell you, although it is hard to speak ill of my – of Madame's – no, of Monsieur,' stammered the boy, suddenly confused by the knowledge which he believed he alone possessed.

'Your father, not my husband. I know all, Lito; for your mother came to Valrosa for you, I learned the truth and came away at once; Phillip is nothing to me now. Go on, I'll tell my tale afterward.'

Holding her hand and stopping now and then to caress it with a mute expression of the love and sympathy which he knew not how to speak, Lito told his story.

'The day he found the letter and was so angry and sent you away he threatened to kill me if I would not promise to write a letter saying I preferred to stay with him. I knew then he was my father, though the letter said nothing of it, but I would not promise and that night Baptiste carried me away to a gloomy monastery far back among the hills and there buried me alive.'

'Ah, that was what he meant by speaking of no one's suspecting that you were buried there when he looked toward the hills. But the mystery of the olive grove? I found a new-made grave there, Lito, and an ornament from your fez, and I thought you were gone, dear.'

The boy smiled, then sighed and answered sadly, 'No, it was my great hound's grave. I loved him, but Baptiste killed him because he hated me. That night poor Leo followed me, I begged to have him but Baptiste shot him before my eyes and afterward buried him there, I fancy, that it might be thought the dog was with me. The filigree image of my patron saint, which I missed and wanted because you gave it, must have fallen out as I struggled with Baptiste when he killed my dog in the grove. That is the mystery which alarmed you, Rosa.'

'Thank God, it is made clear to me! Go on, Lito.'

'It was horrible at San André; they were so stern, so grave and cold I could not bear it, and nearly a month ago I ran away. I had tried before and failed, for it is like a prison, but old Tomaso, the gardener, pitied me and yielded at last to my prayers. He let me slip away one evening as we worked together, and bade me find a certain friendly peasant in the valley who would help me on. I did find him, but he was poor and could only give me a suit of coarse clothes as a disguise. I had no money but I met kind people along the way and so got on to Paris. My plan is to reach England and my mother; I remember the address she gave me and I will find her. Here in Paris I found by chance a good Italian to whom I told my story; he gave me my harp and sent me with Anton to earn a little money that I may go more quickly to England. I do well and soon I shall see my mother.'

'Happy child, to have a refuge like that!' sighed Rosamond with an aching heart.

'Come with me, dear Madame, no, it shall be Rosa

now. Come to my mother, she will love you for your kindness to me, and welcome you because you are unfortunate. That will be too happy for me if I have you both!'

'No, Lito, I cannot, any woman but your mother may help and pity me, from her I cannot bear it. She is kind I know, for I heard her speak gently of me at Valrosa. I bless her for it, but I cannot ask charity of her.' Rosamond's face was covered with sudden tears.

Boy as he was, Lito felt the sad truth of her words and urged no more, but listened to her plans forgetful of his own, begging to go with her whenever she went and be her protector.

As they talked Honorine said suddenly, 'I must go and order the gates shut; with such precious fugitives in my charge I must fortify my house lest the enemy surprise us.' It was half a pretext to leave them alone, but she was also nervous and excited by the discoveries and plots going on about her, though she enjoyed them with a Frenchwoman's relish for intrigue. Wishing a breath of fresh air, she tripped down to the flowery courtyard and bade Adolph close the gates. As he did so he glanced down the road and muttered with an air of annoyance, 'There he is again!'

'Who?' asked Honorine pausing in her walk.

'It is nothing, Mademoiselle, only an impertinent who amuses himself with riding or walking by every day and examining the house.'

'How long has this been?'

'For three days, Mademoiselle. I observed him because few pass this way and he is neither groom nor gentleman. A bad face, I shall insult him if he comes often,' said the old servant angrily.

'Let me look, Adolph. Leave the gates ajar and affect to be showing me something amiss with the bolts as he passes,' said Honorine quickly, for the sound of hoofs was already near. Adolph obeyed and his mistress used her keen eyes to some purpose. A dark, slight man passed slowly with a careless look about him and the courteous salute without which few Frenchmen pass a lady. The instant he turned the corner Honorine flew into the house and related what she had heard and seen.

'It is Baptiste!' cried the fugitives together, and regarded one another with faces of dismay.

'I will kill him if he comes for you,' said Lito fiercely.

'He shall not keep you from your mother,' answered Rosamond, holding the boy's hand as if she feared another separation.

'You must both go at once. He has discovered you, Rose, of that I am sure. I think he knows nothing of Lito's arrival, for Adolph says this is his first appearance today and the boys were safely in nearly an hour ago.'

'Yes, we must go, but Honorine, I cannot leave Lito to go with you. He must be helped on; my little store of money I give him, and I will go as far as Amiens with him, from there to Calais is not far and once across the Channel he is safe. I must do this as the only return I can make his mother, who judged me so gently and desired to save me. That I never shall forget.'

'And you, Rose?' asked the actress anxiously.

'I shall go to the Convent, for a time at least; it suits me best and leaves you free. Dear friend, you have done enough for me, I will not burden you. Already I can see that this anxiety for me wears upon you and it must not be. No, say nothing I am fixed; my only care is how to get away without exciting suspicion.'

'We must deceive Baptiste and throw him off the track. He will ride to and fro at intervals for the next hour as if trying a new horse, Adolph says; meantime we must devise some stratagem,' said Honorine, when all her entreaties failed to keep Rosamond with her.

For several minutes the three sat silent, then Lito exclaimed half doubtfully, 'Rosa might dress like a boy and go out as Anton if her hair was short. I dyed mine and stained my skin, but her hair is too long to hide and perhaps she would not dare to try that plan.'

'I'll cut my hair and do it!' cried Rosamond at once.

'It is a good idea, but I will improve it. You shall take Anton's clothes, he shall take some of yours and I will carry him to town in my coupé with affected haste and mystery. Baptiste will see and follow, then you two can slip away and go on to Versailles; there change your dress, Rose, and take the train to Amiens. It is capital! But we must lose no time. Fortunately the servants are all at the fête but Adolph and old Margot, who nods by the kitchen fire. I will prepare Anton and buy his silence and his suit, do you go and clip this lovely hair – ah, what a sacrifice! – while Lito helps me with the boy and the coupé is prepared.'

All was excitement and hurry for a time, then the four met in the saloon and in spite of danger could not refrain from a general laugh. Anton in Rosamond's dress, well veiled and cloaked, looked the part well enough but was awkward in his movements, and Honorine drilled him up to the last moment. Rosamond made a charming boy, with short, dark curls about her head and Anton's rusty velvet suit and rough mantle. Her small feet were hidden in big shoes, the brim of the hat shaded her face, and Lito had darkened her fair skin with the pigment which he carried to renew the olive color of his own face.

With the pipe in her browned hands, which she concealed as much as possible under the long sleeves of her jacket, and a pouch slung over her shoulder, she looked like one of the picturesque Italian boys whom artists have immortalized. She was too shy and feminine at first, but Lito taught her to take a larger stride, to look boldly up and swing her arms, now modestly folded.

The actress and the lads entered so heartily into the spirit of the masquerade that the girl could not long resist the infectious merriment, and when the carriage came round she gaily wished the others success as they departed, and, with Lito, peeped from the curtains to watch the effect of the ruse upon Baptiste, who passed exactly as they drove out, though when Adolph looked a moment before he had not been in sight. They saw him lean forward and dart a sharp glance into the coupé, saw Honorine assume an alarmed expression and pull down the curtains, saw them drive rapidly away and heard Baptiste galloping after as if quite satisfied.

'Now we may go, for it is getting dusk and the servants will not observe the change. Come down and thank old Margot, then follow me boldly out and trust to my protection,' said Lito, assuming the man's part though in spite of his fourteen years and a brave spirit his heart beat quickly and his manner was a little nervous as he made his adieux and led his companion out onto the lonely twilight road.

'Have you got your pistol?' was his first question as they hurried away.

'Yes, I never go without it.'

'Good, I have the little dagger I always carry now, so we will fight for our liberty and sell it dearly if need be. Can you walk a mile or more?'

'I can walk twenty to be free, Lito. Where shall we sleep? Or is it best to push on all night?'

'Versailles is two or three miles farther, we can easily reach it and go to some small *auberge* to sleep. If you fear to meet people so soon we can find a barn perhaps; I like them and have slept in them often. We need not go hungry either, for Margot filled my pouch with meat and bread and wine.'

'We will try the barn, I am as yet too shamefaced to see men and play my part; I will practice first. Yet I like it, Lito, and if I were a boy I'd roam the world over, happy with my pipe, my freedom and my little friend.'

'I wish you were, and this reminds me that you have no name. What shall I call you? "Anton" is surest, for I am used to that.'

'"Anton" let it be then, and I think we should talk in Italian, it is safer as few understand it here. I will pretend to comprehend no French and so run no risk of betraying myself by my voice.'

'That is a wise thought. Tomorrow I will teach you an air or two upon the pipe. It is very easy to accompany me on the harp and you will learn quickly.'

So talking and planning the fugitives pressed on, and soon the lights of Versailles shone before them. Near the outskirts of the town a lovely, somewhat dilapidated barn appeared, and, having reconnoitered, Lito pronounced it empty except for a little hay. Here they paused and having arranged two fragrant beds, eaten their supper and had several panics, the wanderers fell asleep to dream serenely until dawn, while Honorine baffled and bewildered Baptiste to her heart's content.

Anton was left at the house of a friend who had a young son; a plausible story of a harmless jest was told, the boy reclothed in proper attire and sent away with a well-filled purse in his pocket and injunctions to execute the desire of his heart and return to Switzerland at once. Then the actress drove home alone, leaving Baptiste to guard the new cage to which he believed the bird had flown.

Early were the friends astir and, after a lesson on the pipe which fitted the mock Anton to play his part if necessary, they went on their way without fear, for already the girl felt at ease and enjoyed her freedom so heartily that she decided not to change but to go on to Amiens in her new costume.

'It is two hours before the train leaves; go, Lito, and buy some breakfast at the house yonder; I will go down and wait for you beside the river, it is sunny and safe there and I am thirsty,' she said as they neared the town.

The boy went and Rosamond followed a little path made by the feet of cattle going to drink. It led her to a quiet nook formed by a curve in the river which flowed on outside the stiller water of the little bay. Stepping on a flat stone, she knelt down and, putting back the rushes, stooped to drink. But no drop touched her lips, for close beside the stone a woman's body lay half hidden in the water. So pale and peaceful was the young face with its closed eyes and breathless lips that Rosamond felt neither disgust nor dread, but looked till tears dimmed her sight.

A paper was pinned on the dead bosom, the sun had dried it since the tide had floated its bearer to that haven, and gently taking it Rosamond read the few pale lines it held.

I pray that whoever finds the body of one driven to her death by a great wrong, will bury it decently wherever it may be found, for I have no home, or friends, and pray for the soul of Madelaine Constant.

'Shall I be driven to this in time?' thought Rosamond with a shudder. With the fear like a flash came a strange design. An instant she paused fancying it too wild, too uncertain to be worth executing, but a strong impulse urged her to it, and obeying the inexplicable feeling she took out her purse, which contained both pencil and paper, and copied the words exactly, except that where the name 'Madelaine Constant' appeared she wrote 'Rosamond Vivian'. Dipping the paper in the water, she refastened it to the dead breast, and as if asking pardon for the act, she bent and kissed the cold forehead with the silent promise to pray for the soul of this sister sufferer whose sorrow had been greater and whose soul less strong than her own.

111

CHAPTER XII

Behind the Grating

Feeling sure that before the day was over the body would be found, Rosamond left the spot to meet Lito and tell him what she had done.

'You are right, she will be discovered and buried as no friends can come to claim her. As you say, it will be put in the papers and Baptiste will see it, he always reads deaths and murders, but a description of the girl will also be put in; did you think of that?' asked the boy, whom danger was making precociously keen and crafty.

'Yes, but I do not fear the description. She had dark hair, and dark eyes probably, was young and slender, with fair skin and delicate hands, well dressed and evidently of respectable birth. I saw this as the plan flashed into my mind and knew that any description would apply to us both. It is a mere chance, but it may succeed for a time at least.'

They breakfasted with such appetite as they could, then took the early train, and at nightfall were set down within sight of the Convent of St Annunciata.

'Dear Lito, here we must part; it is best not to be seen together by these people who are to receive me, lest we endanger each other. Here is money, Calais is near, you have your mother's address and soon may be safe in her arms. God keep you, dearest child, think sometimes of poor Rose, and so good-bye.'

It was a sad and tender parting, but Rosamond would not detain the boy an hour from his mother and by this sacrifice tried to repay the kind words the wife had spoken of her at a time when most women would have felt only hatred or contempt. With tears the two young creatures separated, each to go on their lonely way; Lito hastened at once to Calais and Rosamond to the shelter of the Convent.

Just out of the town it stood, a quiet, shadowy place full of pious women intent on good works and the glorification of St Annunciata. Sending in the letter Honorine had given her, Rosamond was kindly welcomed by Mother Ursula, the Superior, who, though somewhat scandalized at the costume, was only too glad to receive another lamb into her fold.

That night the girl slept in a narrow cell with a sense of peace and safety to which she had long been a stranger. Nothing but the slow, soft footfalls of the sisters passing to midnight mass and the solemn chant from the distant chapel broke the silence, and lulled by sounds like these she sank into a dreamless sleep untroubled by a fear.

On the morrow her new life began. Habited in the black gown and veil of the sisterhood, her beautiful face looked doubly young and lovely, and more than one withered old nun followed the newcomer with eyes that plainly betrayed the admiration women seldom lose for youth and beauty. To none but the Superior was her story known, for sins and sorrows were held sacred there, and she took her place among them unquestioned and unknown.

For six months she led a life of tranquil seclusion, seldom leaving the Convent except upon the errands of mercy which the sisters did among the sick and poor. To these she came like an angel with her words of comfort, her gentle care, and soon 'Sister Agatha's' sweet, saintly face was watched for and welcomed with a love and gratitude very precious in her sight. Her days were spent in learning the dainty art of embroidery by which the nuns earned money for their charitable deeds; she did her share of household labor, none being thought too humble for the highest there; vigils and prayers, penances and confessions had a charm for her now, and Mother Ursula did her best to change the young Protestant into a devout Catholic.

In all those months nothing was heard or seen of Tempest, and Rosamond tried to feel that she rejoiced in the success of her last stratagem. But in that perverse heart of hers would linger a longing to know where he was, what he was doing and if he mourned her death with a grief as strong as his love had been. She tried to forget but it was impossible, for since the knowledge of Lito's safety had freed her from that dark fear, she could not conceal from herself that her affection for Tempest was not dead in spite of deceit and wrong. He was the first, the only love of her life, and in a nature like hers such passions take deep root and die hard. In vain she recalled his sins against herself and others; in vain she told herself that he was unworthy any woman's trust and love, still the unconquerable sentiment that once made her happiness now remained to become her torment.

'Everything is possible to God, but we must help ourselves if we would be helped by Him. I have not asked aright, so my poor prayers remain unanswered. I will take counsel with some of these pious souls who have found peace and they will show me how to earn a like tranquillity,' she said within herself.

Mother Ursula was a kind but weak and narrow woman and Rosamond could not turn to her. None of the sisters, though friendly creatures, were persons to whom she could confide a grief like hers. Two priests belonged to the Convent and to one of them she would apply. Father Ignatius, the younger, was a cold, silent man with a pale, ascetic face and eyes that seemed so bent on turning from the vanities of the world that they were seldom lifted from the ground. But Rosamond had seen them fixed on her more than once with the look of

114

devout admiration which a devotee casts upon a saint, and she shrunk from speaking of her heart to him. Father Dominic was an old, white-haired man, with a benignant face, mild voice and a paternal manner which attracted her strongly. He should be her confidant, and under the seal of Confessional would she lay bare her troubled soul.

Two events delayed her purpose for a time. A contagious fever broke out in the town and many died among the poor, but the rich escaped with one exception. The daughter of the Comte de Luneville fell ill and terror seized the father. He sent to the Convent for a nurse, but all the good sisters were either worn out with other labors or too timid to go. Rosamond alone was ready, and regardless of danger prepared for the task which might be her last. As she stood waiting for the carriage of the Comte in the gloomy parlor of the Convent, Father Ignatius came in, haggard and worn with many sleepless nights and days of care among the poor. There was no sternness in his voice, no coldness in his manner, no melancholy in the eyes now full of an expression warmer than admiration as he said, gently, anxiously, 'My daughter, is this wise?'

'I but follow your example, Father,' was the soft answer as Rosamond put back her veil and looked up with a face full of a reverence never felt before.

A sudden flush rose to the priest's pale forehead and for the first time in many months a smile shone on his face.

'But you are young, my daughter, and to such life is sweet. To me it is but a burden which I am ready to lay down whenever God wills.'

'I also am ready, for life is not dear to me. Let me go, my father, and work while I may.'

The beautiful eyes filled as she spoke, and with a gesture of infinite compassion Ignatius laid his hand on the meek head, saying tenderly, 'May the Holy Mother keep and bless you, Agatha.'

115

With the blessing she went away to her ministry of love and performed it so well that the young girl lived, though death had seemed inevitable. Boundless gratitude and costly gifts were her reward when the task was done, and a few months later the Comte de Luneville added another proof of gratitude, another costly gift.

On returning to the Convent she found Mother Ursula dead of the fever and a new reign begun under a new Superior. Sister Magdalene was a haughty, bigoted woman who had been mortally jealous of Rosamond because the girl was such a favorite with the abbess. Now that her day of power had come, Magdalene revenged herself by every petty slight, injustice and indignity which one woman can show another. Rosamond bore this meekly for a time, but soon the calm life grew monotonous when no friendly influence gave it grace and warmth. She began to pine for freedom, and to remind herself that she had taken no vow to stay. But where go if she abandoned this home?

Suddenly a new care beset her. Father Ignatius began to haunt her like a shadow. If she went out upon some mission of mercy he was sure to cross her path, to follow afar off and watch over her with a silent vigilance that surprised and then annoyed her. If she walked in the Convent garden as the spring came on, he was always there at work, or pacing to and fro, book in hand. In the house she seldom saw him, yet felt conscious that he was often near.

When they met he sometimes passed without lifting up his eyes or uttering a word; usually a grave salutation, a brief glance and nothing more. All these things determined Rosamond to ask counsel of Father Dominic, whose kindness remained unchanged, indeed had rather increased of late as if he saw and pitied her discomforts. She sent word that she desired to see him and he appointed an hour for her to come to Confession.

As the time approached she grew restless, and throwing aside the delicate work with which she had vainly

116

tried to calm herself, she went down into the quaint old garden where the soft May sunshine lay warm on trim beds of herbs and budding fruit trees. The lower wall was close upon the river and in one angle was a stone seat near a narrow opening which framed a lovely picture of the opposite shore, sloping upward to the Comte's Chateau.

Sitting here half hidden by the ivy screen that shut in the spot, Rosamond looked across the water, thinking of the young Comtesse to whom she had that day said farewell before her father took her to the German baths for the summer. Natalie had prayed her to go with them, but she had refused, thinking it a girlish whim. Now she wished she had accepted, for with the spring freshness came an irresistible desire to leave the gloomy cloister and go out into the sunshine. The plash of oars disturbed her reverie, and peeping down she saw Father Dominic approaching from the town. She was about to speak when the sight of Ignatius sitting motionless and watchful on the steps that led down from the garden door to the water's edge arrested her.

With his broad-brimmed hat upon his knees and his white hair stirring in the mild air Father Dominic sat serenely smiling as a sturdy lad rowed him along the quiet river. The smile faded as he saw Ignatius and he shook his head with a troubled look, saying as the younger man advanced to help him land, 'This is not well, my son, flee temptation, chasten the flesh and defy the devil.'

'I do, Father, especially the latter,' and Rosamond heard a grim laugh from lips that rarely even smiled.

'The delusion is strong upon thee, Ignatius, fast and pray, fast and pray, my son.'

'Nay, rather watch and pray, my father,' returned the other, adding to the boy who was about to push off, 'Leave the boat, Jan, I shall have occasion for it shortly.'

'For what purpose?' asked Dominic, pausing with his foot upon the first step.

'The salvation of saints,' was the enigmatical reply as Ignatius fastened the boat and bade Jan go back by the bridge.

The boy ran off along the little footpath by the riverside, and the young priest turned to the old one, saying, with his accustomed deference and a suggestive motion of the hand, 'After you, my father.'

Dominic put on his hat with a benign smile, gathered up the long skirts of his cassock and nimbly mounted the steps. At the top he paused, and as Ignatius reached his side he took his arm with a confidential air. 'I have something upon which I desire to confer with you, my son. There is time before Confession, come with me to the little Oratory, there we can be private.'

What the other answered Rosamond did not hear, but it was evidently an affirmative for they walked away together toward a small isolated building nearby. Leaning forward, she saw Father Dominic produce a key, fling open the door and motion his companion to enter. He did so, Dominic seemed about to follow, but suddenly closed the door, relocked it on the outside and walked away, putting the key in his pocket. Surprise kept the girl motionless as the old man approached. He did not see her as he descended the steps, unmoored the boat and pulling out a silver whistle recalled Jan, who still loitered along the shore.

The boy returned, and having received the brief order, 'Take the boat over and leave it on the other side,' rowed away, looking somewhat perplexed by these contradictory commands. Laughing quietly to himself, Father Dominic returned, and as if weary approached the ivy seat. At sight of the girl he paused an instant, then came on as tranquilly as ever.

'Ah, my daughter, I had no thought of seeing you here, but it is as well. You overheard us, Agatha?'

'Yes, Father, I both heard and saw you.'

'And wondered doubtless at my conduct? It is but natural, yet I could have wished to spare you this.'

'What, Father?'

'The knowledge that a priest can forget the deference due to his superiors, the sanctity of his vows, and the honor of his Order as Ignatius has done.'

'How, Father? I know nothing of this.'

'Innocent child! If I could keep it from you I would, but it will be told by him if I delay and it is better that I utter the sacrilegious truth. Agatha, he loves you.'

She had feared this, had tried not to read the language of those eloquent eyes, the meaning of the sleepless vigilance, the secret of the change which had crept over Ignatius since she knew him first. Looking keenly at her, the old man saw regret and sorrow in the downcast face before him but neither surprise or joy, and an aspect of relief replaced the former one of anxiety in his own.

'I can divine your horror and pain at this, my child, and I will spare you any answer. I simply warn you to shun this unhappy man while he remains, it will not be long. Now give me your arm, daughter, I must see Mother Magdalene and then I shall await you in the Confessional.'

She rose and offered the old man the support he asked, but could not restrain a wistful glance toward the little Oratory, whence no sound proceeded.

'Is he to be left there, Father Dominic?'

'For a time, my child, it is your only safety. He is mad with this temptation of the devil and planned to carry you away this very night. I have removed the boat, and imprisoned him, thus you are safe for a time. It grows damp, let us go in.'

Thanking the kind old priest for his paternal care, she left him with the Superior and retired to her cell to wait and muse over this new trouble. At the appointed hour she repaired to the chapel. Father Dominic's hat lay on the bench beside the door and fearing to have kept him waiting she hurried into the Confessional, two compartments each large enough to hold a single person. In the priest's half was an easy chair, in the other a hassock for

119

the speaker to kneel upon; double doors shut in both parts and in the partition between them was a little wicket with a grating and a curtain before it on the priest's side. To this wicket he placed his ear and the sinner spoke unseen.

Kneeling here, Rosamond said in a low, eager voice, 'My father, shall I speak?'

'I listen, Daughter,' was the whispered reply.

'The chief sin which I have to confess is that I cannot fix my thoughts on heaven as becomes this holy place. I am no nun and no vow binds me, but I would gladly forget the vain world if I could. It seems impossible; I am so young, so full of life, so hungry for happiness that I daily find less and less desire to devote myself to the duties of a cloister. What can I do to cure this? Or is it best to yield to a natural longing and go back to the world? You are wise and kind, tell me my duty.'

'What tempts you back to the world?'

'Chiefly the unconquerable wish to know if a former friend still lives.'

'What friend? Tell me all before I advise.'

'The man I loved. He wronged me and I left him. He followed me, offering to atone for the wrong; I refused and fled; but now like a daily temptation comes the thought that I might go back without sin when he has removed the only obstacle between us.'

'Why call it a temptation?'

'Because in spite of this longing I know that I shall purchase happiness at a high price if I return; that new falsehood may betray me, new tyranny oppress me, and above all I feel that with this man I must lose more and more the love of all good things, so strong is his influence, so unprincipled his nature. My only hope is that I may save his soul and yet not lose my own. Can I, dare I do this?'

'Yes, heartily, and at once.'

'Ah, if I could only feel assured that it was right and not a blind impulse of a weak woman's heart!'

'One thing, my daughter, in spite of all deceit, unworthiness and wrong do you still love this man?'

'Yes.'

Almost inaudible was the low, reluctant answer, so low that she thought the old man had not heard it and was about to speak again when a burst of exultant laughter startled her like a thunderclap, the curtain was pushed aside and through the grating looked the dark face of Phillip Tempest!

CHAPTER XIII

Flee Temptation

Like a bird held by the terrible fascination of a serpent's eye, Rosamond knelt motionless and mute, gazing at that familiar face as if it were a Gorgon's head which had turned her to stone.

'Dearly beloved, you are pardoned, for that last word cancels all your sins,' said Tempest, still smiling. Then, as if impatient of delay, he left his nook, threw open the door of hers and added, as he gently lifted her, 'Sweet saint, come and embrace, not "flee temptation".'

She did not speak but she submitted, for in that moment of surprise her heart turned traitor and cried out within her, 'Let me be happy for a little while, then I will be wise.'

Seating himself on the steps of the Confessional, Tempest drew her to his knee, put off the veil and close coif that enveloped her head so that all the beautiful hair came clustering about her face, changing the meek nun into a lovely girl again. Lifting the startled face, Tempest looked long and ardently into the eyes that could not conceal their happiness, but suddenly he clasped her close, exclaiming in a tone which proved how much he had suffered, 'Oh, my darling, how could you leave me to believe that I had driven you to your death!'

'You found the paper then, you thought the girl was me?' she asked, so touched by his emotion that she forgot to reproach or repel, but put her question with a soft hand against his cheek, the caress he used to like so well.

'Yes, how could I help it? Baptiste saw the story in the paper three days after, and we went to the place at once. The body had been buried, but the note, the name, the description were enough. I would not have your rest disturbed, I left you in the churchyard at Versailles and went away to mourn you for six long months. See, Rose, I have worn this next my heart all this weary while, the last relic of my lost Rose.'

He drew out a little velvet case and in it showed her the worn paper and a bit of cambric with her name upon it.

'My handkerchief! Where did you find it, Phillip?'

'Among the rushes where the poor girl was found.'

'Ah, I remember, I meant to bathe my face that morning but as I looked into the water I saw my olive skin and knew that the color would be washed away; then I saw the dead body and forgot everything else till that strange thought came to me.'

'Baptiste was filled with admiration at the ruse; he is seldom long deceived, but for a time he was entirely baffled and lamented that such an exciting chase should end so soon.'

'What caused it to begin again? How did you find me out? Who betrayed me?'

'Father Dominic.'

'Impossible! You mean Father Ignatius,' cried Rosamond breathless with amazement.

'I mean what I say; my complaisant old friend Dominic, who is open to bribery and a most obliging old rascal. The other is as true as steel and as firm as a rock; but for him I should have found you weeks ago; I have yet to settle that score.'

'Poor Ignatius, how I have wronged him!' thought the girl, and the remembrance of his truth, his fidelity, made her shrink instinctively from one who possessed so little of either virtue. She half rose and looked about her, longing to go and free him yet afraid to increase his danger by betraying any interest in him.

Detaining her gently yet irresistibly, Tempest said, laughing, 'Sit still, sweetheart, you are not the first nun who has met a lover in these walls I fancy. I've much to say and we are safe, for Dominic keeps guard without and your priestly watchdog is safely kenneled for the night.'

'Speak quickly then, it is late and will soon be time for mass.'

'Poor frightened heart, how it beats! They have taken half the spirit and courage out of you, Rose, with their stupid penances and prayers. I'll soon mend that when you are mine again. What shall I tell you first? If you are still a woman and not all saint, you must be curious.'

'Tell how you discovered me, for even now I cannot think that good old man could be so false.'

'You will find that money can buy everything, even the conscience and integrity of a priest,' began Tempest.

'It could not buy that of Ignatius,' she interrupted with a look of triumph, for amidst so much deceit she felt a double gratitude that one man had been found true.

Tempest frowned and shot a quick glance at her with the sudden recollection that Ignatius was younger than himself and that for six months young priest and lovely nun had seen each other daily.

'It would have bought him had not a higher bribe been offered. Well for me that his vows doom him to lifelong celibacy else I might have come too late, for he is a handsome man, Rose, and you *hate me*, you know.'

Stung by the unjust suspicion, the insulting look which accompanied it, she tore herself from his hold, saying passionately, 'I wish I did! I wish I did!'

Conscious of his mistake in rousing her spirit, Tempest changed his tone, and beckoned with a repentant air. 'It was but a jest, forgive it and come back to me.'

'No I will not! The momentary weakness is over now

and you shall see that penances and prayers have strengthened my courage and given me a spirit that you cannot conquer. Stay there, and say what you will, come nearer and I'll rouse the house to defend me in spite of that traitor Dominic.'

She had her hand on the great silken rope that rung the chapel bell and one stroke would bring a flock of indignant women to the rescue. Tempest knew he had invaded sacred premises and felt that caution was wise. Pausing as he strode toward her, he leaned against a pillar and softly applauded her last words.

'Excellent! Honorine must have taught you that pose. I submit, you thorny rose, and I will maintain a distance until you relent, as you will when I tell you what I have been doing while you told your beads and grew more charming than ever. I shall let you wait for that good news till I have satisfied your curiosity on the other point. Mother Ursula died a few weeks ago, and on her deathbed confided you to her successor, who it seems, hates you with the jealous fervor of your amiable sex. As soon as the good Ursula was dead and Madame Magdalene in her place that pious soul took pity upon me, for she had been told your story, and wrote an anonymous letter stating that in Amiens I could find what I had lost. I have had many anonymous letters in my life and should probably have taken no notice of it, but I was in London when the messenger arrived in Paris to find me and the letter fell into the hands of Baptiste. He was idle while waiting for my return, had never recovered from the chagrin of his defeat in not bringing you back to me, and something in the mystery of the thing interested him. He returned no answer but disguised as a peasant came to Amiens and tried to find you. He knew not where to look, for the letter gave no hint, but worked in the dark till a short time ago the praises of Sister Agatha's beauty, piety and devoted courage roused his suspicions. He watched you, but being always veiled in the street and guarded by this Ignatius he found no opportunity of satisfying himself. A week ago as he rowed down the river he saw you in the garden looking out of the ivy window in the wall. You did not recognize him in the blue-bloused boatman with the black beard, but he was enraptured at his discovery and wrote at once to me.'

'Then you came to bribe the priest, and tempt me from the only safe sanctuary left for such as I?'

'Exactly; but I cannot agree about the safety or the sanctity of this refuge. There is a delusion that those who enter here leave human passions behind, yet you find to your sorrow that love, jealousy, hypocrisy, avarice and falsehood exist in the holy shadow of St Annunciata as well as in the wicked world. So the sooner you leave this unsafe sanctuary the better, little Sister Agatha.'

'Have you more to tell me, Phillip?' she asked sadly, for indignation had given place to sorrow, and though she looked calm and cold yet in her troubled heart she was praying for strength to flee temptation.

'Much more, if you will hear me. It seems that Ursula had given Magdalene to understand that you were an injured wife who had fled here for peace. Not knowing this when I wrote to tell her I was come I betrayed the truth and the woman was scandalized, having in spite of her jealousy a trifle of that inconvenient article called principle. She refused to give you up, but dismissed me with the comforting assurance that you should expiate your share of the sin by mortifications of the flesh and humiliation of soul. Having lost that ally I looked about me for another, for in these days one cannot sack a convent as in the chivalrous old times. The world does not give me a flattering character, as you know. Ignatius had heard of me and complimented me by regarding me as a fiend incarnate. He rejected my offers with such scorn that when I am at leisure I shall teach him a lesson he will not soon forget. Father Dominic proved more tractable; he loves money and I bought him body and soul. Desiring to create no scandal, I planned to enter quietly, but Ignatius has thwarted me twice. Tonight, thanks to the old man's wit, I got in unseen and flatter myself that the surprise was a success.'

He paused there, waiting for some demonstration from her, but with her hand still holding the bell rope fast and the dim light of the altar lamps shining on her colorless face she looked back at him, saying coldly, 'What next?'

'Only this: Marion has consented to a divorce, since the boy is dead. I have been busy in the matter and soon I shall be free. Then, Rose, you will become my wife in solemn earnest?'

'No.'

'Why not, most capricious of angels? Did you not confess that you loved me, longed for me, and desired to save my soul. Your Director bade you do it at once and with all your heart, will you not obey him?'

'No; the wish was a weak and wicked one, the answer false and I reject it. I thought I had a wise, kind friend in Father Dominic, but he betrayed me and now I have no one to trust – but Ignatius,' she added within herself, 'he is true, he will help me; I'll stand firm now and ask counsel of him when Phillip goes.'

Tempest eyed her for an instant as her head drooped and her voice faltered. Finding that force and falsehood failed to win her, he had resolved to try generosity and justice. In a serious, frank tone he said, 'Rose, you may trust me, for though I have deceived you cruelly once, now I am in earnest and I will prove it. I do not ask you to go with me yet, I leave you free until I can come to claim you honestly. You doubt me, and I cannot blame you, but it is the solemn truth and time shall convince you. Very soon the divorce will be completed and then, Rose, I shall have the right to demand an answer.'

'You shall have it; meantime I hold myself aloof from you and go where I will unfollowed. You promise me this?' she said firmly yet with an incredulous air.

His manner changed, the malicious merriment came back to his eyes, the imperious accent to his voice and the masterful expression to his face. 'That I cannot promise. I *must* know where you are, but I will not molest nor betray you till the time arrives. Go where you like, assume what disguise you choose, do what you please, except die or marry. I'll stand off and watch the play, but I *must* follow. I like the chase, it is exciting, novel and absorbing. I have tried and tired of other amusements, this satisfies me and I am in no haste to end it. Upon my soul, Rose, it gives a new interest to life and makes my wooing wonderfully varied and delightful. Now I am going straight back to Paris while you lose yourself again, and in a week or two Baptiste and I will take the field for another harmless hunt. Are you too angry to say adieu?'

Sure that it was only a test of her firmness, she offered her hand with a scornful smile. To her intense surprise he kissed it warmly and left the chapel without another word. Still expecting him to return, she followed to the door that looked upon the garden, saw Tempest pause for a few words with Father Dominic, then vanish down the steps, and a moment after the dash of oars assured her that he had really gone.

Agitated and bewildered, she hurried away to her cell and throwing herself on her narrow bed lay there a prey to conflicting thoughts and feelings till the bell rang for midnight mass. Then she rose with her decision made, her plan arranged. Putting her purse and the little pistol in her pocket, she readjusted her veil, threw on a cloak and waiting till the stillness assured her that the house was empty she stole away to the chapel by the garden. Peeping in, she saw the sisterhood devoutly murmuring their prayers and Father Dominic in his robes chanting before the high altar. They were safe; and gliding to the sacristy she glanced eagerly about for the old man's cassock, which he laid aside when he assumed his robes. It hung over a chair and slipping her hand into the pocket where she had seen him deposit the key of the Oratory, she found it. With a glad heart and noiseless step she ran across the garden, full of moonlight shadows now, and tapping at the door called softly, 'Father! Father Ignatius, are you there?'

The sound of someone springing up told her the prisoner still waited, and opening the door she stood before him in the silvery light like an angel of deliverance. He seized both her hands with a face full of grateful wonder, an exclamation of intense relief.

'You, Agatha? Thank heaven you are safe!'

'No, I thank you, and humbly ask you to forgive me for my long distrust. I know all now, Tempest has come and gone, and for a time I am free again. One favor more I ask of you, help me to reach the Chateau.'

'Tonight?' he said regretfully.

'Yes, at once. I cannot stay among those who have betrayed me. The Comte will befriend me and I must go.'

'But this man, what will he do? Why has he gone?'

She told him rapidly, for now she clung to this one faithful heart with a child's confidence, forgetting for a time that he loved her and remembering only that he was 'true as steel; firm as a rock'. He listened, detected the secret weakness of the girl's love, and resolved to save her from it if he could. He had drawn her out of the moonlight into the little room and still holding the hands that unconsciously clung to him he said, imploringly, 'My child, never go back to this man. I know him and if I dared sully your innocence with such knowledge I would tell you the history of his life. You love him still and struggle against your love, feeling that it will undo you. He knows this and he will tempt you by every lure he can devise, every deceit he can employ. Sorrow and sin will surely follow if you yield; happiness never can be yours with him; doubt, remorse and self-reproach will kill love, and a time will come when you will find that in gaining a brief joy you have lost your peace

129

forever. Oh, Agatha, be warned in time, do not listen to your own weak heart but to the conscience that nothing can bribe or silence. Child! child! You *must* be saved, listen to me and let me keep your white soul fit for heaven.'

In his earnestness Ignatius had flung himself upon his knees before her, passionately pleading not for a return of the love which look, touch and tone unconsciously betrayed, but that she would save herself. It was as if her own conscience had taken human shape, for his voice eloquently uttered the fears, the feelings that had filled her heart that night. She had wavered, for love was sweet and life looked desolate without it; but the example of this man who asked nothing for himself and was as true to his own soul as he would have her to hers, touched and inspired her with a brave desire to be worthy his respect, to emulate his virtue.

The first tears she had shed that night fell on the forehead of the priest as, kneeling at her feet, he looked up and waited for an answer. Broken by emotion yet humbly trustful was the quick reply, 'Father, I am weak but you are strong, into your care I give my soul; help me to do the right and save me from myself.'

'I will! Thank God for this!' Up he sprung, his face shining with sudden joy, his manner full of a cheerful courage which sustained and comforted the girl with a confidence that never failed.

'You will go with the Comte? It is well; they leave tomorrow and he will befriend you faithfully. Come, we will cross at once and leave no trace behind.'

With unquestioning faith she let him lead her down the steps to the little landing below. No boat lay there and she looked about her wondering till Ignatius, with that rare smile of his, said, glancing over the stream, 'Have faith and wait, I shall work a miracle for your deliverance.'

Going on a step or two he threw off his cassock and plunged into the river. Rosamond uttered a stifled cry but he never turned, and with a beating heart she watched the strong swimmer cross the wide, rapid stream, unmoor the boat upon the other side and with no pause for rest come rowing swiftly back. It was a feat to stir a woman to that admiration of manly strength and skill which men most love to win; Ignatius saw it shining in the girl's eyes as she welcomed him and his barren life seemed suddenly to blossom like the rose.

'Ah, that was a brave miracle bravely wrought! It reminds me of the days of romance. You should have been a knight and not a monk,' she said, smiling up in his face as he stretched out his hands to help her in.

'I will be for an hour. Lie there, detested thing!' and he flung the cassock like a cushion on the seat where she was to sit.

Something in his impetuous manner, his vehement tone recalled to Rosamond's memory the fact that this man loved her. Gathering her veil about her, she sat silently watching him as he plied the oars, and for the first time fully realized that he was both young and comely. The priestly garb was gone, for he had torn off the bands about his throat and left his hat behind him. Thin and pale with thought and suffering was the fine face opposite her, but as she looked color came into his cheeks, fire kindled the melancholy eyes, a happy smile softened the lines of that firm mouth and as he shook the thick, dark locks off his forehead there was no sinister scar to mar the beauty of the broad, benevolent brow. A noble, true and most attractive face she found it, and the moments which followed that bold act did more to win regard for Ignatius than months of quiet intercourse had done.

As the boat touched the shore and they stepped out, Rosamond threw off her cloak and offering it, said with the air of soft command which in her was peculiarly charming, 'Knights wore cloaks; take mine, you will be cold.'

He gave her a smile that warmed her heart, but

wrapped the cloak about her with a gesture which she could not resist, and said decidedly as the smile faded, 'Not when ladies needed them. No, I will be a monk again, it is better not to forget the truth even for an hour. Come, my child, there is no time to lose.'

Infinitely tender were the words 'my child', but a sigh followed as if he said within himself, 'She can be nothing more to me, I must remember that.'

CHAPTER XIV

A Glimpse of Happiness

In one of the balconies of the Hotel of the Four Seasons at Wiesbaden two beautiful women were walking to and fro, one apparently, the other really unconscious of the admiring glances fixed upon them from above and below, for the street was full of young officers and the windows of the great hotel of loungers. One was a pretty blonde French girl of seventeen, vivacious and gay though evidently an invalid, for she was wrapped in a great shawl and leaned on the arm of her companion.

The elder and much lovelier of the two was a slender, graceful woman of one or two and twenty, with the perfect outlines of neck and shoulder which one sees only in England. The delicate face was pale, the lines of the mouth betrayed past suffering, and the eyes were full of melancholy beauty. In looking at her one involuntarily said, 'That woman has known great sorrow, but it will not kill her,' for there was an indefinable air of strength and courage about her which wonderfully enhanced the spell of her beauty.

'You will know it tonight, Rosalie,' exclaimed the girl, with a pretty affectation of mystery after a few silent turns had been taken.

'What shall I know, dear?' asked the other, showing no sign of curiosity.

'Ah, that I must not tell and you will never guess it. But you must promise to agree to it when you do know because it is such a charming plan and will make us all so happy.'

'I think I dare promise, Natalie, for I guess it.'

'Has Papa told you then?' cried the girl, looking disappointed.

'No, but when I found a costly dress in my room with my name on the card that accompanied it, how could I help knowing that it was a friendly hint to be ready for the ball at the new Kursaal?'

'Wrong! Wrong! It is not that, though you are to go in spite of all refusals, and I thank you for your meek obedience. It is something far better than balls, something I have wanted and waited for all the three months you have been with us. Two days ago Papa said I should have it if you were willing and tonight he is going to arrange the plan.'

'It is to spend the winter in Paris? I agree, but I do not think you strong enough for that gay place.'

'Wrong again, it's not Paris. You waste time in trying to guess and I shall be tempted to tell if I stay, so I'm going in to leave you the torments of suspense. Blind Rosalie, not to see what I have seen so long.'

With a mischievous laugh Natalie stepped into the salon through one long window just as her father stepped out at the other. The Comte de Luneville was a tall, soldierly man of five and forty; slightly gray, but with a handsome patrician face which age would only soften and refine. Intensely proud but too well bred to show it except by the cold courtesy of his manner; very jealous of the honor of his ancient name, and fiery as a boy at any insult offered it; fastidious and reserved, yet chivalrously compassionate to weakness or want, and passionately fond of his one motherless child.

Rosamond he had received into his heart and home without a question, for in her he saw the savior of his daughter and he felt that that debt could never be paid. For three months they had wandered through Germany, devoted to the invalid who now was almost restored, thanks to the healing waters of the Spas and Rosamond's untiring care. No mother could have been more tender and the girl loved her with the ardor of a grateful heart; no father could have felt greater pride and affection for her than the Comte, no lover showed his regard in ways more delicate and charming. A happy trio, for so guarded and cherished, Rosamond could not but recover cheerfulness and heartily enjoy the sweet atmosphere of home which now surrounded her.

Ignatius was the Comte's spiritual Director and through him she often heard of her friend, though he never wrote to her in spite of all temptations. Following this example Rosamond employed every device to banish Tempest from her thoughts, and succeeded better than before. No sign had he made, and having resolved to renounce him she schooled herself to rejoice at this silence on his part; yet at times a vague disquiet possessed her and she felt an unconquerable foreboding that no power but death would force him to relinquish his claim upon her. This hidden fear had haunted her of late so strongly that she often asked herself how she could escape, and looked about her for some help which should end her anxiety forever. From a source the most unexpected and in a guise the most tempting it came to her at last.

Along the balcony approached the Comte with extended hand and the cordial smile which he gave only to his daughter and her friend. He had heard Natalie's last words and a slight flush rose to his cheek as he said, offering his arm, 'You shall not suffer long, Mademoiselle Rosalie. Permit me to seat you here to briefly tell the little plan which so delights Petite.'

Most men would have been both awkward and confused at that moment; a Frenchman is never awkward and can conceal emotion with consummate skill if he chooses. Rosamond felt the Comte's hand tremble as he placed her in a chair just inside the window, but as he stood beside her his face was quite calm and there was no change in his manner except a slight additional deference as he addressed her.

'Mademoiselle, you have already conferred upon me an obligation which I never can repay, yet I cannot resist the desire to ask of you another and a greater favor. I know well how little I can offer to one so rich in beauty, youth and goodness as yourself, but I am presumptuous enough to hope that you will make a grateful man proud and happy with your love, for his heart is wholly yours.'

Surprise and emotion left Rosamond no power to answer for a moment. The delicate generosity and respect of the offer touched her to the heart. Putting aside all he could give, rank, wealth, protection, honor, and with no hint at her poverty, friendlessness or the shadow on her life, he had offered the one gift that made both equal, his love, and sued for hers as humbly as if she were a princess of the land. Such things win women, and though she did not love him Rosamond could find no courage to refuse him, no words warm enough to thank him.

'You are too kind – I am not worthy – you do not know my past—' she faltered with full eyes and grateful heart.

'I do know it, Rosalie,' he answered with unchanged tenderness. 'Forgive me if I erred in asking of another the truth which I would spare you the pain of telling me. To Father Ignatius I first told my love and asked if it was wise to nourish it with hope.'

'You told *him* this! What did he answer?' Rosamond forgot both her lover and herself in pity for the hard task the unconscious Comte had given poor Ignatius. Well pleased at her eagerness, the cause of which he utterly mistook, De Luneville put a letter and a note into her hand, saying hopefully, as he stepped into the balcony to leave her free, 'Read it and let your answer be as kind, *ma chère.*'

It was a long letter telling her story in the truest yet

the kindest language. Giving her no blame but dwelling eloquently on her innocence and ignorance, the courage with which she had shunned temptation, and the penitence by which she had striven to atone for her unconscious offense. He encouraged the Comte to hope, assured him that Rosalie was worthy to be the wife of any man, begged him to pardon the past, the sin of which lay not on her shoulders, and to make her future happy with every blessing she deserved. Tears dropped upon the paper as she read, for, knowing that the writer loved her, every generous word, every kind wish was doubly precious and yet doubly sad. Even in speaking of the man who was his rival Ignatius had been just, had given no name and spared Tempest the Comte's detestation.

The note was to herself, very brief and very beautiful, for in it he bade her freely accept the good gift offered her and forget a dangerous passion in a true and happy love. No word of himself except to assure her of his approval and his prayers for her peace. That note she put into her bosom with a long sigh and the words, 'I gave myself into his hands, he bids me do it, and I will obey him.'

Then, as De Luneville glanced in wistfully, she said, steadily though tears still lay on her cheeks and her eyes were full of a touching humility, 'Monsieur le Comte, I will be frank with you, for such great kindness inspires me with a wish to be worthy of it. You know the truth now and yet you offer me your honorable name, your noble heart; I never can prove my gratitude for this, but my life shall be spent in the service of you and yours. Nay, do not thank me, I am not done. Forgive me if I confess that I do not love you as I should; my heart is full of affection, reverence and thankfulness; these I can give you gladly, but no more. I have suffered much, I think I can never love again, but if this daughterly regard contents you, take it and let me live for you.'

The Comte smiled and eagerly accepted the hand she offered him, for, manlike, he felt sure that a woman so young and tenderhearted would not long remain insensitive to love. But even as he did so something in her face made him pause and ask anxiously, 'Is this a sacrifice, Rosalie? Can you be happy with me? Does no tie still bind you? Will no secret regret poison your peace hereafter?'

As he spoke her eyes fell, the color died out of her face, her head sunk and with a sudden tremor she drew her hand away, answering slowly, 'It is no sacrifice, I shall be happy, but I cannot utterly forget.'

Remembering all she had suffered, the Comte saw in this demonstration only the humiliation of a woman wronged as she had been, and pity deepened his love. 'It shall be my care to efface the past and make you forget the bitter in the sweet. This hand is mine, and I claim it now, the heart I will win hereafter.'

As he retook it, Rosamond bent and kissed his own with a mute gratitude which he would have answered like a lover in defiance of French etiquette, had not Natalie peeped in, and seeing the act, clapped her hands, crying with an April face as she embraced Rosamond, 'Mamma! Mamma! You have said yes! Papa is happy and I'm your little daughter now.'

So wooed, so welcomed, it was impossible for Rosamond to regret her promise or to fear the future. Seeing the happiness it was in her power to give, feeling the love which surrounded her, and knowing that no deceit would ever wreck her peace in this safe home she yielded to the gentle power that controlled her and lived in the joyful present. At her desire the Comte consented that the marriage should be very private, and at his desire she consented that it should be a speedy one. A secret presentiment possessed Rosamond that it would never take place at all and in spite of every effort to banish it this feeling remained unchanged.

The trousseau was ordered from Paris and the Chateau prepared to receive its new mistress; Natalie was in a perpetual rapture over her beautiful Mamma, the Comte devoted and supremely happy, the day fixed and everything prepared, yet still Rosamond said within herself – 'It will never be.'

In spite of orders and entreaties to servants and Natalie the secret took wind and the fashionable loungers at Wiesbaden knew well that Comte de Luneville was about to marry Mademoiselle Rosalie Varian, his daughter's friend, for Rosamond had thus disguised her name, hoping the longer to elude Tempest and Baptiste.

The grand ball came two days before the wedding, and to gratify his daughter, who was sadly disappointed that there were to be no public festivities in honor of the marriage, the Comte had promised to give her a glimpse of the new Kursaal in its evening splendor. Rosamond had consented, and Natalie would not release her, though she desired to be left at home.

She was standing before her toilette while the maid put the last touches to her dress of the richest black lace (for she had worn no colors since she left the convent) when Natalie came flying in with a velvet case in her hand. Very charming did she look in the elegantly simple costume which French girls wear with such grace, and having taken a look at her pretty self she turned to Rosamond, saying gaily as she opened the case, 'Papa begs that you will wear these for his sake. He is very proud of you, my lovely Mamma, and though you reject all other ornaments I know you will wear these.'

With a consenting smile Rosamond bent her head to receive the bandeau of bridal pearls, and allowed Natalie to decorate neck and arms with the jewels that only enhanced their beauty.

'You are ravishing now, come and thank Papa as he best likes.' Following the girl, Rosamond went down and, advancing to the Comte, whose eyes were full of tender admiration, she put a white arm about his neck, a soft cheek to his and whispered with a shy first kiss, 'Gustave, I thank you.'

'Monsieur le Comte, the carriage waits.'

With a thrill of terror Rosamond turned to see standing at the door, in the Luneville livery, Baptiste!

CHAPTER XV

Madame La Comtesse

He was gone as she looked and in the hurry of departure no one observed Rosamond's pallor. As she descended she tried to persuade herself that it was a phantom conjured up by her own fears, but at the carriage door appeared the real Baptiste. Without the slightest sign of recognition on his expressionless face he put her in with the respectful care of a well-trained servant and she sunk back feeling that all was lost. As they were about to drive off he put his head in at her window, saying with a meaningful smile and an obsequious bow as he offered a glittering object, 'Madame la Comtesse dropped her fan.'

Natalie laughed, and the Comte pulled up the window looking half amused and half annoyed, but Rosamond clutched the fan, feeling sure that it concealed some threat or warning for her eye alone.

'Who is that man?' she asked, trying to speak naturally.

'A new valet whom I engaged today. It is evident he wished to propitiate his new mistress, and so imitates the other servants in giving you your title somewhat prematurely.

'He has a bad face, I do not fancy him.'

'He is merely on trial, I shall dismiss him if he does not please you,' replied the Comte with all submission.

'We will arrange that tomorrow.' But even as she spoke, Rosamond thought drearily within herself, 'What may not have happened by tomorrow?'

While De Luneville waited for them at the door of the cloakroom and Natalie arranged her curls, Rosamond examined the fan. As she expected, a tiny paper was folded in it; only a line in Tempest's hand:

Meet me as a friend and fear nothing.

He would be there then! Her heart sunk within her, for the shadow of his presence seemed to fall darkly over all her future. What would he say? Where would he meet her? A feverish anxiety at once took possession of her and her usual graceful quietude was replaced by a suppressed excitement which heightened her beauty and made her seem gayest when most miserable.

The immense Saal was filled with a brilliant throng made up of all nations; some dancing, some sitting in the recesses between the marble pillars that alternated with tall vases heaped with flowers, some roaming in and out from the lighted gardens where the lake shone, music echoed and lovers whispered in the linden walks. But the chief attraction were the gambling tables. Several of these occupied the small rooms adjoining the grand hall and were always surrounded, for at Wiesbaden every one plays and no one reproves. Men and women alike take their places at the green tables, stake their napoleons and lose or win as the impassive croupier turns a card and rolls a ball.

Natalie, full of girlish delight, hung chattering gaily on her father's arm, and Rosamond, scarcely knowing what she said, talked as gaily while her eye eagerly scanned every face that passed them as they promenaded slowly round the hall. Quite unconscious of the glances that followed her, the whispers interchanged as she went by or the Comte's satisfaction at her debut, she went on searching for one face with ever-increasing excitement. Her altered demeanor first surprised, then pleased, then disturbed De Luneville, for he could not understand it. Her usually pale cheeks burned with an unnatural color, her glittering eyes roved restlessly to and fro, she talked at random, turned almost rudely to look after passers-by, started and breathed quickly sometimes, and often seemed about to break away and follow some uncontrollable impulse. She evidently tried to conceal this strange excitement and seem like herself, but failed to do so and the consciousness of her failure added to her trouble.

De Luneville was on the point of speaking to her about it when Natalie begged to see the gambling, and, hoping a quieter scene might compose Rosamond, the Comte led them into the nearest room. The table was filled and a double row of spectators surrounded it, but several gentlemen at once gave way and permitted the ladies to draw near. A curious scene, for princes, barons, women of rank, adventurers, actresses, and disreputable characters of both sexes sat side by side in perfect silence watching the cards, laying down their gold or raking up their winnings with such a variety of expressions that the faces alone were an absorbing study.

De Luneville watched the game, Natalie became interested in the fortunes of a pretty French Marquise who in full ball costume sat playing recklessly with a group of young adorers behind her chair. As if still possessed by the same unrest, Rosamond glanced eagerly round the long table, and suddenly her eye caught a glimpse of something at the far end which made her color change and her heart beat fast. Forgetting everything but a desperate desire to see, she leaned forward, quite unconscious that her arm touched the shoulder of the gentleman sitting before her. He turned with a frown to rebuke the rudeness, but at sight of the beautiful arm the frown melted to a smile and leaving his napoleons to their fate he sat looking up into the eager countenance above him.

At the other end of the table, with averted face and head leaning on his hand, sat the man who had arrested her attention. Short black curls covered the head, and the hand that hid the face was shapely and white, with a signet ring on the third finger. Was it Tempest? Would he never turn? Trembling with suspense, Rosamond bent nearer till the gentleman over whose shoulder she leaned could hear the rapid beating of her heart. Her anxiety was almost unbearable when the man turned, and with a long sigh of relief she saw that it was *not* Tempest.

Pressing her hand upon eyes weary with that long strain, she stood so till a warm breath on her arm made her look up to see the dreaded face close before her, smiling with a smile of satirical satisfaction that nearly drove her wild.

Neither spoke for an instant, but Tempest touched his lips with a significant gesture and assumed the air of a stranger. Scarcely knowing what she did, Rosamond drew back with a hasty '*Pardon, Monsieur,*' which he answered with the bow and smile of a gallant man and a glance at the white arm as he said, '*Merci, Madame.*'

A moment after, the Comte, turning to speak to Rosamond, was startled at the entire change which appeared in her. Pale and motionless as a statue, she stood with a strangely absent expression in the so lately eager eyes, and the look of a woman who waited to receive some impending blow. Glancing about him to discover any cause for this entire metamorphosis, the Comte saw nothing but the busy crowd and most absorbed of all was the peculiar-looking man just before her.

'You are tired, come and rest, *ma chère*,' whispered De Luneville, drawing her arm through his with tender anxiety. She fixed a blank look on him as if she had not heard or comprehended, then roused herself by a strong effort and passed her hand over her eyes with a nervous shudder as she said softly, 'Yes, take me away, the crowd distracts me.'

'Papa, Papa, I entreat you to let me stay a little longer,

it is so fascinating.' cried Natalie, who was a spoilt child and ruled her father like a pretty tyrant.

Before he could explain, Rosamond said, with all her usual self possession and in her usual clear tone, 'Stay with her, Gustave, here is Madame Duval and her son going to sit in the garden, I will join them, the air will refresh me and you can meet us at the Pagoda.'

With a decided gesture she withdrew her hand and was gone before De Luneville could detain her. Perplexed and somewhat annoyed, he submitted and remained to guard his daughter, quite unaware that the peculiar-looking man was observing him with keen but covert scrutiny till he rose and mingled in the crowd.

Madame Duval and her party were soon absorbed in ices and gossip, but as Rosamond cared for neither she was politely allowed to rest somewhat apart from the gay group. She had purposely left the Comte, had purposely raised her voice as she spoke of the Pagoda, for she knew Tempest would haunt her till he had spoken and now she waited for him, resolved to have no meeting or explanation before the Comte if possible. She did not wait long; soon Tempest appeared, and having said to Madame Duval with the utmost suavity in his perfect French, 'I am an old friend, I have news from England for Mademoiselle, is it permitted that we take a little promenade by the lake?' and without waiting for a reply he offered his arm to Rosamond, adding under his breath. 'Will you come, or shall I speak here.'

She went at once, leaving Madame to shrug her shoulders and lament the unwise freedom allowed their young ladies by 'the mad English', as they are called abroad.

Leading her into a shadowy path lighted only by the moon and deserted for livelier walks, Tempest said, almost sternly though he held her hand with a warm grasp, 'Why did you break your promise?'

'I made none,' was her equally stern reply.

'You forget, I told you that I left you free to amuse yourself as you chose; two things only I forbade you, death and marriage; yet I find you on the point of becoming Madame la Comtesse.'

'You have no right to forbid me anything.'

'Perhaps not, but I have the power.'

'I doubt it and defy it.'

'I warn you to beware, Rose, I am in earnest and I *always conquer*.'

'*I* am in earnest and I *never yield*.'

He paused and examined her face in a streak of moonlight which fell across the path. It was very pale but perfectly emotionless, and the eyes she fixed steadily on his were full of a dauntless determination deeper and stronger than defiance. His own eyes kindled, his ruthless mouth grew grim, and his whole air showed plainly that he felt the crisis had come and held himself ready to meet it.

'Rose, do you love this man?' he asked vehemently.

'As a father.'

'And he is satisfied with that cool affection?'

'Yes.'

'You are ambitious, you marry him for his rank?'

'I am friendless, I marry him for protection.'

'Against whom?'

'You.'

'He will not protect you when he knows my claim upon you,' sneered Tempest, stung by her words.

'He knows the truth and still loves me.'

'All, does he know all, Rosamond?'

'Everything but your name. Ignatius spared you the added shame of a good man's contempt.'

She had withdrawn her hand and with folded arms, head erect and the carriage of a queen she walked beside him through the light and shadow of the flowery path. Tempest ground his teeth as he watched her, conscious that some invisible barrier had risen up between them to baffle and defeat him. What it was he could not tell, but felt it, and the subtle resistance roused passion, pride and will to conquer it at all hazards.

In a tone of concentrated wrath and hatred he said, 'I understand, the handsome priest has wrought this change. He is the Comte's confessor and Madame la Comtesse will become a devotee. Chateau and convent are not far apart and Englishwomen soon learn that French customs permit a young lover as well as an old husband.'

She answered not a word, never turned her head, and betrayed no sign of having heard the insult except by, with a sudden, disdainful gesture, gathering back the sweeping skirt that brushed against him as if he were some noxious thing. It was an involuntary act, a womanly retaliation, but it wounded him more deeply than the sharpest word, for he loved her the more intensely the more she repulsed him, feeling sure that, in spite of all, her heart was his and would yield at last.

That little touch of silent contempt stung him to the soul and harassed him with the fear that her coldness was real, not assumed. With an expression that would have daunted any woman he placed himself before her and was about to speak when, finding her passage barred, she turned and swept slowly back again, outwardly untroubled but inwardly intensely grateful to be nearer help in case of need, for he looked as if a word would goad him to any violence.

With a stifled oath he sprung to her side and put out his hand to arrest her, but something in her face restrained him and walking at her side he said low between his teeth, 'You will marry this man?'

'I will.'

'You no longer love me then?'

'Not a whit.'

'You utterly reject me, do you.'

'Yes.'

'You refuse my prayers and defy my warning?'

'I do.'

'Then it is war to the death! Are you prepared for the consequences of your act?'

She turned now and looked at him, for his frightful calmness made her blood run cold. 'What will the consequences be?' she asked, half pausing.

'A bullet through De Luneville's heart is one of them.'

At this threat, uttered with a look which plainly proved that it would be mercilessly executed if she defied him, all her courage failed her. Any insult, wrong or danger to herself she could bear, but death to the man who loved her, Natalie's beloved father, her generous friend, that was impossible, that sin must never lie at her door even if she killed herself to prevent it.

Tempest saw his power and used it well, for as she stretched her clasped hands toward him in mute entreaty, before words could come he drew back as if implacable and answered her with a relentless voice, 'No, I will not be cajoled nor bribed again. I have waited long and patiently, have left you free and let no word of mine betray the tie that binds us. I have no desire to kill this man but if you persist in putting an insurmountable barrier between us I swear I will have his life, and his blood will be upon your head.'

'If I submit, what then?' she whispered with a terror-stricken face, for in the shadow that other face, swarthy, fierce and fiery-eyed, recalled the night when she saw it first and likened it to Mephistopheles.

'Then I vanish, unknown as I came. I leave you free and wait till this cursed divorce is won. A month more and my chain is off; I am glad and ready for another then, and surely I can give no better proof of my love than that, when after fifteen years of slavery I give my freedom into your keeping, Rosamond?'

His voice softened as he spoke, and he laid his hand upon her head as if he claimed her by an inalienable right. The proud head drooped at once, the chaplet of pearls fell at her feet, and all the peaceful, happy future vanished in the gloom of the shadow on her life.

Tempest lifted the jewels, guessed their giver and with a dark smile said, 'See, Rose, your bridal crown drops away at my touch, for it is none of mine. Accept the omen and promise that in a month I shall put another in its place.'

'I cannot promise! Phillip, be merciful! Let me make this good man happy; I owe him so much, I can show it in no other way the gratitude I feel for him. You have done me bitter wrong and I pardon it, but for God's sake do not haunt and ruin my whole life.'

Regardless of time or place, Rosamond had sunk upon her knees as she implored pity of the pitiless. He loved her, but it was a selfish love and he was glad to see her proud spirit broken, for he thought that her defeat was his victory. She had forgotten everything but her despair, he was watchful and wary even at this excited moment. He desired to remain unknown if possible, to work behind the scenes and avoid bloodshed, knowing well that Rosamond would find many defenders if the truth was known. To work upon her fears was the safest course, yet not to drive her too far lest he lost all.

Steps and voices approached before he could reply, and hastily raising her he led her on, saying in a tone she could not forget, 'Go and think of this; I give you till tomorrow night. Escape is impossible, for Baptiste watches in the house and I watch without. Your woman's wit will devise some pretext for retracting your promise to the Comte, or deferring its fulfillment for a month. Then I shall appear and this long struggle must end happily. Be wise and decide as I would have you, else—'

He did not finish but the pause was terribly significant, and bowing her head in mute assent Rosamond quitted his side to glide into a seat at the door of the Pagoda where Madame Duval still sat.

Tempest vanished and when the Comte came to look for his fiancée he found her waiting for him with the same unnaturally quiet, absent look on her colorless face. Natalie begged for one more promenade through the great salon where the ball was now at its height and Rosamond assented for the child's sake, though De Luneville desired to take them both away. As they fell in with the gay procession which eddied round the hall, he felt the hand that lay on his right arm clenched with sudden force, and looking down saw Rosamond's face flash into life and color in the drawing of a breath. Pride, defiance, scorn and hatred mingled in that briefly brilliant expression. It was gone as quickly as it came and she walked on like a beautiful automaton again.

Looking up with a bewildered glance, the Comte saw the peculiar, scarred face of the man at the gaming table, now arm in arm with a friend of his own who bowed in passing, while the stranger fixed his eyes on Rosamond with a singular look.

'What a repulsive person De Launoy has with him. Did you observe, Rosalie?' asked the Comte quickly.

'Yes, he was horrible,' she answered with a shiver.

'He had magnificent eyes, Papa. Some hero I am sure by the great scar on his forehead. I shall ask De Launoy who his romantic-looking friend is tomorrow,' said Natalie, all unconscious of the tragedy going on so near her.

As the carriage door closed upon them Rosamond leaned forward to put down the window, when a mocking voice whispered in her ear, 'Adieu, till tomorrow night, Madame la Comtesse.'

CHAPTER XVI

Mad

The spacious gardens adjoining the Kursaal were usually
filled with fashionable loungers by twelve o'clock, but
on the morning after the ball they were deserted by all
but a few gentlemen who had spent the night at the
gaming tables and were breakfasting under the trees
before the great Café. At one of these tables sat Tempest
and his new-made acquaintance, De Launoy, enjoying
coffee and cigars. Up and down a distant walk a tall
soldierly figure was marching in the September sunshine
with bent head and absorbed expression. From time to
time Tempest glanced that way and presently his companion's eye followed his.

'Ah, the poor De Luneville! He tries to dissipate his
impatience by an early promenade. My faith! He is as
ardent a lover as if his head was not gray. One would
think he had had enough to keep him from a second
experiment of this sort.'

'Might I ask what misfortune beside the death of his
wife has afflicted the Comte?'

'It is well known and I may speak of it. Madame la
Comtesse was mad for years before she died, and De
Luneville suffered so intensely that we never allude to
the unfortunate lady. Any discussion or hint of insanity
drives him half distracted, for he is haunted by a fear
that Mademoiselle may inherit her mother's malady.'

'Ah, – yes, – thank you.'

The words fell slowly from Tempest's lips and for

many minutes he sat so still that De Launoy fancied he was half asleep. Had he seen the eyes behind those downcast lids he would have known that some purpose was absorbing the man's mind so intensely that he was unconscious of everything else. A sudden laugh broke the silence and seemed to recall Tempest to the fact that he was not alone. Checking his mysterious merriment, he accounted for it by relating some ludicrous incident of the night before and had just finished the story when De Launoy said, 'Here is De Luneville, do you know him?'

'No, I desire to, pray present me.'

The Comte approached, but in no mood for introductions, and when his friend presented Tempest it required all his native breeding to receive him courteously. De Launoy made him sit and having started an agreeable subject of conversation pleaded an engagement and slipped away to bed. Tempest smiled as he went, and eyed the Comte as a cat might eye a mouse before she tortured it. A word had inspired him with a diabolical plot and chance seemed to favor its execution, for even while he hesitated how to take the first step accident befriended him. He dropped the cigar which he was about to light and stooping to recover it a little locket slipped from his vest pocket and rolled toward the Comte. The spring was broken, and as it fell it opened, causing the Comte to exclaim in the act of taking it up, 'Mon Dieu, how like Rosalie!'

'It is my wife,' was the quiet answer as Tempest stretched his hand for the miniature.

But De Luneville kept it, saying with an air of haughty surprise mingled with anxiety as his eye fell on two letters, 'I do not doubt your word, Monsieur, but permit me to ask the name of this lady whose initials and face are so wonderfully like those of Mademoiselle Varian?'

'Rosamond Vivian is the name of the lady whom I married nearly three years ago, and who, I have the unhappiness of informing Monsieur le Comte, is the same person as Mademoiselle Rosalie Varian.'

'It is false!' De Luneville flung down the picture as if it were a battle gage.

With the same calm air, the same pitiful glance, Tempest took up the trinket and opening the other side displayed a curl of dark hair folded in a little paper on which in a hand the Comte knew well was written, 'For Phillip from his Rose.'

As he looked the angry color forsook the unhappy man's face, he dropped into the seat from which he had started, and laying a trembling hand on Tempest's arm he whispered hoarsely, 'Tell me what it means?'

'I will. For this I came hither, hoping to be in time to save you from the terrible misfortune which rumor whispered you were about to bring upon yourself.'

A look of relief swept over the Comte's face as he exclaimed like one who caught at a clue to the mystery, 'I know the story of her life and I forgive it.'

'Ah, Monsieur, you are nobly generous but you are deceived; you believe that romantic tale, you pity and forgive. God knows the poor girl needs pity and pardon for the fraud, but you will thank me for the truth, bitter though it be, which saves you from marrying a madwoman.'

Tempest's voice dropped low and his lips trembled as he uttered the black lie that was to doom the Comte's happiness to a sudden death. De Luneville's face blanched with unutterable grief and horror as he listened and believed even while repelling the dreadful fact.

'No, no, it is impossible! It cannot be my Rosalie, she is as sane as I. It is some terrible mistake; for God's sake tell me anything but that,' he cried in tones that would have touched a heart of stone.

They did touch Tempest's, hard as it was, but having staked much upon the venture he would not retract, seeing how strong an adversary he had in this man's love, and feeling that De Launoy's hint was the best

153

weapon to use against it. With well-feigned compassion he soothed the Comte's anguish and seemed to share it as a fellow sufferer.

'My poor friend, I beseech your pardon for this blow, but it was inevitable. Listen while I tell you the sad tale of my bereavement and her malady. I loved her passionately, nay, still do in spite of all, and yearn to win her back.' No acting there, real love in the voice, real longing in the eye, real sorrow in the sigh that followed. This touch of nature struck the listener with the force of truth and gave weight to every word of the artful story. With a groan the Comte pulled his hat over his brows and listened in despairing silence.

'We were married hastily, I have the proofs of the act and can produce witnesses, though the poor girl denies the whole. For a year we were very happy, but at times a strange restlessness tormented her and troubled me. I indulged every whim, led a wandering life to gratify her, and devoted myself soul and body to her pleasure. In the beginning of the second year the vague fear which had haunted me was confirmed by her sudden flight. I followed and found her, a sad wreck in Paris where some kind Providence had thrown her into the hands of friends. I could no longer conceal from myself the dreadful truth, for she was the victim of one of those monomanias which baffle the skill of the wisest and lie unsuspected till some mysterious impulse betrays them. She denied that I was her husband, accused me of deceiving her by a false marriage, firmly believed that I had a wife living, and was in a hopeless state of mental confusion. I did my best, not wishing to use force, but while I waited for some change in her she fled again to Amiens.'

'Yes, it is true, the story is the same; go on, go on, I will hear all,' murmured the Comte, leaning his head upon his hands in an attitude of desperate patience.

'At times she is quite herself, so lovely, mild and winning no one would suspect the sad malady till a word from me, a hint of the past, or some inexplicable mood brings back the mania in its stubborn or its frantic form. At the Convent she was apparently well, and this Ignatius having won her confidence espoused her cause with the blind devotion of a lover. It is true, priest though he be, and Rosamond will not deny it. She was touched by his passion but knowing that it was vain, and possessed with a never-dying fear of me, she took refuge with you. I knew whither she had gone for I never lost sight of my poor afflicted girl long, yet cannot find the courage to confine her lest it confirm the malady past cure. While she was useful, well and happy I remained passive, but when tidings of your approaching marriage reached me I could no longer hold my peace, and as an honorable man I came to confide the heavy secret to you, regretting deeply that I could not have spared you from all suffering.'

'Too late, too late!' groaned the Comte.

'It afflicts me to the heart to learn this, but I had never dreamed that you would love my Rosamond other than as a friend, a father. Your gray hairs deceived me and now I can do nothing but offer you my thanks for past kindness, my respectful sympathy for present pain, and remove my unhappy wife as soon as possible.'

The thought of parting seemed to calm De Luneville by the very weight of his grief, and though overwhelmed with the sudden shock he still tried to delay the end. Looking up he asked, as an ominous recollection returned to him, 'Monsieur, allow me to ask how often these paroxysms occur, and how their approach is manifested? I have had cause to know and dread this terrible malady and I have never detected any of its symptoms in Rosalie – till last night,' he added to himself.

'Hers is a peculiar case and every physician I have consulted assured me that it is incurable, though time may mitigate its violence. Once or twice a year this restless mood comes over her, beginning with melancholy, increasing to excitement which usually ends in some outbreak. She is conscious of her affliction, tries to hide it and forget, but feels its approach and if possible she seeks to save herself from the fear and pity of others by flight. Have you observed none of these signs of late?'

'Yes,' and with that one hard word the Comte fell into a state of passive despair.

In answering the question Tempest had described a case of insanity which he had known, shrewdly suspecting that an impetuous, demonstrative creature like Rosamond had passed through many changes of feeling and demeanor during her sojourn with the Comte. He remembered that her manner the previous evening had been excited and must have seemed doubly so to one who possessed no key to the mystery.

His reply had confirmed De Luneville's fear and banished his last doubt. Rosamond *had* been melancholy; there was something peculiar in her manner when he offered her his hand; the events of the evening were fresh in his mind and now seemed strongest confirmation of the story he had heard. On reaching home she had gone hastily to her room, and there he had heard her walking half the night. She had refused breakfast, and Natalie reported that she looked like a ghost lying dressed upon her bed with everything in unusual disorder round her. All this the unhappy man recalled as he sat there with hidden face while his tormentor waited to finish the wicked deed he had begun.

Presently he looked up, deathly pale but very calm, and said, rising like a man suddenly grown old, 'Monsieur Tempest, I thank you, I relinquish all claims of course, I put the unhappy lady into your hands and leave Wiesbaden at once for my daughter's sake. Here is my address, you will find me there at any hour and may freely ask any assistance in my power. Pardon, that I leave you now, I have much to do, for tomorrow was to have been my wedding day,' and bowing with sad dignity the Comte went away to hide his sorrow from all eyes.

Tempest sat in deep thought for several minutes and then hurried away in an opposite direction, for he also had much to do.

De Luneville was a brave man, but the frantic scenes he had passed through with his mad wife had given him an intense fear of insanity, and much brooding over the sad memory had not lessened its horror. As he wandered through the most desolate portions of the park he went over his interview with Tempest. At times he doubted the whole story and resolved to demand proofs; then he recalled Rosamond's strange moods and felt sure that the malady was there. Again he thought of her past and shrunk as he had not done when Ignatius told its history, for since he had seen Tempest an instinctive repugnance came over him at the idea of marrying the girl who once had loved this man. The longer he thought of it the firmer became his resolution to relinquish all hope of Rosamond and save his name from any stain, his daughter from any harm, by the sacrifice of his own love. Whatever the truth might be he would end his own part in the tragedy and break loose from the entanglement before it was too late, sparing himself as much as possible from public criticism and censure by timely flight, for the thought of facing the world's pity or contempt made the proud man writhe.

Full of this determination he turned toward his hotel after hours of solitary meditation, and was approaching home when his attention was arrested by the erratic movements of a lady hastening on before him. A thick veil hid her face and she carried a small parcel in her hand. She walked quickly down the long street, often glancing nervously behind her; once or twice she paused and seemed undecided which way to go, then dived into a shop till some one passed, and emerging cautiously, retraced her steps a little way to cross and return more rapidly than before as if anxious to reach some distant point unobserved. Something in the figure and the gait of the lady made him follow her, and just as she was stepping into a fiacre he touched her arm with a quiet 'Rosalie!'

She sprung back, threw up her veil and after a startled glance, laughed nervously as the color dyed her haggard face, and said hurriedly, 'Where have you been so long? Why do you follow me?'

'I have been in the Park, and I follow to know where you are going in such haste,' he answered soothingly.

'Home, will you come?' and she stepped into the carriage with the expression of one baffled in some secret purpose.

'She meant to escape; Tempest is right,' thought De Luneville, marking her restless eyes, her eager manner, as with a quiet, 'Thank you, yes,' he seated himself beside her.

She leaned back and put down her veil without a word till the parcel slipped from her lap. She snatched it up before he could reach it and holding it fast, said rapidly, 'It is nothing, I had a little plan, a surprise for you, but I cannot do it, I must wait. Ask no questions, and don't tell Natalie I came out, she thinks I am asleep. I wish I was!'

The wish broke from her with a heavy sigh, and touched with pity, the Comte took her hot hand in his, observing that she wore no gloves and was dressed with strange simplicity.

'*Ma chère*, you should rest after the fatigue of last night; it was too much for you,' he said kindly.

'Yes, too much, too much!' she answered with a sudden tremor and a quick glance from the window as Baptiste, still following her, passed leisurely by unseen by De Luneville.

'Come home and let me send for Dr Geuth; I am sure you are ill and need advice,' began the Comte, already terribly anxious, for her pulse beat faster than he could count and her whole appearance frightened him. As he spoke she caught her hand away to drag down both curtains, saying abruptly, 'I hate to be stared at!'

She had caught a glimpse of Tempest driving rapidly in an opposite direction, and fearing some harm to the Comte had hidden him by that unfortunate act. Mad people dread and avoid the eyes of the sane, knowing that they cannot meet them; this speech of hers and the veil held close made the Comte's heart sink as no peril would have done. He said no more, but having seen her safely to her room bid her maid keep her quiet and shut himself up to arrange for a speedy departure.

The half hour before dinner is the quietest of the day even in hotels, for then everyone is dressing and salons and halls deserted. Taking advantage of this time, Tempest went to the Comte's apartments; Baptiste received and showed him into the private parlor, and took up a written message to Rosamond. She came at once, as preternaturally calm as she had been excited a few hours before, for she had resolved upon another means of escape, having failed of the first.

'Have you decided?' was Tempest's brief greeting, still bent on moving her through fears for the Comte.

'Yes, I submit; I will delay the wedding and wait if you will have no mercy.'

'I do not accept your submission, I distrust you, for in spite of your promise to meet me now and here you would have broken your engagement but for Baptiste. Where were you going in that wild way? Back to the priest perhaps.' He wished to rouse and agitate her and used the taunt that seldom failed.

It succeeded now, for every nerve was strung to the utmost and she looked like a hunted creature driven to bay. Her white face flushed with indignant color and her eyes darkened and dilated with strong excitement as she said, almost fiercely, 'Utter his name again and I will take you at your word. In defending me he will forget he is a priest and teach you to respect and fear him as you never feared and respected man before. Say what you have to say and go.'

Her mood alarmed him, and a sudden dread of

making her a madwoman in dreadful earnest checked the scornful answer which rose to his lips, for the thought of Ignatius angered him more than he would confess even to himself. Taking out a case of pistols he laid it open on the table, saying calmly as he pointed to it, 'Choose one of two things. Go with me *at once* or see me insult De Luneville and shoot him; I never miss my aim.'

At this instant the Comte appeared upon the threshold. Forgetting everything but his danger, Rosamond clutched the pistols and rushed toward him crying wildly, 'Go! Go! he will murder you!'

In her despair she spoke in English, which De Luneville did not understand, and seeing her fly toward him with out stretched hands so armed he fancied the frantic paroxysm possessed her, and with an exclamation of horror turned and fled.

'He does not fear *me*; it is *you* he flies from. I told him you were mad, he believes it and renounces you. Now choose.'

As the words left Tempest's lips she turned on him with a look of superb defiance and disdain, saying only, 'I do choose – this!' and placing a pistol to her side she fired.

CHAPTER XVII

Torment

When Rosamond recovered the consciousness she lost as the bullet entered her side she looked about her in amazement, for everything was strange. She lay on a narrow bed in a large, comfortable, but somewhat bare-looking room. The windows were barred, the fire burned behind a tall, wire screen, and on the wall hung a shapeless garment with many straps and buckles. Rain beat on the panes, glimpses of a dark pine forest were seen, and the wind sighed drearily down the mountain passes. Strange sounds met her ears, loud laughter, discordant singing, incoherent voices, and now and then a terrible, shrill cry as of one in mortal pain. Beside the bedside sat a strong, sober woman in a sort of plain uniform, gray gown, white cap and apron, a whistle hung from her neck and a badge on her shoulder. Knitting busily, she sat with half-shut eyes, but no movement of the girl's escaped her vigilance.

'Where am I?' asked Rosamond when she had collected her feeble senses and recalled the past up to a certain point.

'Madame is quite safe, rest tranquil,' was the brief reply.

'Is this a hospital?' asked the faint voice again.

'If Madame likes to call it so.'

'What name has it?'

'The Refuge, Madame.'

'Where is it? Near Wiesbaden?'

'A few miles south, Madame.'

'Who brought me here?'

'The husband of Madame.'

'When?'

'Last night, asleep and ill.'

'Is he gone?'

'Yes, Madame.'

'Thank God for that!'

The woman who had eyed her curiously smiled at the fervent ejaculation and said, as if to test her sanity, 'Monsieur was in despair at leaving Madame but it was best as Madame could not travel. He left orders that everything should be done for Madame's comfort, and his valet remained to serve Madame.'

'Baptiste here to wait on me? I understand, he watches me till I am well lest I escape, cruel, cruel!'

'Madame did not see the grief of Monsieur when he wept over her and saluted her tenderly as he went. It was not cruelty but great kindness to leave Madame in so safe and excellent a home.'

'Home!' echoed Rosamond, but at the instant a cry so loud and terrible rung through the place that she sprang up exclaiming, as the truth flashed on her, 'Great heaven, it is a madhouse!'

'Madame is right,' replied the woman coldly.

With a moan of mingled pain and horror the poor girl fell back upon her pillow, not unconscious but over-whelmed by the dreadful truth. Sick, helpless, friendless, guarded by Baptiste and in Tempest's power, what could she expect when this outrage was the first step he took to win her back? Mute and tearless, she lay feeling utterly forsaken by God and man. The calmness of despair came over her and saying, 'I have done my best, I can do no more,' she resigned herself to whatever fate had in store for her. One thing she resolved and remained true to throughout all her coming trials; Tempest desired to make others think her mad, in that she would thwart him and by no look, word or act confirm the lie.

A sharp pain in her side roused her from a bitter reverie and looking down she saw that it was bandaged. Speaking in a quiet tone, she said civilly, 'Will you kindly loosen these things, I cannot breathe.'

'Certainly, Madame,' and laying down her work the woman skillfully unwound the bandages.

'A little wound to give so much pain. Did Monsieur tell you how I received it?' asked Rosamond, looking at the tiny purple mark on her white flesh just below her heart.

'Yes Madame, he sadly confessed that in a paroxysm of delirium Madame essayed to destroy herself, but happily the ball wounded no vital part and is not dangerous though painful. To prevent such misfortunes he brought Madame hither for a time, which was wise.'

'Did he leave any message for me?'

'Yes, the servant of Madame has a letter when Madame is able to receive it.'

'Bring him at once, I am able now,' commanded Rosamond and Manton went to find Baptiste, after vainly urging that Madame should wait.

The man appeared with a face as inscrutable as his master's, respectfully delivered a note and informed her that he was at her service whenever she chose to ring for him. Seizing the paper she dismissed him and eagerly read what Tempest had left for her:

My dearest,

You cannot tell how it afflicts me to treat you with such seeming harshness, but you leave me no alternative. I cannot lose you and your desperate act prevents my taking you with me as I long to do. The Comte has gone, renouncing you entirely after I told my tale, for his pride rebelled and he was glad to escape. Let him go, he is not worth a tear, for such lukewarm affection is not

*love. For a time you must devote yourself to recovery;
the instant you desire to be free inform Baptiste and he
will bring you to me.*

*I am forced to be in England, for the divorce is
passing through its last forms. Soon I shall be all your
own and then I claim you. Make haste to recover your
bloom, my little Rose, and come soon to reward the
constancy of one who loves you faithfully as master,
lover and husband.*

Phillip

'No hope there.' Dropping the note Rosamond hid
her face to conceal the tears that disappointment, suffering and indignation wrung from her. The paper fell open
at Manton's feet and without stirring she read it,
glanced at the girl and shrugged her shoulders as only a
Frenchwoman can, expressing by the gesture sympathy,
doubt and determination.

Rosamond said no more and for a week lay quietly on
her bed waiting for strength and spirit to act. So calm,
rational, patient and sweet was she that the woman's
heart was touched, and Dr Gérard treated her with the
utmost respect in the daily call he made. An unscrupulous, skillful charlatan who made money by lending his
house for any illegal imprisonment of inconvenient
people, he was all suavity, smiles and compliments, but
underneath as ruthless as a savage and as crafty as a fox.
Rosamond disliked him at once, but hid her repugnance
and obeyed him with a docility for which he was
evidently unprepared.

By the second week her bed became insupportable,
and she sat at her window looking out upon the Black
Forest and the lovely valley at its foot. She never sent for
Baptiste but often saw him sitting in the garden or busy
among the autumn flowers of which he sent her up a
delicate bouquet each morning as if to remind her of his
presence. Manton was her only society and she was not
loquacious though kind. Books were denied her, also

pen or needle and she was left to brood over her unhappy fate.

Tempest proved his wit in leaving her no employment, thus forcing her to think, knowing well that she could not fail to contrast her present dreary solitude with the gay, luxurious life which might be hers with a word. She did think of this, but for a time it was no temptation and she made no sign of relenting, though she felt sure by Dr Gérard's manner that he reported her state to Tempest and received directions from him.

The third week she was moved into another wing of the house and a new torment began. She was surrounded by lunatics; in the court below they roamed and moped so that she could not look from her window without seeing sad or frantic figures. Above and around her shrieked, laughed and chattered maniacs and idiots, making day wretched and night terrible. Sleep, appetite and spirits forsook her, life was unutterably dark and heavy to her, hope seemed to die within her, and the future to show no gleam of light. Still she held fast to her resolve, sent no message, showed no sign of madness, and clung to one faint possibility; Ignatius would remember her, would seek for her and might save her. He was her only friend and to him she cried for help in her despair, but no answer came.

So wan and wild-eyed did she soon become in this dreadful place that Manton rebelled and implored the doctor to remove Madame before her health gave way. After some delay he complied, and Rosamond was allowed to walk in the private garden where Baptiste watched her, but so unobtrusively she scarcely knew it.

Even Baptiste was shocked when he saw her, and plainly showed his sympathy by mute tokens of respect and goodwill. At first she took no heed of this, but as time wore on and no help came, she began to watch Baptiste with the hope that pity might soften his heart, or money bribe his vigilance. Pausing near him as he worked one day, she said, with her eye upon his dark expressionless face, 'Baptiste, for how much will you let me escape from this dreadful prison? I might try to flatter and blind you but it would be in vain, therefore I boldly ask the price of your fidelity.'

'Madame is wise, she understands me well; but I regret that my fidelity cannot be sold. It is the Master's and I dare not betray his trust.'

'"Dare not." I thought you feared nothing human, Baptiste.'

'It is not fear but gratitude which binds me to him, Madame. He saved my life once and I swore to devote it to him. I cannot forfeit my word, much as I may long to do so.'

'But if he orders you to commit a great wrong, does your gratitude require you to do it?'

'Yes, Madame, a crime even; my life is his and he may use it as he will.'

'Ah, if I had a faithful servant like you how grateful I should be, for in all the world I have not a single friend.' Rosamond turned away to hide the tears that would not be restrained.

Baptiste's eye followed her and softened as he looked. So young, so lovely, so wronged and so forsaken, it was little wonder the man's heart smote him and duty grew repugnant to him. He worked in silence till she came round again and was about to pass in silence when he looked up, touched his cap and asked below his breath, 'What would Madame offer for liberty?'

'Everything I own. Tempest sent all my possessions to me. I have many trinkets, for the Comte's gifts are there; I have a little money and I can add the blessings of a grateful heart saved from despair.'

'Where would Madame go?'

'Anywhere to escape from Tempest. Once free from this place I can find a refuge and be happy. Baptiste, do not torture me! Is it possible? Will you relent?'

166

'I will think of Madame's proposal, and however I may decide Madame may be assured of my respectful sympathy.'

'Oh Baptiste, be generous, be pitiful! Let me go and I will pray for you all my days,' cried Rosamond stretching her hands to him imploringly.

He dropped his spade, pulled off his cap and pressing his hand on his heart bowed deeply, saying only, 'Madame I thank you,' but as he spoke he glanced toward the barred gate, the key of which he held and smiled significantly.

'I understand, if I find it open I am free! Do not deceive me, is it so Baptiste?'

'Madame must give me time. Tomorrow the doctor goes to town, perhaps Madame goes also by another route; I do not promise, I only suggest,' and with a second smile Baptiste departed, leaving his mistress in a state of suspense hard to bear.

The morrow came and saying not a word to Manton, Rosamond left a ring and written thanks in her room, placed the rest of her jewels and money in her pocket and at the usual hour went down to walk in the garden. Baptiste was not there, the gate was locked as usual and nothing appeared but her nosegay on the stone seat where she sometimes sat.

Angry and heartsick with disappointment she threw it from her and as it fell something dashed on the flagged walk. Darting to the spot, she found the key half-hidden in the flowers, and with a cry of joy she seized it. This garden opened on the quiet and lonely road that wound away through the valley, and led through the outskirts of the forest to Wiesbaden. Stealing to the gate, Rosamond opened it noiselessly and shut it after her unseen, for no one thought of watching Baptiste, whose fidelity was so well known. Scarcely daring to believe the truth Rosamond hurried away, intent on reaching the nearest town where she could inquire of boat or train.

No one followed or met her, and with increasing hope

she kept on till a picturesque old mill appeared with a motherly woman spinning in the doorway. Feeling faint with her unusual exertion Rosamond ventured to ask for bread and wine, explaining her lonely state by saying she had lost her party in the forest and desired to get on to Wiesbaden as soon as possible. The good soul gladly fed the wanderer and sent her on in the charge of her son, who gallantly led the mule she rode and beguiled the way by tales of the famous forest in which he was a *Forstmeister* or keeper. Avoiding the fashionable part of Wiesbaden, Rosamond desired Ludwig to take her to some humble Gasthaus where she could pass the night and take boat for Coblenz in the morning. Alarmed at Tempest's last act, she had decided on seeking the only refuge where she could be safe, and with this purpose she turned her face toward England.

Away early in the morning in one of the cheap steamers that ply up and down the Rhine, she spent an anxious day floating down that lovely river, and in the twilight landed at Coblenz. Having been there before, she felt less forlorn than if it had been utterly new, and going to a quiet inn was trying to eat a hasty meal when a pretty, somewhat bold-eyed girl came in and ordering wine sat down to enjoy it.

Being anxious to husband her small store of money lest she should incur suspicion by trying to sell the jewels, which were very valuable, Rosamond had not ordered a private room but sat a little apart at one of the tables in the eating-saal, which chanced to be empty when she came. At first she was grateful that the newcomer was a woman, but presently the girl's manner annoyed her, for she stared pertinaciously and had a sharp, inquisitive expression which alarmed the fugitive. Hastily finishing her supper she desired to be shown her chamber and was about to lock herself in when the girl appeared, and offering a letter, said she would wait below for a reply. Taking it with fear and trembling, Rosamond read,

Chère amie,

I am here, I recognized you in the street but made no sign lest I should do harm. I long to see and speak with you, will you not come to me and let me be as of old your faithful friend?

Honorine

No address, no date but the peculiar handwriting was genuine and the monogram on the dainty sheet was familiar to Rosamond. Here was a happy chance, a hope of help and comfort too precious to be lost. Calling up the girl she said eagerly, 'Where is Mademoiselle?'

'At her little chateau just beyond the town.'

'She sent you for me?'

'Yes, Madame, I am her *femme de chambre*, I know the place and when Mademoiselle saw you pass not long ago she said, "Annette, follow that lady and give her this note unperceived. If she consents to visit me, bring her quickly to the chateau, if she cannot come, return bringing me permission to join her if possible."'

'I will go with you, call a carriage.'

'One waits at the corner for Madame.'

They went, and entering the comfortable English coupé which waited for them they were rapidly driven away over the bridge toward the famous fortress that commands the town. Spirit and hope renewed in the poor girl's breast as Annette spoke of her mistress's delight on seeing her friend and her eagerness to welcome her. She was reposing here before another winter at Berlin it seemed, and Rosamond half resolved to go with her if Honorine repeated her offer. Full of confidence and courage, she listened to the maid's chat and followed her up the steps of the pretty chateau perched on a green slope overlooking the town.

She was led into a charming boudoir, and Annette begged her to repose a moment while she informed Mademoiselle of her happy arrival. Being left alone she looked eagerly about her, seeing many signs of her

169

friend in the embroidery frame drawn to the window, music scattered over the instrument, a mask and pair of foils, a pet dog and a profusion of exquisite flowers. A pair of man's gloves lay on the table and as her eye fell upon them Rosamond smiled, thinking to herself, 'Perhaps Honorine is married and plans a surprise for me. Happy the man who wins her.'

A burst of laughter from below made her pause where she stood. A woman's laugh, and soon the rustle of a woman's dress was heard as if some one hastily approached.

'Honorine!' cried Rosamond as the door opened, and with a cry of joy threw herself into the arms of Tempest!

CHAPTER XVIII

One Friend

'Welcome *"chère amie!"'* cried Tempest embracing her
warmly. 'I did not expect so kind a greeting, little
sweetheart – but, good heaven! Rose, how terribly you
are changed!'

Well might he say so and look dismayed, for she
stood like one turned to stone, regarding him with a
wild and woeful air that made her haggard face more
tragical than death itself. The surprise and betrayal
were so sudden, so treacherous, it half bewildered and
wholly overwhelmed her. Baptiste's perfidy, Tempest's
triumph, her own despair crushed her, and when he
waited for an answer she had only strength to break
from him and stagger toward the door. Her limbs
failed her before she reached it and he laid her down
utterly spent with the fruitless flight, the bitter disappointment.

'Curse Gérard, he exceeded orders; I bade him break
her spirit and he has destroyed her health,' muttered
Tempest wrathfully as he rung for Annette.

'Bring wine and recover her without delay. Then beg
Herman to take Ludmilla away for a time, my poor girl
cannot bear such society yet,' he said in a tone of
command, and Annette obeyed with the utmost meekness, for he was evidently master here.

Rosamond was soon herself again, but, seeing how her
condition alarmed Tempest, she concealed her strength
and lay mutely waiting while she girded up her courage

for the coming conflict of wills. Kneeling by her when Annette left them, he watched her with a face full of remorseful tenderness as he caressed her wasted hand and sought to excuse his past cruelty.

'My darling, forgive me! I never meant that you should suffer like this. Gérard promised to deal gently with you, Baptiste to guard you carefully. Both shall atone for their negligence, I swear it to you. Speak to me, Rosamond, I cannot bear to see your face so white and stony, to feel that your heart is hardened against me. I seem a brute, but it is my love which drives me to such harsh measures; when you relent I shall be your slave again.'

But Rosamond never moved nor spoke; like a lovely, pale statue she lay as if deaf to his prayers, unconscious of his caresses, blind to his regret and love. Her immobility frightened him; it was so unlike her, so different from the scene he had anticipated and prepared for. Thinking to rouse and interest her he talked on, telling her what she longed to know but would not ask.

'This last plot was Baptiste's; I knew nothing of it till he telegraphed to me to come on at once as you were ill but would not yield and purchase freedom at the price I set. I hurried away at once to find you gone, but Baptiste told me his plan and I was forced to be satisfied. He said your entreaties would have won him but for his vow to me. Wishing to serve us both, he permitted you to escape but sent a spy after you and followed by rail in time to be prepared for you here. He chanced to have a note sent by Honorine while you were at Wiesbaden with the Comte. For reasons of his own he did not deliver it then but kept it as he does all such trifles, for he knows how to use them. Having tracked you here he bade me wait at this chateau belonging to a gay friend of mine who lends it for a time. He lured you quietly from the inn with the note, and now you shall wander no more but rest here till I am free, when we will be married and go where you will.'

172

She gave him a look which proved that however weak her body might be her soul was unconquered still, and turned her face away without a word. It angered him but he controlled himself and rising, said with real solicitude in voice and manner, 'Perverse child, why torment yourself and me when we might be so happy? You are weak and weary now, you shall rest tonight and tomorrow wake to find yourself at home.'

Taking her tenderly in his arms he carried her into a luxurious chamber adjoining the boudoir and, laying her down as if she were a suffering child, he called Annette to wait upon her.

'She will stay with you, love, so sleep tranquilly while I guard the spot that holds my treasure. Have you no word for me, no kinder look, or kiss of pardon, my little Rose?' he asked, bending over her so wistfully and with such love in his face that few could have denied his prayer.

But Rosamond's delusion was utterly destroyed, that last act of his had steeled her heart against him and as he spoke she shrunk away with a shiver of detestation, saying only as she hid her eyes, 'Leave me in peace, the sight of you is abhorrent to me.'

Pale with anger he turned from her, pointed to the closely shuttered windows with an imperious, 'Remember your orders,' to Annette, and left the room, locking the doors behind him.

The long night passed slowly; Rosamond lay sleepless on her bed. Annette read novels by a shaded lamp and Baptiste slept before the door. With morning came Tempest, grave and kind but very unlike his usual self. With no greeting but a quiet bow he approached and said, 'Rose, I come to propose a truce. You need rest and care for a time. I have a brief holiday and want to enjoy it here with you. Let us be friends and bear with one another. You shall be free to go where you will in this little kingdom which Herman lends me; I will demand nothing but the privilege of seeing you daily, will devote

173

myself to you and spare no efforts to win your heart again before I have the right to claim it.'

'When will that be?' she asked abruptly.

'Unavoidable delays have arisen, but a week or two will see this tedious business ended. Till then I will wait and prove the sincerity of my love by my patience. Do you doubt me still?'

She did, but concealed the distrust and answered sadly, 'If you proved your love by generously giving me my liberty I could not doubt its sincerity. It is a selfish passion which will give me no rest till I die, for it can never win again the heart it has broken.'

'I am arrogant enough to think it can both win and heal. Be wise, Rosamond, sign the truce and do not rouse the devil in me by opposition. I will keep my word and you will lose nothing but a week or two of liberty by staying here with me.'

He offered his hand, she gave him hers and he sealed the compact with a kiss upon it, looking well pleased as he smiled and added, 'Now let Annette make you comfortable and when you are refreshed go and lounge in the boudoir, no one will disturb you there.'

He left her looking as if he had won an unexpected victory, and Rosamond obeyed him, resolving to feign submission for the sake of peace and to escape if possible before the treaty ended. She rose, bathed, and let Annette dress her in the simplest of the rich garments hanging in the wardrobe of the unknown Ludmilla. She ate and drank, and then, feeling too unquiet to rest, she went to the boudoir, trying to while away the weary hours by examining the beauties and comforts that surrounded her. As she sat listlessly at the window which overlooked the river and the town Tempest entered.

'Ah, this is well! Now I shall amuse you,' he said, eyeing her with unfeigned satisfaction and delight.

'I am past that.' She turned her wan face away as if no power could ever recall its smile again.

174

'You once said everything was possible to love. I shall prove it and show that you are not past amusing, for Phillip Tempest never yet failed to charm a woman when he gave himself to the task.'

Rosamond looked coldly incredulous, but he was right and she was forced to own it in the end, for he did give himself to the task of charming *this* woman.

Well as she thought she knew him she was surprised at the discovery of unsuspected resources, accomplishments and traits of character. Before he had not been obliged to exert himself to win her young heart, and even when fondest had also been imperious. Now the task was harder, for the heart was shut against him; time had only made it more precious in his eyes and both love and pride united to recover the lost treasure. All that day he was devoted to her, a slave now, not a master. Gentle yet gay, lover-like yet not presuming, he read, talked and entertained her with untiring pleasure. Wrapped her up and drove her out along the mountain roads, beguiling the way with legends of ruin and river, or leaving her to enjoy in silence the loneliness which no words could describe.

At dinner he let no one wait upon her but himself, tempting her to eat by playful artifices which she could not resist. In the evening he established her on a nest of pillows and whiled away the twilight hours with music, singing song after song with a power and passion which would have melted the heart of any woman. Vainly did Rosamond endeavor to resist the spell, but it was too new, too sweet and subtle to withstand, for never had he sung to her before.

In the old time it was for her to serve and amuse him, now the parts were changed and after her late unhappy experience such love, and entire devotion were dangerously welcome and alluring. In spite of her efforts to remain cold and indifferent that tender music touched her, bringing tears even while it soothed her by its magic. A stifled sob betrayed her to the quick ear alert to catch any sound of hers, and, satisfied with this test of his power, Tempest went to sit near her while he talked of things which could not fail to interest and amuse her.

So skillfully did he play his part that more than once Rosamond smiled against her will and involuntarily broke the silence she had imposed upon herself by an impulsive question, or an exclamation when he artfully paused in the middle of some exciting adventure, romantic incident or witty anecdote.

So rapidly did the evening pass that she looked up at the pendule with surprise when Tempest rose, saying regretfully, 'Ten o'clock so soon! My invalid must keep early hours, so good night and happy dreams, my Rosamond.'

'Good night, Phillip,' was the unexpected answer as she put out her hand in momentary forgetfulness. Instantly she caught it back and warned him off with a forbidding frown. He laughed, bowed with mock humility and left her, saying to himself, 'That "Phillip" had the old sound, patience and a week of this treatment will make her mine more entirely than ever.'

It surely would have done so had Rosamond been unchanged, but the years that had passed since they first met had strengthened the woman's nature by suffering, experience and that long struggle against temptation. Even now she might have yielded to the subtle power of the man once so beloved had not another and a nobler sentiment, half unknown and wholly unconfessed even to herself, guarded her heart from treachery and defeat during that skillful siege. When most tried and tempted, most weary, weak and wavering, some inexplicable impulse always made her turn away, crying within herself to that one friend of hers, 'Ignatius, help me, save me from myself!'

Day after day went smoothly, swiftly by at the little chateau on the Rhine. Tempest never forgot the new role he played, never wearied of his devotion or changed the purpose, which had become the ruling passion of his life. Rosamond could not help reviving, so cherished and beloved, yet despite her seeming submission she was still unwon, though often a desperate desire to cease struggling and be at peace came over her.

She still called upon Ignatius, but her good angel never answered her prayer and she believed he had deserted her. This sad fear did more to destroy her hope and courage than all Tempest's beguilements, for if no one in the world cared for her why should she care for herself?

With this gloomy thought in her mind she sat one day wondering how the tangle of her life would end when Tempest entered with a letter in his hand. He watched her keenly before he spoke, and his face cleared, for he divined her mood and felt that it was an auspicious moment for the proposal he had come to make.

'Rosamond, I am free at last! Read for yourself and tell me you are glad.'

He gave her the letter, she read it, knew that it was true, and looked up at him as if trying to realize the fact which might make such a change in her own fate.

'I *am* glad, not for your sake or mine, but for hers. What comes next?' she said slowly.

'The first use I make of my liberty is this.' He went to her, knelt down upon the cushion at her feet and offering her his hand said with an earnestness she could not doubt, 'I have a right to do it now, accept it, Rose, and save both of us from further sin and suffering. You alone have power to make me what I should be, I alone love and cling to you through everything; be my wife and you shall find me what I have proved I can be, faithful and fond. Let me atone for past wrongs, let me recall past happiness and in an honest, honorable future find salvation for us both.'

Coming at a moment when she felt unutterably feeble, forsaken and forlorn the ardent words sounded sweet to her, the eager face looked very winning, and the thought that this act would in the world's eye atone for her disgrace seemed to make it possible. She hesitated, scanned Tempest's upturned face with eyes made clear by many tears, and yielding to the passionate entreaty of the lover, the unconquerable yearning for affection so strong within her, and the temptation withstood so long, she sighed, half smiled and was about to accept the offered hand, when in putting out her own it touched a little rosary that always hung at her belt. She had worn it since she left the convent as a talisman, for Ignatius had given it and she loved it for his sake.

As her hand touched it her eye fell on it and the memory of her good angel saved her, for she thought of that hour when Ignatius knelt to her in the moonlight warning her to beware of her own weak heart, imploring her never to go back to this man, and, putting by his own love, praying her to save herself from sin. Clear and strong as an actual presence, that remembrance flashed upon her in an instant, that example upheld her, and the true love defeated the false.

Holding fast the ebony crucifix she drew back and gave her answer steadily yet warily, for sad experience taught her to beware of rousing the devil in Tempest by opposition.

'It is too late, Phillip. I have no heart to give you. I will be your friend, I cannot be your wife.'

Still keeping his place Tempest received her reply with a slow smile stealing to his lips. He had expected this, fancied pride and resentment restrained her, and was sure that another appeal would succeed, for he marked the sudden change which softened and beautified her as she spoke, and believed that she loved him still.

'If I must I will be content with that for a time. I see it is too much to hope for pardon so soon and will expiate my sins by patient waiting. You refuse one prayer, will you grant this? I am recalled to England, let me take you with me, Rosamond.'

Only an instant did she hesitate, for with the word 'England' came the thought, 'Once there I am near my haven – my chances of escape are infinitely better than here.' – 'I'll go.'

The last words were uttered aloud, and Tempest could not restrain a glance of exultation as he rose, feeling that one great step was gained.

'Thanks for such gracious granting of my request. But tell me why you spoke out in that decided tone? What wicked little plot do you harbor now, you cruel, crafty girl?' he asked, puzzled by her prompt acquiescence.

'None, I only hope to see my grandfather, I only plan to be a true friend to you, and try to earn my liberty by giving all I can to one whose love makes a tyrant of him,' she answered, still in that changed tone.

'A slave you mean; by my soul! I never served a woman as I have you, Rosamond. Jacob's seven years were boy's play compared to what I have undergone and will yet bear for you, tyrant that you are. If I stay with you much longer I shall be completely subjugated and you will rule me with a rod of iron.'

'May that time come soon. To prove the truth of your assertion I'll venture to ask you to take me out for a sunset stroll as in the old times. Will you, Phillip?'

'I'll take you anywhere on the face of the earth if you will ask me in that tone. Here are the wraps laid ready, come at once before the night wind rises.'

With the devoted air fast becoming natural, not feigned, he folded her cloak about her, tied on the graceful hat provided for her, and insisted upon fastening the furred overshoes he made his invalid wear. Catching up his own hat on the way, he led her out along the winding road that stretched over the hills.

'When can we go?'

'At once. Tomorrow if you will. Now come and let me get some color into these pale cheeks before I show my wife in England.'

She went, and leaning over the low wall that separated the garden from a deep ravine, stood musing happily while Tempest, always restless, roamed here and there talking of the future which he fondly believed now lay before him. Coming to her side, he looked into her face, wondering at her long silence. Her eyes were fixed on a pretty blue flower growing just below on a narrow ledge of rock.

'Shall I get it for you?' he asked, 'Nay, there is no danger, surely I can venture here when you run much greater risks for a girlish caprice.'

Anxious to preserve her gracious mood and prove his docility, Tempest quitted her side and, grasping a sturdy shrub, swung himself over the cliff, which was not perilously steep. As he stooped to seize the aster, a man sprang from some unsuspected hiding place and uprooted the shrub with one blow. Losing his hold, Tempest went crashing down into the ravine below.

Rosamond opened her lips to utter a shrill cry but a firm hand stifled the sound and a voice said in her ear, 'Hush, have no fear, it is Ignatius!'

CHAPTER XIX

'My Daughter'

Waiting for no reply, Ignatius caught her up and hurried her away through the open gates into the wood. Too bewildered and happy for anything but broken exclamations Rosamond clung to him with the perfect confidence of a child. A short rapid walk brought them to a little hut near which stood a traveling carriage as if waiting for someone. Placing her in it he gave an order to the postillion, sprung in himself, and they drove swiftly away along the lonely road. Drawing a long breath, Rosamond seized the hands of her deliverer with an expression of gratitude that warmed him to his heart's core.

'I knew you would come!' she cried, 'I was sure of my one friend, and though the time seemed long I never lost the hope that sooner or later you would remember me. How can I thank you, Ignatius?'

If she had ever feared that he would cease to love her she now saw how unchanged that true heart was. Love, stronger, deeper warmer than before, shone in his eyes, glowed in his face and sounded in his voice, though by no word did he confess it. Looking at her as a man might look at the treasure of his life newly rescued from danger, he answered eagerly, as he placed cushions behind her and wraps about her feet, 'My child, I never for a moment forgot you; I thought of you by day, I prayed for you by night, and when the Comte wrote me of your removal by Tempest I set out at once to find and protect you at all hazards. It has been a long task but this moment is worth years of effort and suspense.'

'Tell me more, Ignatius, talk to me and make me forget the dreadful scenes I've passed through since we parted. Your voice always soothes me, your presence cheers and comforts me like a charm, and you are indeed my good angel as I call you.'

Still like a child she looked and spoke and clung to him, feeling nothing but a blissful sense of safety, rest and happiness. He saw how weak and wan she was and was paternally tender with her, conscious the while of a satisfaction and delight too deep for words.

'When I reached Wiesbaden the Comte was gone, you had disappeared, and no one could give me any clue to your prison. All I could discover was that Tempest had returned to England alone, that you had been carried away mortally wounded and guarded by Baptiste. Various rumors sent me hurrying from place to place till I at last discovered Gérard's asylum. For a week I vainly tried to enter, and at length managed to catch Manton, only to find you gone. I traced you here and have haunted the place trying to see or give you a hint of my presence. Many times have I followed you in disguise as you walked or drove, and once actually passed the gate as a beggar, but you were so well guarded I could do nothing, so waited for chance to help me, as it has, thank God! That new carriage was driven in, I slipped in behind it and have been hidden here for hours.'

A sudden fear shot through Rosamond's heart and she turned to him with a shudder.

'Have you killed Phillip?'

Ignatius clenched his hand and his eye grew fiery, for neither prayer nor penance had subdued the native spirit of the man.

'No, the cliff is not steep; the fall may maim but will not kill him. Better for the weak and innocent perhaps if it did. Do you hate me for what I have done?' he added, with sudden humility and an imploring glance.

182

'Nothing could make me do that, I think. No, my faithful friend, I could not blame you had the fall been fatal. I should have regretted that you had stained your hands with a bad man's blood. But a sense of freedom would have come to me with tidings of his death. It is sinful, but only natural; I have suffered so much, he is so false, so cruel and selfish I wonder that I ever loved him.'

'Then you no longer love, Agatha?' he asked earnestly.

'No, no! I detest, despise, hate and discard this man forever. My delusion is gone, I know him now, and nothing can restore love, respect or confidence. He is my evil genius, and long ago when as a reckless girl I said I'd sell my soul to Satan for a year of freedom little I knew that I should be taken at my word in such fearful earnest. I've been happy, I've paid a high price for it, and now I have no desire but to expiate the impious wish by patience and submission.'

There was a momentary silence broken only by the steady roll of wheels and tramp of hoofs. As if the sound recalled her thoughts from past to present peril she said suddenly, 'Where are we going? I never thought to ask.'

He smiled and answered with a mixture of deference and doubt, 'I can desire no better proof of confidence than that. We will go wherever you wish. I am your courier as well as friend; name any refuge and I will take you to it and guard you in it as long as you remain. I'll not trust you to the care of others again – if you permit me to protect you.'

'I do, so gratefully, so gladly! I will tell you the plan I made when I escaped, but if you think it unwise you shall direct me, I leave all to you. I meant to seek and ask the protection of Mrs Tempest.'

'His wife?'

'Yes, strange as it may seem I turn to her as my safest refuge now. I'm humbler than I was, I remember her kind pity for me at Nice, her wish to save me, and I also remember that Phillip said once in speaking of her that he shunned her like the plague. If she consents to befriend me I am safe, for he will never dream of my going to my rival. Shall I do it?'

Ignatius mused a moment, and impatient at his silence Rosamond added, with a womanish satisfaction in the fact, 'She is not his wife now, they are divorced and she is free.'

'Then it was true that Tempest wished to marry you?'

'Yes, who told you that?'

'Herman, the friend whose chateau was lent for your temporary home. I met him and drew several important reports from his careless conversation.'

'And Ludmilla was his wife?'

'No, she should have been. Did you see her, Agatha?'

'Phillip sent her away when I came and never called her back, though I asked for her thinking she might help me.'

'He had more regard for you than I believed if he spared you the insult of that woman's presence,' muttered Ignatius with a frown.

'You forget what I have been,' she said, turning her face away with an expression of intensest pain.

'More sinned against than sinning, I never forget that, my child.' The words were infinitely tender as he laid the homeless, weary head on his shoulder as if she were indeed a suffering child. To divert her mind from that sad thought he added in a hopeful tone, 'I like your plan, and we will try it. You need the protection of a good and friendly woman; Mrs Tempest cannot forget your kindness to the boy, and if she be the creature you describe your mutual wrongs will draw you closer to each other. In order to perplex and elude our pursuers, who will be sure we have escaped by boat or rail, we will travel by unfrequented roads to Cologne or Düsseldorf, there take steamer to Rotterdam and so across to England without loss of time.'

'Excellent! I care little how long we are on the way, it is so pleasant to be free and with you—' she checked herself suddenly, colored, and gently drew away from the supporting arm as if at last she recollected that the priest was a lover and herself no longer a child.

He feigned unconsciousness of the change and busied himself in making her comfortable, saying as he did so, 'We must travel several hours before we reach Mülheim, where we rest till morning. Can you bear a rapid drive like this? I have made all possible preparations for your comfort but you are very feeble still, I see.'

'I feel strong now, I enjoy the air, the motion, and the thought that each step takes me farther from that man gives me new power and spirit. It is dark and strange, but I have no fear.' She looked from the evening gloom without to the staunch friend within with a brave bright smile long a stranger to her lips.

With playful pride Ignatius showed her the unsuspected treasures of the well-arranged carriage. The seats were converted into a couch, a lamp was lighted, a delicate supper appeared and was eaten with much quiet merriment by the pair, who heartily enjoyed the romance of the flight, and each felt the potent charm of the unspoken passion hidden in either heart. For an hour or two they planned and talked with increasing cheerfulness and confidence, then Rosamond's strength began to fail, her lids grew heavy and after vain efforts to conceal her fatigue she was forced to own it and allow herself to be wrapped up and lulled to sleep by the murmur of her companion's voice as he read aloud in a soothing tone.

Soon she slept, then Ignatius dropped the book and, leaning forward, feasted his longing eyes upon the beauty of the beloved face lying so pale and peaceful on the pillow opposite. Every line and shadow made by pain and care, every remembered charm of expression, shape or color, every flitting smile or frown as dreams passed through the sleeper's brain were seen, enjoyed and pondered over with unwearied interest and delight, for now he dared indulge his love with a brief holiday. Once she whispered his name and stretched her hands imploringly as if beseeching him to come. Several times she clutched the little crucifix he had given her, and through all her troubled sleep he saw that she held fast a fold of the cloak he wore. Dangerous hours for Ignatius, and a dangerous awakening for Rosamond as she suddenly looked up to see his heart in his eyes and to give involuntarily a mute but eloquent reply.

Neither spoke and both were glad that the lights of the little town appeared before them a moment after. Not till the postillion came to ask at which inn to stop did a sound break the silence. Having given his orders, Ignatius turned to Rosamond and said, 'We must decide on our names before we encounter curious eyes and gossiping tongues. Who and what shall we be?'

'Anything you please. Do you know it never occurred to me before that you had any name but Ignatius? May I know it?' Leaning on her elbow, she gave him a half-timid, half-curious glance which conquered his reluctance to confess.

'Bayard Condé was the name I bore before I became a monk.'

'A brave and noble name! I remember hearing my grandfather read with admiration of a young Duc de Condé who led the gallant students in the last revolution. He was my hero and I longed to know what became of him. Was it any relative of yours?

'Yes.'

'Tell me about him that my romance may be complete. There was something about a lovely girl whom he adored and whose coldness drove him so recklessly into danger. Did he marry Léonie and enjoy the happiness he deserved?'

'No, he disappeared and never wooed or fought again.'

Something in his tone made Rosamond start up, exclaiming with mingled wonder, joy and reverence, 'Ignatius, it was you! I know it now, I am so proud, so glad to find my hero is my friend. *Mon Dieu*, to think that under the priest's gown is hidden a Duc, a man whose name was famous once and of whom it was predicted that he would rival his great ancestor!'

Seeing her pleasure, he no longer tried to deceive her but with a half-sad, half-amused expression gratified her curiosity.

'Such predictions always fail. I tried love, glory and pleasure; none satisfied me, and, weary of the world, I left it. It was a mistake, but being young and enthusiastic I felt that I should give my best to God and not wait till I had but the dregs of life to offer. Youth, rank, fortune, and fame I could dedicate to His work and I did it heartily. A time came when I rebelled against my choice, hated my vows and struggled to be free; that is over now and with Heaven's help I will be faithful to the end.'

'And Léonie?' faltered Rosamond, longing to know all.

'Married and dead long ago. A cold, proud woman whose memory I neither cherish nor respect. Now forget that I am anything but a poor priest and hereafter call me Father. It is safest and easiest for both.'

'You are too young for that and I too old.'

'I am growing gray as the daylight will show you, and many furrows have come of late; these short curls, your simple hat, and your late illness make you look more girlish than you know. We are Swiss gentlefolk going to England for your health; Monsieur Salzburg and his daughter, Minna. Does that please you? Shall it be so?'

'Yes, Father, I have played so many parts that I shall not fail now but enjoy the masquerade, since I have a partner in it,' answered Rosamond, laughing with a little of her old gaiety as she gathered up her curls and prepared to meet strangers, for now the inn was reached.

A quiet night passed, and a glad awakening came with the thought, 'I am safe and Ignatius is here!' Leaving her room early, Rosamond went down to the little salon and finding it empty amused herself by looking down into the courtyard, where the carriage stood ready. A gentleman was talking to the postillion and she watched him a moment before in the elegant stranger she recognized her friend. No sign of the priest remained and the modern costume, though perfectly simple, was worn with the indescribable air of ease and grace which marks the gentleman born.

Scrutinizing him with the keen eye of a woman, she saw, as he stood uncovered to enjoy the autumn sunshine, that the gray hairs *had* come and that deep lines marked the brave forehead; yet in spite of this she thought she had never seen a comelier man, for happiness made him young and the eyes that watched him were those of a lover. She smiled at the idea of his impersonating her father and turned to the glass to resmooth the curls that clustered round her face, and gave to her dress those little touches which add charm to the plainest costumes. As she did so she sighed, and said to herself with a conscious blush at the fervency of the wish, 'I wish he was not a priest!'

In spite of all resolutions Ignatius wished so also when he came in and saw the beautiful face brighten as it turned to him, heard the happy, 'Good morning, Father,' which greeted his coming.

'Good morning, Daughter; are you ready for another flight today?' He smiled as he spoke, but dropped her hand with a heavier sigh than hers had been.

All day they traveled on through unfrequented roads, enjoying the ever-varied panorama of forests, mountains, ruins and picturesque valleys which makes the Rhine the loveliest river in the world. Early next morning they took steamer to Cologne and for several days went floating downward toward the sea. Wonderfully calm and happy days they were, for the mild October days were cloudless, the nights made magical by moonlight, and each hour increased the charm that made the little voyage so memorable to both.

One care annoyed and yet amused them; a party of English came on board at Arnhem and among them two inquisitive old ladies who beguiled the way by speculating on their neighbors. Ignatius and his pale charge attracted their attention and excited their curiosity, for there were few other passengers and the river below Cologne has little to vary the monotony of its low green shores. Believing themselves quite safe in speaking English, they sat chatting together one day with frequent glances toward Rosamond, who lay, apparently asleep, under the awning, and at Ignatius who sat beside her with a book in his hand.

'Jane, I know I'm right, it's nonsense to say that man is her father. He's barely forty and unless I'm much deceived she is past twenty. It's not illness alone that makes her look a woman, it's an indescribable expression of mental suffering which girls don't have, unless their lives have been uncommon.'

'But, Mary she calls him "*mon père*" and he calls her "*mon enfant*". I must confess I never saw a father so devoted, but if he is not hers what is he?'

'Her husband or lover, my dear. These French are so odd and romantic one sees all sorts of curious marriages. They are evidently newly married, that accounts for his devotion and her docility, for a girl with eyes like hers has a will and is not ruled by anyone but a lover. He adores the ground she treads on, and she worships him though she conceals it under that shy calm manner.'

'You are as full of romance as a young girl, Jane. It's very interesting to hear you go on!'

In the earnestness of the discussion their voices became audible and the pair heard distinctly words which agitated both. A sad yet happy day followed as they went floating down the Rhine; for both delighted in being together, and both dreaded the separation hourly drawing nearer. As they approached Cologne, silence fell between them, and presently Ignatius began to pace restlessly to and fro, while Rosamond feigned to read.

CHAPTER XX

T.F.

Well for both that events of an exciting nature absorbed the last day of their voyage, for in the morning neither looked the other in the face and for the first time seemed happier apart. Rosamond affected to be absorbed in a book and Ignatius roamed restlessly about, pausing occasionally to say a word lest the sudden change in his manner should attract attention.

In one of these aimless wanderings to and fro Ignatius was surprised to see a little, gray-headed, mild-looking gentleman start forward suddenly, as if about to accost him, but stop halfway, glance at him from head to foot, catch up a chair and return to his place as abruptly as he left it. A vague fancy that he had seen that gentleman before caused the priest to return stare for stare, and presently, when the fancy took a shape and name, he approached the stranger, who sat apart, and entered into conversation with him.

Rosamond, who lost no movement of her friend's, wondered much who the person could be whose chat so interested Ignatius, for though somewhat stiffly begun the conversation soon grew easy and animated, and when Ignatius left the little man he came at once to her, asking in a low tone, 'Who do you think that is, Minna?'

'Some learned professor grown dry and dusty digging in the graves of dead languages to judge from his appearance,' answered Rosamond, glad to have the truant back.

'He is Vetréy, the great Chief of Police in Paris. He is on the track of an escaped criminal and thinks the person is on board in disguise. He thinks – pardon, Madame,' and he stepped aside to let a lady pass.

She was a tall woman in deep black with dark curls about her face; a respirator hid her mouth and a crepe veil partially concealed her face. Fine black eyes and a pale olive skin were all a hasty glance could discover. Acknowledging his courtesy with a stately bow, she passed on to a seat which commanded a view of theirs.

'I've not seen her before, who is it?' Rosamond did not say 'my father' nor did Ignatius say 'my child', for both felt what empty phrases they had now become.

'She came on board at the last stopping place. A handsome, fierce-looking lady, Spanish I fancy, and a widow. Will you come and walk, or is the book too captivating?'

She threw it down, took his arm, and they went away together, looking so like lovers that Miss Jane nodded triumphantly at Miss Mary and whispered, 'You'll see I'm right in spite of all their pretense.'

As they passed from sight the lady in black crossed the deck and paused near the seat Rosamond had left. Her sweeping skirts concealed the bench and while affecting to look pensively down into the water she opened the book and read the name on the flyleaf, 'Minna Salzburg.' A smile passed over her face but died suddenly as, gliding on, she addressed a courteous remark to the garrulous old sisters. Glad to talk with anyone, they readily gave the stranger all the gossip they had collected about their fellow travelers and dwelt with particular relish on 'the mysterious couple' as they called Ignatius and Rosamond. The lady listened with polite attention and seemed to enjoy the conjectures of the inquisitive spinsters till Monsieur Vetréy came up to offer his glass for a fine view of a distant ruin. Sudden paleness overspread the lady's face as she turned and saw him;

for an instant her eyes flashed and she set her teeth, then smiled, murmured her thanks and accepted the glass.

Nothing could have been more tranquil and bland than the Frenchman, or more gracefully self-possessed than the lady, yet as they stood quietly criticizing the ruin Vetréy was exulting within himself that he had found the criminal, and the Spaniard was feeling stealthily for the stiletto hidden in her breast.

From that moment Monsieur Vetréy devoted himself to Madame Montez, much to the amusement of the other passengers, who fancied that the little gray man was fascinated by the handsome Spaniard. Ignatius and Rosamond, being in the secret, watched them with interest and rather wondered at the evident annoyance of Madame at their observation, for she occasionally darted a fierce glance at them. As the boat approached Cologne, her disquiet seemed to increase and Vetréy's assiduous attentions increased likewise.

They were standing side by side near the gangway, Madame leaning on the bar which guarded the opening and Vetréy leaning near her, talking in a low tone. Suddenly, as if burdened by its weight, the Spaniard untied her long velvet cloak and hung it on the railing. An instant afterward the bar gave way and both were precipitated into the rapid stream. As she fell the woman uttered an exclamation more like a laugh than a cry, and disappeared, leaving both bonnet and respirator to float down the stream.

All was confusion at once; the boat was stopped as soon as possible and Vetréy picked up nearly exhausted, not by the struggle, for he swam well, but by a wound in the shoulder. He was soon himself again, said the wound was made by some part of the wheel, and seemed to forget everything but the loss of Madame. No sign of her appeared and after a long delay the steamer went on.

At the moment of the fall Ignatius felt Rosamond clutch his arm and, looking down, saw her pale and trembling.

'It was Baptiste!' she whispered in a terrified tone. 'He threw off the bonnet as he leaped and I knew him. Oh Ignatius, what shall we do?'

'Nothing but rejoice that he was disposed of before he had time to annoy us. Vetréy tells me he is an escaped convict whose disappearance caused much excitement some years ago, for the escape was a most daring and mysterious one. He vanished and no one has been able to discover a trace of him, till a short time ago in Paris Vetréy caught a glimpse of him. He never forgets a face, and trusting the work to no one, he set out himself and will yet succeed, I have no doubt.'

'I hope so. The mystery of Baptiste's escape and disappearance can be explained I think by the fact that Tempest found him concealed somewhere, took him away on one of his voyages, and has befriended him ever since. Baptiste is grateful and serves Phillip with blind fidelity.'

'They just suit each other. But why do you look so troubled? What do you fear now?'

'I fancy Tempest must be dead else he would follow, and that Baptiste's fierce looks were caused by his secret purpose to avenge his master's death.'

'No fear of that now. Vetréy will daunt him and while he is with us we are safe. I must go and offer my services to the poor man, that desperate *forçat* tried to drown him, and that failing, to stab him underwater.'

In a few hours they landed, and as no train left for England till next day at noon they devoted their evening to Monsieur Vetréy, who promised to protect them in return for the information they gave him. He left them at ten, not to sleep but to work, and early next morning came in radiant as they sat at breakfast.

'You are right!' he exclaimed, 'That rascal has braved the danger of capture that he may obey his master by securing you. He is actually here, I have seen him in the dress of a workman down yonder in the Square. He did not observe me, for I was in a carriage, but I am not to be deceived. Now, Mademoiselle, I must ask of you the favor to help me take him.'

'Me, Monsieur, how is it possible?' Rosamond drew nearer to Ignatius as if seeking protection from her old enemy.

'No danger to you, Mademoiselle, I give you my word. My idea is this: The fellow desires to speak with you, for that he watches and waits; you will give him an opportunity by going down into the garden as if for a stroll. Monsieur goes with you, but you send him back for a shawl, a book or some trifle. Nothing escapes the quick eye of Baptiste, he seizes the moment, he accosts you, we watch our time unseen and take him. Will you do this for me and so rid the world of as black a scoundrel as ever walked in it?'

'I will.' Rosamond's native courage returned to her, for years of danger had not entirely broken her spirit.

Peeping from behind the curtain of a back window, Vetréy pointed out among a group of blue-bloused workmen one who wore a thick black beard and a cap slouched over his eyes. He was not working, but stood half leaning on a stout staff as if just in from the country in search of work. Vetréy surveyed him with satisfaction.

'I entered unseen and bade the porter say if anyone inquired for me that I was ill of my wound. That will reassure him – ha! He is coming, as I thought he would. He addresses the porter – see, he smiles and looks well pleased. Now he will lounge in that alley till you appear. Wait a little, then saunter out and leave the rest to me.'

They obeyed him and presently went down to walk in the garden, which always forms a part of a Continental hotel's attractions. A pretty green spot, well kept and full of little tables not yet occupied. Choosing one near a thick low hedge behind which he meant to conceal himself, Ignatius left Rosamond there whiie he returned at her desire to bring a parasol.

When alone, her heart beat fast and an uncontrollable desire to glance about her made it difficult to assume an unconcerned demeanor. Several minutes passed and no one came; a faint rustle behind the hedge assured her that Ignatius was near, and so guarded she soon became impatient to see the much-dreaded Baptiste appear. Presently a lad came down the path, arranged the seats and returned after a glance at the solitary lady. A moment later the blue blouse came out slowly from a cross alley with a rake in his hand. When opposite Rosamond, he lifted his cap as is the custom with the rudest peasant when passing a lady, and at the same instant gave her a glance of recognition so fiery and threatening that her start of fear was perfectly natural.

'Hist!' he said reaching her in one stride and barring her way with outstretched arms. 'Madame must hear me or I shall be forced to compel her.' One hand went to his breast with an ominous gesture.

'I will hear you, what have you to say, Baptiste?'

'Merely a message from the Master. He lies dying at Coblenz and pines to say a farewell word to Madame. He fears you will not come, but he implores, he promises freedom and safety, he only asks for one word, one look before he dies. You will grant this prayer or I—'

Rosamond was spared an answer, for as Baptiste bent toward her, speaking in a low, rapid tone, Ignatius leaped the hedge and seized him. With the quickness of a practiced wrestler he freed himself and turned to find Vetréy and three gendarmes behind him. The suddenness of the thing took him by surprise, but he fought like a tiger to escape and yielded only when bound hand and foot and held down by the men.

'*Chut!* He is the same devil as ever,' exclaimed Vetréy, rubbing his hands with an air of supreme satisfaction. 'A thousand thanks, Mademoiselle, for this service. All goes admirably and now you are safe. Stay, Monsieur, will you satisfy yourself that this amiable valet is in truth a *forçat*? Behold our mark.' Pulling aside the torn blouse, he showed on the brown shoulder of Baptiste the letters 'T.F.' (*travaux forcés*), the brand of the galleys.

Rosamond turned away with a shudder and the men eyed him with glances of detestation, but Baptiste smiled scornfully and said to Vetréy tauntingly, 'You too, Monsieur le Chef, have a mark upon your shoulder which you will not soon forget.'

Vetréy laughed good-humoredly and answered, 'Yes, by my faith, the souvenir of Madame Montez is a mark to be proud of. Have you anything to say to that charming creature before she goes, Mademoiselle?'

Rosamond looked at the convict as he lay there panting, bound and bleeding; womanlike pity conquered resentment, and bending over him she tied her delicate handkerchief about his wounded head, saying softly, 'I forgive you and entreat you to leave me in peace hereafter for your own sake if not for mine.'

'Mademoiselle, you are an angel!' exclaimed Vetréy. 'Have no fear of further molestation, this gentleman's time is up, he'll never trouble you again for I shall guard him till he is shot tomorrow. A convict's doom, Mademoiselle, and from it there is no escape.'

The face of Baptiste had softened as the woman he had hunted so mercilessly bent over him, but as the Chief spoke it hardened again as he said maliciously, 'The Master is neither dead nor dying; he is unhurt, he is on your trail and he will avenge me. Madame, permit me to offer my congratulations.'

And with a grim laugh and a significant glance at Ignatius, Baptiste disappeared from her sight forever.

CHAPTER XXI

Mrs Tempest

In the most secluded room at the Priory sat Mrs Tempest, a handsome but worn-looking woman of five and thirty. An open letter was in her hand and as she read it her eyes filled, her lips trembled, and her whole face betrayed the presence of some half-pleasurable, half-painful emotion. In the window lounged Lito with a book, which he neglected in order to watch his mother's face. As she put down the letter and looked at him with a fond smile, he hurried to her, exclaiming as he caressed her with a protective air, 'Mamma dear, what is it that makes you sigh and smile and look at me in that way? I'm the head of the house now and I ought to know everything that troubles you.'

'It is about your Rosamond, my boy, she is coming to us. Her good and faithful friend Father Ignatius writes to prepare me, that the poor girl may not fail to receive a cordial welcome. He thought I might have forgotten, or time perhaps changed my feeling toward her, and so with the most delicate kindness he tells me her hopes, her trials and virtues, unknown to her, making me more her friend than ever.'

'Oh, Mamma, now I have no wish ungratified. It will be perfect heaven to live with you and Rose. I know you'll love her as I do and she will be so happy with you, for she always spoke of you as the sweetest woman she had ever known, though she saw you but once. When will she come, Mamma?'

'At any moment, dear; the letter was written at Cologne but has been delayed and it is already past the time when Father Ignatius spoke of arriving.'

'I wish I could run down to the gates to watch for them. I'm not afraid, Mamma, the danger is over now I think.'

'Not while your father has a right to claim you, Lito. As yet he does not suspect your presence here, but I never know how near he may be and never cease to fear losing you again. Hark, there is a carriage! You'll not have to seek for your friend. No, dear, wait here, let us meet her in private, it is kinder.'

A few moments later Ignatius entered the room alone. Mrs Tempest had expected to see an old man and was somewhat embarrassed at the sight of the elegant stranger, but a few words from him set her at her ease and completely won her heart. Waiting for no introduction, Lito greeted him enthusiastically and then rushed into the anteroom to embrace and welcome Rosamond with all the warmth and rapture of a loving heart. Rosamond could only lay her head on his shoulder and weep, longing yet fearing to meet the mother.

Before she had recovered herself, Mrs Tempest came to her, took her in her arms and, kissing the tearful face, said in a tender motherly tone, 'My child, you are very welcome. I hoped you would one day find me out and let me give you a safe home.'

'Oh, Madame, I am not worthy of such kindness, but in my despair I turned to you, remembering your beautiful compassion long ago. If I may stay a little and serve you in the humblest way I shall be more grateful than words can express.'

'We both have suffered, let us comfort one another,' was the sweet answer to her prayer, and falling on her knees Rosamond thanked heaven that after many dangers she was safe at last.

Ignatius had drawn the boy away and when, after a long hour spent in unburdening their full hearts to each other, the women joined them, the priest saw with a glance that a friendship had begun which would end only with their lives.

The Priory held a happy family that night, for the newcomers were not strangers long, and sitting round the fire they told their various adventures and made pleasant plans for their future. Lito was in the gayest spirits and amused Rosamond with an account of the panics he had suffered for a long time after he was safe at home. All the servants in the house were old and faithful and there was no fear of their yielding to bribery. But Tempest never went down into Staffordshire, the Priory being his wife's property and the neighbors regarding him as a fiend incarnate. He so firmly believed in the boy's death that he made no inquiries and endeavored to forget him, so Lito was doubly safe and led a quiet life with his mother, never venturing out alone and being provided with several hiding places should any unexpected danger arise.

'See, Rose, here is my refuge when strangers come or when Mamma is off guard,' he said, touching a spring which caused a mimic library to revolve upon unseen hinges and disclose a closet lighted by a narrow window and furnished with a seat, books and sundry comforts and amusements to make the boy's temporary captivity endurable. Rosamond examined it with interest and playfully promised to share his refuge with him, little dreaming how soon she would be driven to do so.

A tranquil week passed by with but a single care to disturb the wanderer: Ignatius took lodging in the town and only came up to the Priory for an hour in the evening. A wise arrangement, but Rosamond missed him sadly and unconsciously betrayed herself to Mrs Tempest by the change which came over her on his arrival. Ignatius never varied in the grave friendliness of his manner, yet the elder woman read his secret as well as the girl's and wondered anxiously how it would end.

Sitting alone with Rosamond, one day they fell to

talking of love and marriage as women often do and Mrs Tempest told her something of her own past life.

'My father married a Greek lady and I was born in Greece and lived there till my mother died when I was nineteen. Soon after Phillip came, made me love him and obtained my father's consent to our marriage. For two years I was very happy, for Phillip was devoted and my baby was the joy of my life. My father died, Phillip wearied of everything and roamed away in his restless fashion to be gone months together. He wanted me to go with him, but I clung to the child and would not expose him to the dangers of travel. Now and then I went on a little voyage and on returning from one of these was told the boy was dead. No tie bound me longer there and I went with Phillip. But time rapidly changed him for the worse, I learned to know him better and after bearing many slights and insults I left him.'

'Why were you not divorced then, dear Mrs Tempest?' asked Rosamond, with a face full of sympathy.

'Because I still hoped to reform him and when that hope died a new one had sprung up. Years had passed since I was told my baby died and I believed the tale, but by the merest accident a friend passing through Nice saw at Valrosa a boy so like Phillip that he was sure it was a son of his, though he denied it. Willoughby mentioned it to me when he wrote to England and I at once went to find the child. He was gone, taken away by his father, and since then I have vainly tried to recover him. The law gives Phillip a right to keep him, and I had no hold upon him except so long as I remained Phillip's wife. He desired a divorce but could not get one without my consent, for his infidelity was well known and it was for me to demand a legal separation. I would not unless he gave up the boy. That he refused and it was only after Lito came to me that I agreed, for my lawyer is sure of getting a promise from Phillip that I shall have the child should he ever appear. He was thought to have been lost in the boat that left Nice for Genoa and as Phillip has heard nothing of him he is sure of his death and will consider my request a woman's foolish clinging to hope when hope is gone.'

A bell rang as Mrs Tempest paused and a servant brought up a card. The name on it was Phillip Tempest.

'Where is Lito?' was her first thought and word.

'Here, Mamma' The boy came in from the next room, where he was waiting for Ignatius.

'Quick! Into the closet and make no sound for your life. You also, Rose; have no fear – I can meet and foil him.'

In breathless haste the two ran into the refuge, the false door closed upon them and the lady of the house was found alone when Tempest and two gray-headed lawyers were shown in. Husband and wife met with the coolness of strangers, and with merely a word of greeting they sat silently apart while the old men explained certain papers which were to be signed as the last formalities of the divorce.

When this was done, Mr Furnival, Mrs Tempest's lawyer, said with a glance at her, 'Mr Tempest agrees to your wish, Madam, though he cannot but think as I do that you feed yourself with vain hopes. Here is a written promise made in due form which gives you the sole right to the boy *if* he ever appears.'

'You know nothing of him, Marion, to this you can swear?' asked Tempest, with a keen scrutiny of her pale, firm face.

She looked him straight in the eye with well-feigned eagerness, which changed to sorrow as she answered with a bitter sigh and an impetuous, 'I wish to heaven I did!' – adding to herself, 'God pardon me for the lie I tell to save my son.'

'So do I,' and with a momentary sadness on his hard face Tempest signed the promise to which he attached no importance; the lawyers witnessed it and Mrs Tempest received it with a joy almost impossible to conceal.

A few words more and the interview was about to

close when a half-stifled laugh made Mrs Tempest start and turn so pale it attracted the attention of the three gentlemen. She recovered herself instantly and murmured something about the giddy maidservants, but Tempest's suspicions were aroused, for the laugh was a boy's hearty 'Ha! ha!' and sounded familiar to his ear. Without a word he strode to the spot whence it had come, examined the false door and tried to open it. In an agony of alarm Mrs Tempest assured him that it was only the little footboy and begged him to believe her.

'Not till I satisfy myself. I understand the meaning of your absurd request now. The boy is here and I will find him if I raze the house to the ground.' And exerting his great strength he shook the door till it cracked in his grasp.

The old men interfered and Mrs Tempest implored, but, heeding none of them, he was about to give another blow when the door flew open and Rosamond appeared in the refuge alone. Tempest fell back as if a ghost had confronted him. Mrs Tempest sank into a seat with a fervent thanksgiving that the boy was safe, and the lawyers stared, alert to catch a clue to the mystery.

Quite calm and with no sign of agitation but the indignant fire of her eyes, Rosamond demanded imperiously, 'By what right do you violently break upon my privacy? The house is not yours and on me you have no claim; I place myself under the protection of these gentlemen, and that they may comprehend the case I shall explain my appearance here.'

Tempest seemed literally unable to reply, and while he stood speechless she rapidly and forcibly recounted her wrongs, her sufferings and her firm resolution to discard him forever. The truth, eloquence and fire of her recital thrilled even the cold hearts of the old men, made them her champions at once, and when she ended with an appeal to them, both heartily assured her of their protection and support.

'Surely there is some redress for me, some safety in

this land of law and liberty. I claim entire freedom from this man's persecution; I will hide no longer, here I shall remain and let him molest me at his peril.'

Never had she looked so beautiful, so dauntless and determined, and never had Tempest loved her so passionately as when she cast him off with womanly contempt and defiance. As if nothing should be wanting to make his defeat galling and complete, Ignatius suddenly entered the room and, uttering a little cry of joy, Rosamond went to him with such confiding freedom it needed not the protecting gesture or tender glance of Ignatius to betray how much they were to one another. The sight of a rival roused Tempest to fury, for it not only stung his man's pride but it convinced him past all doubt that Rosamond was lost forever.

White and trembling with wrath, he turned on them with a terrible face, exclaiming in a tone that made Rosamond cling closer to the arm of Ignatius, 'I read the riddle now and admire the art with which you have allied your forces against me. But it will not succeed. Plot, lie and defy as you will, I'll conquer yet, for no man ever defeated Phillip Tempest. You have heard the artful story of this girl, gentlemen, let me add that she brings these charges against the man who loves her that she may be free to give her fickle heart to this false priest, this low adventurer whom no one knows—'

He paused for breath; and Ignatius smiled a smile of mingled pity and contempt but uttered not a word. Rosamond spoke for him and disregarding his warning glance broke out eagerly, 'Is Bayard Condé, whom you once said you admired beyond any man, a low adventurer whom no one knows? Is he a false priest who gave up fame and fortune, youth and love to serve God with all his powers in their prime! It is *you* who are false and base, *you* who should pray to be unknown, for in all the world no human creature loves, trusts or honors you.'

Something in her kindling face, her proud smile, her clear glad voice carried instant conviction to Tempest's mind and daunted him with sudden shame before the man whose noble life made his own seem doubly despicable. Fearing to disgrace himself by some outbreak of the passion fast becoming ungovernable, he clenched his hand and cast on Ignatius a look of deadly hatred as he left the room, saying between his teeth with a gesture of insolent significance, 'Monsieur le Duc, I shall not forget you.'

CHAPTER XXII

Twice Conquered

With hasty assurances of help the lawyers followed, and as the door closed on them Mrs Tempest exclaimed, 'Lito? where is he?'

'Safe in one of his other hiding places. We listened, and when the paper was signed he could not repress a triumphant laugh. I was dismayed and made him slip out by the window at once, and remained to divert suspicion, for I heard Phillip's threat.'

'He forgot the boy in his wrath and now that you have the paper Lito may venture to appear; though I should advise prudence for a time,' said Ignatius.

'I will be careful, but now I must find him.' Holding the precious promise fast, Mrs Tempest hurried away to assure herself of her darling's safety.

'Baptiste was right, the fall did not injure Phillip. I should be glad of that and yet I am not. It's wrong, but I did wish it might cripple him for a time that we might be safe. I'm growing hard and wicked and this persecution is destroying me body and soul. Ignatius, I hate that man with a mortal hatred.' Rosamond looked darkly toward the spot where he had stood.

'You would be more than human if you did not. Even in a generous nature like yours love will turn to hate when wrong follows wrong and insult is added to insult. What will he do now?' answered Ignatius, hoping to draw her thoughts from herself for her dark mood troubled him.

'Do! He will haunt us, waylay, entrap and torment us as he has done. He has the subtlety of an evil spirit and though Baptiste is gone he will devise some scheme alone more treacherous than any yet. Oh, beware of him! He will destroy you if he can, his wrath falls heaviest on you and I can do nothing to defend my defender. Stay here where we can watch over you, I entreat you to let me repay a little of my great debt in this way, Ignatius.'

'It is impossible, my child'

'But why?'

'This house is more dangerous than any other to me.'

'He will not return, he dares not.'

'I have no fear of him for myself.'

'Who do you fear, then?'

'You.'

She understood him now and drooped before his sad but steady gaze. He looked down at her with an expression of the deepest suffering, but when he spoke it was in a cheerful tone, and his parting glance was cheerful also.

'I shall not change my way of life for him. It is my duty to guard you and I shall do it at all costs. If he molests me or threatens you, let him look to himself.'

Rosamond was right, Tempest did haunt them, not in person but by means of spies, he kept himself acquainted with their movements till an effectual stop was put to his surveillance. Three days after his visit one of the old servants came to Rosamond with an anxious face.

'Please, Miss, as Mistress is out I make bold to tell you that a strange man has been hanging about the place off and on all day, and just now I caught him talking over the garden wall to Margery, the new girl.'

'What was he saying, Barbara?'

'He was flattering her at first and then when she was a bit fluttered with his soft speeches he asked about the foreign gentleman, Miss. What time he came up here usually, where he lived and so on. I put a stop to it before Margery answered and sent him about his business with a warning not to show himself here again.'

'Thanks, Barbara. Father Ignatius has enemies and we must do our best to guard him. Mrs Tempest and Lito are away for the day so I must go and warn him. Let the pony carriage be ready as soon as possible and ask John to go with me.'

Without loss of time Rosamond was on her way to the lodging of her friend, bent on preparing him to meet whatever danger impended over him. Ignatius had a modest set of rooms over a shop, and entering below as if to make purchases she went up by a private way at the rear.

He was alone and asleep, looking as if worn out with wakeful nights and restless days. A book had fallen from his hand as he lay on the couch, and lifting it Rosamond saw that it was the life of Martin Luther. It opened at a certain page which seemed to have been much read, for several paragraphs were marked and the leaf was worn by frequent turning.

It was that part of the story where the great reformer practiced as he preached, and, boldly affirming that priests might marry, confirmed his sincerity by wedding his beloved Katherina. Rosamond's eye went from the book to the sleeper and an irrepressible hope sprung up within her, for the circumstance had a joyful significance to her.

Softly touching him, she breathed his name, and opening his eyes he stretched his arms to her as if he fancied her a vision of his sleep. Even in the act he woke and sprung up, exclaiming with wonder and pleasure in his voice and face.

'You here! I dreamed it but never thought to find the dream fulfilled. What is amiss, dear child?'

He never called her Rose, for the sound of it on Tempest's lips had made it distasteful to him. She told her fears, implored him to be careful and insisted on hurrying away again lest too long a stay should excite suspicion. He let her go, but before the pony carriage had climbed the first hill he was following and kept it in sight till it turned safely in at the Priory gates. Then, with an air of satisfaction, he retraced his steps entirely regardless of himself.

Halfway across the wide, desolate moor a man appeared from behind one of the great stones scattered among the gorse. A tall, powerful man, who lifted his hat as he approached as if distaining concealment. For an instant Ignatius paused, remembering his utterly un-armed and helpless condition, then with a smile at his hesitation he went on as tranquilly as if about to meet a friend.

In the middle of the lonely moor the two men met, and pausing face to face, eyed each other silently for a moment. If Tempest had detected the slightest symptom of fear in his rival's face he would have been better able to begin the interview. But so perfectly cool and calm was the bearing of Ignatius, so clear and steady his glance, so almost indifferent his tone that Tempest was impressed in spite of himself.

'You seek me, I am here,' was the brief greeting of the priest as the other did not speak.

'I do, we are well met and will settle this question before we part. If you were what I thought you I should have shot you like a dog as you passed me not long ago. Knowing you to be my equal, I offer you a chance for your life and demand the only satisfaction you can give me. Here are weapons, take your choice and do your best, for but one of us shall quit this spot alive.'

Speaking sternly, Tempest offered a pair of pistols with a grim smile which increased as Ignatius took one of the weapons, saying quietly, 'I possessed some skill once, let me see if I have entirely lost it,' and turning without any apparent pause to take aim he fired at a bird perched on a tall gorsebush some yards distant The bird fell dead, and returning the pistol Ignatius said in the same quiet tone, 'Do not trouble yourself to reload. I shall shoot nothing else today.'

Entirely taken by surprise at his skill and his reply, Tempest made no answer till Ignatius moved as if to go, then he broke out savagely, 'Stay, this bravado will not save you; skillful as you are, I am your match and you *shall* shoot again or share the bird's fate. This is a revolver. Take it and stand off; I'll not be balked this time but have revenge for the Coblenz affair if nothing more.'

Standing erect before him, Ignatius folded his arms and answered with calm decision, 'I decline your challenge.'

'Coward! I'll force you to accept it.' Tempest lifted his hand as if for a blow, but the steady eye and commanding figure opposite restrained him.

'It will avail nothing to insult me, I shall not fight.'

'I demand your reason for refusing.'

'I deny your right to do so, nevertheless I comply, that you may understand me better. If I were what I once was I should say "Bayard Condé fights only with gentlemen"; being what I am I reply, "Father Ignatius as a priest of God may use only spiritual weapons and needs no other."'

Tempest laughed contemptuously, but his face darkened terribly, for the answer stung him to the soul. Stepping back, he raised his arm and said tauntingly, 'Defend yourself with either weapon you choose, for by the Lord I swear I will shoot you as you stand for this last insult.'

Unfolding his arms and turning so that his breast offered a fair mark for the other's aim, Ignatius replied with perfect composure touched with scorn, 'Fire, and deepen Rosamond's detestation by adding another murder to your list of crimes.'

The pistol dropped from Tempest's hand and an unmistakable expression of fear passed over his face as he demanded in an unsteady voice, 'What do you mean?'

'I mean that the man who shot the husband of the unhappy Lady Clyde and lured Robert Willoughby to his death is a murderer whom it would need little to convict and publicly condemn. Well for him that the confidences of the Confessional are held sacred, or the name of Tempest would be disgraced forever.'

The last words seemed to reassure the listener, for his former hardihood returned, and as if anxious to forget the past he said abruptly, 'If you will not fight, will you answer a few questions?'

'Out of pity for your desperate state I will, if they are such as I have a right to answer,' was the mild reply.

'Tell me then, do you love my Rose?'

'Yes.' Only a word, but it spoke volumes.

'And she loves you?' asked Tempest between his teeth.

'That I have no right to say.'

'Bah, it is plain, why make a pretense of doubting it?'

'If it is plain, why question me?'

'Because I choose. You will get absolved from your vows and marry her?' he went on eagerly.

'I shall do neither.' A stifled sigh heaved the broad chest of the priest.

'Ah, I understand, Rose has profited by my teaching and having found marriage a failure will dispense with it now as I would have had her in the beginning—'

He got no farther, for with one step Ignatius caught him by the throat exclaiming in a tone of suppressed wrath, scorn and disgust while his face blazed out suddenly with the passion controlled so long, 'Breathe a word against that innocent creature and I'll throttle you as I would a venomous reptile!'

The instant his hand touched Tempest he grappled with him and Ignatius forgot everything except that he was a man avenging the wrongs of the woman he loved. In fierce silence they struggled together like two wrestlers, each feeling the power of the other and exerting every muscle to conquer. They were well matched in height but not in strength, for Tempest's life had been one to undermine the most perfect health, while Ignatius, temperate in all things as an anchorite, possessed the superb muscular power of manhood in its prime.

Tempest soon perceived Ignatius's superiority and fought with the desperation of despair, for now he knew that his rival's blood was up and that he was not a man to be subdued in spite of his seeming gentleness. It was a short struggle but a deadly one, for Tempest would not unloose his hold though thrown more than once. The third time his head struck a stone in the heath and he lay stunned, still grasping his enemy with the tenacity of a wild beast.

When he recovered, his head lay on the priest's knee and with all the passion gone out of his face, Ignatius was bending over him as he loosened his cravat. For several moments he lay looking blankly up at that compassionate countenance and his first words were the wondering question, 'Why do you restore me and not rid yourself of me when I am in your power?'

'I will not stain my hands with blood nor send you out of this world till you are fitter for another. Can you stand? So! Lean on me and sit with your back against this stone, the air will revive you.'

Lost in wonder, and docile from weakness, Tempest obeyed and sat moodily leaning his dizzy head upon his hand while Ignatius went to fill his hat full of water from the pool nearby. There is a saying, 'If you knock an Englishman down in a fair fight he will respect you ever afterward.' It was so now. Few men had ever conquered Tempest in anything and he felt superior to most, but this man surpassed him in strength, skill, courage and magnanimity, for, hard as he was, Tempest still felt the beauty of a generous act, a noble word. Ignatius had conquered in love and war; had borne insult meekly for himself, had avenged it manfully for another, had given compassion for contempt, and having won the victory generously spared his enemy. It galled Tempest terribly and yet it touched him also, for the noble sincerity of the man impressed him and the influence of real virtue could not be resisted.

As Ignatius came back, offering the water with a friendly air, Tempest rather startled him by asking abruptly, as if the words lingered in his mind ' "Fitter for another world" – is that possible?'

'Yes, greater miracles have been wrought.'

'By you?' In Tempest's haggard face there was a momentary expression of hope struggling with a nameless fear. Before the other could reply it was gone and he dropped his head impatiently on his hand again, saying half angrily, '*Chut*, what a fool I am to talk in that maudlin style. Say what you have to say and leave me.'

'I have only this to say, "Go and repent." '

'Stay, one more question,' cried Tempest, as Ignatius turned away.

Pausing, the priest wiped his flushed forehead and said with a smile as he glanced from the trampled heath to his own disordered dress and the desperate-looking man before him, 'I listen, I repeat your own phrase, "Say what you have to say," and add, let your words be carefully chosen, for I have no desire to make a brute of myself again, and I assuredly shall if you insult Rosamond.'

'Tell me one thing; you love Rose and are beloved yet cannot marry; how will it end?'

Tempest needed one more lesson and he received it when Ignatius turned on him a face full of love and longing, full of a man's dearest and strongest passion, yet answered steadily though his cheek paled and his eye darkened with intensity of feeling, 'I shall love her all my life, shall be to her a faithful friend, and if I cannot remain loyal to both God and her I shall renounce her and never see her face again. You call this folly; to me it is a hard duty, and the more I love her the worthier of

212

her will I endeavor to become by my own integrity of soul.'

With that they parted, and Ignatius left Tempest sitting on the lonely moor, twice conquered in an hour.

CHAPTER XXIII

Retribution

Tempest went back to London and tried to take up his old life again, but soon found that for him as for all sinners the inevitable hour of retribution had begun. The divorce had laid bare his past and honest men shunned him, modest women shrank from him as from the plague, old friends dropped away, the world condemned him, and he was set apart among the black sheep of society. It annoyed him intensely and he would have gone abroad again to some of his former haunts but for Rosamond. He could not take her with him so was forced to remain in decorous England, where his disreputable life and wild freaks found no support.

He grew moody and sat much alone brooding over many things, for now pleasure palled upon him and companionship grew distasteful. For the first time in his life he felt remorse, not for the sins committed but for the untoward consequences of the sins. He was in the power of Ignatius and often worked himself into a fever trying to discover how the truth of his evil deeds had come to the priest, and if it was true that the secrets of the Confessional were kept sacred. Health too was failing, for the fall at Coblenz, though it left no outward sign, had injured him, and being too impatient to take proper precautions at the time, the injury was augmented, and a constant weary pain in the chest wore upon him terribly.

The loss of Baptiste was another thorn; he dared not

openly inquire, but by clandestine means learned that the convict had been shot without betraying anything. He did not regret him as a man but as a tool, for the unscrupulous fidelity of Baptiste was invaluable and it seemed impossible to fill his place.

Tempest never for a moment relinquished his purpose of winning back Rosamond, but waited to find some way of safely accomplishing his design. In England he could not abduct the girl or use forcible means of getting her into his power without danger, scandal and opposition. He hated Ignatius with a mortal hate, feeling that he was the greatest obstacle in the way, and the most insurmountable, for the priest was a rival to be wary of approaching. The scene upon the moor had proved his power and its memory still rankled in Tempest's mind.

Day after day he roamed the streets or sat in his rooms trying to devise some way of accomplishing his double purpose. That Rosamond no longer loved him he could not doubt, and with his own unabated passion was now mingled a resentful desire to make her expiate her contempt by fresh humiliation or suffering.

Accident befriended him. A letter came from old Vivian through Tempest's lawyer. News of the divorce had reached him, and he commanded Tempest to atone for the wrong he had done Rosamond by marrying her or he would compel him to so do by legal proceedings; he also added as a bait that the aunt of the girl was dead and the fortune passed to his granddaughter, subject to his control. Not knowing where Rosamond was (for all her letters had been suppressed by Tempest), he wrote to him for tidings of her and desired him to bring her home at once.

Armed with this letter, Tempest ventured to return to Staffordshire, thinking it would afford an excuse for seeing Rosamond if nothing more, and might make some impression upon her. It was evening when he arrived and entering the gates unseen he was attracted by the brilliant light of a certain window. Stealing up the bank, he swung himself onto the balcony and putting by the vines that curtained the window, looked in upon a scene which forced a bitter malediction from his lips.

Rosamond, more beautiful than ever, was the central figure of the group, and about her were gathered the other three, as if she drew all hearts to her by the spell of her unconscious grace and loveliness. She had been singing and was just reseated at her work with the glow called up by commendation still on her cheek. Ignatius sat opposite and pushing away his book leaned forward talking earnestly while she listened, apparently forgetful of everything but the eloquent dark eyes that told so much.

Nearby sat Mrs Tempest, much of the youthful cheerfulness restored to her comely face, and leaning on the arm of her chair stood Lito, tall and handsome, talking gaily as he spoilt her embroidery like the petted boy he was. The start Tempest gave when he saw his son would have betrayed him had not a general burst of laughter at some sally of Lito's drowned the rustle of the leaves as they escaped from the watcher's hand. He loved the boy, and real thankfulness filled his heart as he saw him safe and well, for he had felt his loss keenly and repented bitterly of his harshness.

A moment he gazed at him with genuine delight, then came the remembrance of the promise he had given and the thought, 'He is no longer mine.' As if the recollection of the deceit practiced on him recalled him to his former self, he turned and left the balcony, saying with a sardonic smile, 'I need amusement and shall find it by walking in among them unannounced.'

He knew the ways of the household, and slipping in without ringing he glided to the door of the room where sat the happy group. He meant to wear his usual air of cool audacity, but as he entered and saw the sudden terror that fell on all at sight of him, the longing to be kindly welcomed was so strong he could not resist it, and with a humility that surprised himself as much as

216

them, he said gravely, as he bowed to Mrs Tempest, 'Pardon for coming unexpectedly, but I have good news for Rose and could not deny myself the pleasure of bringing them. May I wait for your reply?'

Neither of the women spoke, for Mrs Tempest clung to her son and Rosamond disdained to answer. Ignatius, with undisturbed composure, rose and offered the unwelcome guest a seat, saying courteously, 'It is an inclement night, you are wet and weary; sit and rest while Mademoiselle receives your tidings.'

Tempest laid the letter before Rosamond (who beckoned Ignatius to come and read it with her as if she feared some treachery lurked in it), and sat down, feeling an alien and an outcast in his own home.

Lito eyed him defiantly at first, but when his father with an uncontrollable impulse stretched out his hand and exclaimed imploringly; 'My boy, will you not come and speak to your father?' he broke from his mother's grasp and putting his hand in Tempest's looked fearlessly at him. Something in the haggard face, the warm clasp of the hand, the sound of that last word touched the generous heart of the lad, and forgetting the past he remembered only that he was a son. Putting his arm about his father's neck he kissed him, saying affectionately, 'I'm glad you own me at last, Papa.'

Regardless of everyone, Tempest held the boy close, muttering fervently in a broken voice, 'Thank God you are safe, my Lito!'

Pale and agitated with an ominous fear, Mrs Tempest drew near, longing to withdraw the boy yet touched by the emotion of the man. She laid her hand on Lito's shoulder with a warning touch and Tempest looked up. Steadying his voice, he said beseechingly, 'Let me keep him for the little while I stay, Marion; you have made him yours for life.'

'You will not claim him then? You abide by your promise, Phillip?' she said eagerly.

'Yes, though won unfairly I will keep my word, dear

217

as the boy is to me. You are a fitter guardian than I; keep him and let me now and then remind him that he has a father. Tell me, Lito, how you vanished so entirely? I have searched and mourned for you, believing you were dead.'

Grateful yet half incredulous, Mrs Tempest drew back, and leaning on his father's knee, Lito told his little story. While listening, Tempest's eye often wandered to the pair who sat apart, bending their heads together over the letter and discussing its contents in low tones. He had forgotten the terrible indelicacy of making any appeal to Rosamond in that house. His wife had long ago become a stranger to him and the divorce widened the breach between them almost as entirely as if death had sealed the separation.

In his impetuous haste, his selfish love, he thought only of supporting his claim by the old man's command and waited impatiently for her reply. Soon it came, cold, brief and decided.

'Thank you for your tidings. I shall go to my grandfather at once. There is but one reply to his other command, you know it and this is not the place to repeat it.'

Her tone and manner were equal to a dismissal and putting Lito away Tempest rose, feeling that any importunity now would injure his cause.

'I may at least be permitted to congratulate you on your good fortune, and to hope that your Grandfather's wishes will have more weight with you than mine.' Here his respectful manner changed to one of ironical politeness as he turned to the priest and Mrs Tempest.

'Father Ignatius, as you have absolved Mademoiselle from past sins; perhaps you can win her to a Christian forgiveness of the chief sinner, and soften her hard heart as a pious Confessor should. To you, Madam, I leave the boy, though I might claim him easily, for your moral influence will exceed mine if I may judge by the example of truthfulness you have already given. Lito, good-bye, in a few years you will be of age and free to join your father and enjoy life. I'll wait till then,' and with a mocking laugh, a bow of affected respect, Tempest retired, solacing himself with the thought that he had made them all as unhappy as was possible in so short a time.

A servant saw him out and barred both door and gates behind him, but in spite of wind and rain he haunted the spot for hours, unable to tear himself away. It was an inexpressibly bitter moment when he stood alone in the bleak November night, shut out from the warmth and friendliness of the home which now held the only creatures whom he loved. Rose and Lito were there; neither money, treachery nor power could restore them to him and their guardians were the persons of all others most detested by him. This added a subtle sting to the retribution already darkening over him, for he who had won and wasted love so wantonly all his life now pined for it with a longing which nothing could appease, and pined in vain.

As he wandered to and fro before the gates that shut him from his Paradise, he raged against fate and swore to conquer yet. The memory of Ignatius leaning side by side with Rosamond over the letter, her soft hair touching his cheek, her eyes looking confidingly into his, her whole air betraying how deep and perfect was her love and honor for him, was torture to Tempest, and as he recalled the picture again and again all his short-lived regret and humility changed to a savage desire to destroy that happiness in which he could bear no part.

The sound of opening doors arrested him as he stood shaking his clenched hand at his unseen rival in a paroxysm of mute wrath.

Lito and Rosamond were saying good night to the priest and, gliding into a shadowy angle of the wall, Tempest heard the happy voices reiterating farewells, entreaties to come early on the morrow, and charges to ride carefully across the moor. Then the gates were opened and a horseman rode away, followed by a last adieu in Rosamond's sweet voice.

Tempest set his teeth with an oath and hurrying to the spot where his own horse was tied, cautiously followed the unsuspecting man with a black thought in his mind. The night was very dark and the tempestuous wind roared over the bleak moor as the two riders crossed it. No sound warned Ignatius of the approaching danger and nearer and nearer came the man who thirsted for his blood.

Tempest rode warily lest the clash of his horse's feet on the road should betray him, and had nearly reached his rival when the quick tramp of hoofs echoed behind them. Pausing, he heard the newcomer pull up beside the priest, saying in a hearty voice, 'Miss Vivian sent me, Sir, being fearful you might lose your way or come to harm this wild night. It's John, Sir, and I'm entirely at your service.'

'Foolish child,' the listener heard Ignatius say in a tender undertone, then added cheerily, 'Thanks, my man, let us ride on that Miss Vivian may not be disappointed.'

So, guarded from impending danger, Ignatius crossed the moor.

CHAPTER XXIV

The Vision Verified

The sojourn in England was all too quickly over and the point reached when they must set sail for the Island. The day had been mild and clear, but a warm wind rose, clouds began to gather and the sky looked so threatening that Ignatius advised delay. But Rosamond was feverishly eager now to be at home, for the thought that Tempest was still on her track filled her with such alarm that all lesser fears were forgotten. Her will was law, and leaving her to rest in the parlor of the little inn he went out to secure a boat. He was delayed a long time and when he returned it was with an anxious face which his first words explained.

'Tempest is here.'

'Here, impossible! Are you sure?' she cried, turning very pale.

'Beyond a doubt. He must have followed us rapidly. His yacht is here and while I was inquiring for a boat I discovered it. You had just been telling me about the *Circe* and there she lies, ready to sail at a moment's notice.'

'Let her sail or let her stay. I shall not be turned aside by this unfortunate meeting. Phillip may follow. I shall go straight on and defy him to the last. Is the boat ready?'

She spoke almost fiercely and put her question in a tone as imperious as Tempest's own, for her patience was exhausted and for herself she no longer feared anything. To prevent another meeting between the two men was her purpose and she longed to be safely away upon the sea.

'Yes I have found a little craft and pair of skillful sailors to man it. They tell me it is but an hour's sail with a fair wind and we shall reach the Island before dusk. Shall we go?'

'Yes.'

Smiling at her resolute air, Ignatius took her away at once and placed her safely aboard the *Osprey*. Everything was ready and they were just about to start when Ignatius discovered that his purse was gone. Having a vague recollection of laying it on the hotel table when he put on Rosamond's cloak, and the place being close at hand, he returned to find it, fearing to trust any strange messenger.

It was nowhere to be seen and after some delay he gave it up, with a strong suspicion that the officious waiter knew something of it. Fearing to waste the daylight, he hastened back to the pier to find to his dismay that the boat had sailed. Though still in sight and within sound of his voice the men paid no heed to his signals nor his shouts but kept steadily on and soon vanished, leaving him in despair. Hastily hiring a boat, he offered a sound sum to the men if they would overtake the other.

'The *Osprey* is a fast sailor, sir, but we'll do our best,' was the reply and away they went with all sail set. The men were right; the *Osprey* left them far behind and they soon lost her in the gathering fog which blew up from the sea as day declined.

Meanwhile Tempest watched and waited, exulting in the success of his impromptu plot. He had followed close and as he heard Ignatius engaging the boat a terrible thought struck him. Accidents were frequent, why not let one rid him of his rival. The presence of Rosamond alone interfered with his plan. This obstacle was surmounted by bribing the men of the *Osprey* in the

222

absence of Ignatius to sail without him, and detaining him by the loss of his purse, which was easily managed by the waiter, who received a hint that a disgraceful elopement would be prevented if he would lend his aid and pocket a rich reward.

Bad men often prosper miraculously for a time at least, and all went well; the *Osprey* sailed with Rosamond safe in the cabin, Ignatius followed in a little cockleshell, and the *Circe* glided after both like a great white ghost through the deepening mist. Night fell early, the wind rose, the fog thickened and as he made his way with difficulty Tempest comforted himself that the quick-sailing *Osprey* was safely in harbor by that time. He ordered lights hung from the bow and went slowly on, waiting and watching for the little boat. As the tide turned the fog lifted now and then, and in one of these clearer moments a faint spark appeared not far away, and a shout was heard.

'Good, they see my lights and they think I will help them. Wait a little, holy father, and I will show you I don't forget all I owe you.'

Tempest smiled a terrible smile as he spoke and calling one of his men to him he gave an order. The man had been a pirate in his youth, but hardened as he was he shrunk back and looked incredulous as the emphatic whisper met his ear, 'Run down that boat!'

'You wish to take them aboard, Master?' he asked, as if slow to comprehend.

'Not alive! No folly, man, you've done worse deeds than this, and you know how it fares with those who disobey me,' was the stern reply.

Muttering the disgust he dared not show, the man doggedly obeyed. Straight for the doomed boat steered the *Circe*, looming darkly through the mist with her lights like the fiery eyes of some monster bearing upon its prey. At the bow stood Tempest, a fit pilot for such a voyage. As they neared the boat a clear voice rung warningly through the night. He knew the speaker, answered with a decisive shout, and a moment after rising in a great wave the *Cirrce* plunged down on the little boat, which vanished amid the despairing cries of its affrighted crew. Never pausing, the yacht swept on and Tempest stood immovable, muttering with white lips, 'No fear of his betraying me now, for no one will live to tell the tale. Sleep tranquilly, Ignatius, I go to comfort Rosamond.'

He laughed yet shuddered as if a colder touch than that of the chilly mist was on him, and went to give the last orders for the night. Dropping anchor in the little bay, he sent ashore to ask if the *Osprey* had come in and received an answer in the affirmative. Feeling in no mood to meet any human creature, Tempest locked himself into the cabin and tried to sleep.

But he had 'murdered sleep', and every object his restless eyes encountered reminded him of Rosamond. Never before had these memories failed to soothe and satisfy him, but now they harassed him terribly, for a strange shadow seemed to have fallen on all he saw. His thoughts tormented him increasingly; every evil deed rose up to daunt him and a nameless dread chilled soul and body which nothing could lessen or banish. Snatching a vial from the table, he put it to his lips and recklessly swallowed a strong dose of laudanum. Then, throwing himself onto his berth, he resolutely closed his eyes, thinking, 'It is that fall that has unstrung my nerves. Once ashore I'll take care of myself and Rosamond shall nurse me.'

With frequent starts and mutterings he at last fell into a sleep which held him fast till the sun was high the next day.

He woke with a throbbing head and at first did not recall the past, but suddenly the night's work flashed on him and he sprang up as if his pillow was of thorns, his bed of fire. Rapidly arranging his dress, he steadied himself with the strongest stimulant in his liqueur-case and went on shore.

Heeding no one, he trod the well-known path to the old house on the cliff and entered quietly. Not a sound broke the deep hush except his own footfall as he stole along, saying to himself, 'I'll see Vivian first, assure him of my willingness to atone, and enlist him in my favor.'

His cautious tap woke no answer and peering in he saw that the room was deserted. With an astonished gaze fixed on the chair seldom empty, he muttered 'Is the old man dead or asleep?' and passing through the dreary room where he had first seen Rosamond, he entered the bedchamber beyond. Empty also and showing signs of unusual confusion.

'They are together in her little nest above. I'll creep up and surprise them.' Still talking to himself as if the silence oppressed him, he stole away to be again met by solitude and the unmistakable evidences of some unusual event.

'Deuce take the people, where are they all?' After a thoughtful pause he hurried again to the great drawing room, fancying Rosamond had gone to the spot where her early love dream first began.

Yes, she was there, lying on the low couch where they had often sat together, her damp hair clinging dark about her fine pale face where shone the smile seen only upon countenances on which death has set his seal. Beside her, with his white head bowed upon his hands, the old man sat alone; a piteous sight. A smothered groan from Tempest made him look up. Instantly he broke into a frenzy of passion, crying in a voice shrill with age and terrible with grief and wrath, 'Have you come to look upon your work? Here she is safe and free at last. You said you would hunt her to her grave and you have done it. Are you satisfied?'

'For God's sake hear me! I thought her safe, I knew nothing of this, the boat came in last night, what happened? Oh! What killed my Rosamond?' and like a man suddenly gone blind Tempest groped his way toward the pale wreck of the creature whom he had loved so well.

But as if endowed with strength by his intense emotion, the old man half rose on his long helpless limbs, and, clenching his withered hands, waved him back, shrieking out the dreadful truth with an awful exultation in the retribution the man had brought upon himself.

'You killed her, you wrecked her and left her to die in the cruel sea! The priest followed and compelled your tools to give her up, and would have brought her to me without harm but for your black deed. Wring your hands and groan till your hard heart breaks, you are too late for any word of hers.'

The shrill voice quavered and died out in a burst of tearless sobs as the old man bowed his white head again, exhausted with emotion. Standing where the truth had transfixed him, Tempest stared straight before him with a stony face, for in the solemn silence which filled the room he saw the vision of the Venetian mirror verified.

Opposite him hung the great glass, reflecting the beautiful dead woman, the old man mourning beside her, and the likeness of himself standing near wearing an expression of unutterable remorse and despair.

'Why are you here?'

Tempest turned and saw Ignatius on the threshold of the door. But for the living eyes the priest looked as if he too had received the peace of death, so colorless and calm his face, so emotionless his voice, so far removed from human pain or passion did he seem as he passed slowly to his place beside the dead girl, and standing there repeated his brief question, 'Why are you here?'

'Because I thought to find her living and you dead,' was the stern answer as Tempest advanced, in spite of the old man's feeble warnings, to claim her even now. 'Stand back. She is mine and I will have her,' he said fiercely, confronting the tranquil figure opposite.

'She is mine and you can never take her from me, for

in time I shall rejoin her in a blessed world where such as you cannot enter. Nothing can part us long; our love was true and pure, and though forbidden here it will unite us forever in the beautiful hereafter.' Ignatius spoke with the joyful confidence of a perfect faith and in his face shone the serenity of a true heart strong to love, patient to wait.

Like a fallen spirit shut out from eternal life, Tempest looked at him a moment, then, as the old fire blazed up within him for the last time, he drove a hidden dagger deep into his breast and, dropping on his knees, gathered the dead woman in his arms, saying with mingled love and defiance in his despairing voice, 'Mine first – mine last – mine even in the grave!'

A NOTE ON THE TEXT

The manuscript of *A Long Fatal Love Chase* consists of 290 pages (recto and verso) written and subsequently revised by Louisa May Alcott. The revisions appear to have been an attempt to make the novel less sensational, but resulted in a far less powerful book. This is evident in a much-truncated version to be found in Harvard University's Houghton Library, catalogued under the title of its first chapter, 'Fair Rosamond'. It is a fair copy in the hand of Louisa's sister, May, and includes many of the author's changes. While incomplete – its seventy-three pages cover Chapters 1–4, 9–10, 17 and 24 – it has been helpful in filling the rare gaps in the manuscript published here. My intent has been to restore the original, more vibrant text that Louisa submitted – unsuccessfully – to her publisher. I have made a few (unacknowledged) emendations to clarify certain portions of the novel, and corrected spelling and punctuation errors. Apart from this, *A Long Fatal Love Chase* appears as the author wrote it.

Kent Bicknell
New Hampshire, 1995

ACKNOWLEDGEMENTS

Because Louisa May Alcott wrote *A Long Fatal Love Chase* to help alleviate the financial plight of her family, it seems particularly fitting that a portion of the royalties earned by this book be donated to Orchard House, the home of the Alcotts in Concord, Massachusetts, which is maintained by the Louisa May Alcott Memorial Association. Alcott's father, Bronson, was dedicated to educational reform, and Louisa, too, was a visionary, as evidenced in her classics on the new education, *Little Men* and *Jo's Boys*. It therefore seems appropriate that an equal share of this book's proceeds be given to support curricula that teach both reverence for life and the awareness that the goal of knowledge is service to others.

The editor wishes to thank the following kind friends, without whom this book would not have come to light: Tim Mather, Lane Zachary, and Ann Godoff.

Along the way, much help and encouragement came from Tom Blanding, Chris Francis, Victor Gulotta, Fritz Kussin, Louisa Kussin, Bruce Lisman, Kevin MacDonnell, Jean-Isabel McNutt, JoAnn Malinowski, Cheryl Needle, Charles Pratt, Frederick Pratt, John Pratt, John Pye, Elaine Rogers, Leona Rostenberg, Whit Smith, Madeleine Stern, Linda Turnage, Ike Williams and the Palmer & Dodge Agency. Thanks also to the administration, faculty, students, parents, and board of the Sant Bani School, the staff of Orchard House, and the Houghton Library at Harvard.

The editor gratefully acknowledges the loving support of his family – Karen, Christopher, and Nicholas – and the grace and patience of Sant Ajaib Singh Ji and Raaj Kumar Bagga.

230

ABOUT THE AUTHOR

LOUISA MAY ALCOTT was born in 1832 in Pennsylvania, but came of age in Concord, Massachusetts, at a time when it was home to a group of passionate dissidents, the transcendentalists. One of the most radical of these was Louisa's father, Bronson. But passion was no substitute for basic necessities, and it fell to Louisa to help support her family by her writing, which she did from an early age. She wrote several other novels in the years prior to gaining fame and financial fortune with the publication of *Little Women* in 1868 – one of these being *A Long Fatal Love Chase*. Alcott was an ardent believer in women's rights, and was actively involved in campaigns for women's suffrage until her death in 1888.

ABOUT THE EDITOR

KENT BICKNELL is the principal of the Sant Bani School, a private day school in Sanbornton, New Hampshire. In 1993 he became aware of *A Long Fatal Love Chase*, which Louisa May Alcott wrote in 1866 but never published. Good fortune and a generous backer enabled him to purchase it the following year, and he at once set about rectifying the editorial neglect imposed on it for so long.

Bicknell and his wife, Karen, share the Concord group's affinity with the East, and make frequent visits to India. They have two grown sons, and live in New Hampshire with a Norwegian elk-hound and a black cat.